TRANSITIONS

HALF A CENTURY OF SOUTH AFRICAN SHORT STORIES

Compiled by

Craig MacKenzie

Department of English
Rand Afrikaans University

Francolin Publishers
Cape Town

Francolin Publishers (Pty) Ltd
5 Surbiton Road
Rosebank 7700, Cape Town
Fax: (021) 686-8249
Email: francolin@iafrica.com
Reg. No. 1994/09406/07

First published 1999
Tenth impression 2006

ISBN 1-86859-048-8

Editor: *Jacqueline Douglas*
Design and DTP: *Abdul Amien*
Cover design: *Abdul Amien*
Cover illustration: *Roxandra Dardagan*

Imaging: Image Mix, Cape Town
Printing and binding: Clyson Printers, Maitland

Contents

iv | Acknowledgements
iv | Editorial note
v | Preface

1 | Herman Charles Bosman, 'Old Transvaal Story' (1948)
6 | Nadine Gordimer, 'Six Feet of the Country' (1956)
16 | Richard Rive, 'Rain' (1963)
23 | Es'kia Mphahlele, 'Mrs Plum' (1967)
52 | Bessie Head, 'Heaven is not Closed' (1977)
58 | Ahmed Essop, 'The Hajji' (1978)
70 | Christopher Hope, 'Learning to Fly' (1981)
77 | Sheila Roberts, 'This Time of Year' (1983)
86 | Njabulo Ndebele, 'The Test' (1983)
104 | Zoë Wicomb, 'A Trip to the Gifberge' (1987)
117 | Ivan Vladislavić, 'Journal of a Wall' (1989)
133 | Maureen Isaacson, 'Holding Back Midnight' (1992)

137 | The South African short story: A historical overview
144 | Notes on the authors and commentary on the stories

Acknowledgements

The publishers and compiler are grateful to the following for permission to reproduce copyright material:

Human & Rousseau for 'Old Transvaal Story' by Herman Charles Bosman, published in *Unto Dust*, Human & Rousseau (1963). A. P. Watt Ltd on behalf of Nadine Gordimer for 'Six Feet of the Country' by Nadine Gordimer, published in *Six Feet of the Country: Short Stories*, Gollancz (1956); and *Selected Stories of Nadine Gordimer*, Jonathan Cape (1975). David Philip Publishers for 'Rain' by Richard Rive, published in *Advance Retreat: Selected Short Stories*, David Philip Publishers (1983). Es'kia Mphahlele for 'Mrs Plum' by Es'kia Mphahlele, published in *In Corner B*, East African Publishing House (1967); and *Renewal Time*, Reader's International (1988). Ravan Press for 'The Hajji' by Ahmed Essop, published in *The Hajji and Other Stories*, Ravan Press (1978). John Johnson (Authors' Agent) Limited for 'Heaven is not Closed' by Bessie Head. From *The Collector of Treasures*, William Heinemann Ltd., London. Copyright © The Estate of Bessie Head, 1997. Rogers, Coleridge & White Ltd. for 'Learning to Fly' by Christopher Hope. Copyright © Christopher Hope 1982. Reproduced by permission of the author c/o Rogers, Coleridge & White Ltd., 20 Powis Mews, London W11 1JN. Sheila Roberts (a former South African who now lives in Wisconsin and teaches creative writing in the English Department at the University of Wisconsin-Milwaukee) for 'This Time of Year' by Sheila Roberts, published in *This Time of Year and Other Stories*, Ad Donker (1983). Njabulo Ndebele for 'The Test' by Njabulo Ndebele, published in *Fools and Other Stories*, Ravan Press (1983). Virago Press, a division of Little, Brown and Company (UK) for 'A Trip to the Gifberge' by Zoë Wicomb, published in *You Can't Get Lost in Cape Town*, Virago Press (1987). David Philip Publishers for 'Journal of a Wall' by Ivan Vladislavić, published in *Missing Persons*, David Philip Publishers (1989). COSAW Publishing and Maureen Isaacson for 'Holding Back Midnight' by Maureen Isaacson, published in *Holding Back Midnight and Other Stories*, COSAW (1992).

Editorial note
The stories in this anthology have been reproduced exactly as they appear in the source publications, but certain typographical features, such as quotation marks and ellipses, have been standardised across the stories.

Preface

As its title suggests, this anthology of short stories encompasses the notion of change. The stories selected were first published in the years between 1948 (which marks South Africa's descent into the dark years of institutionalised apartheid) and 1992 (the beginning of the country's transformation into a democratic state). The stories all explore private moments in the lives of characters living through this troubled half-century.

The profound social change of this period is reflected in the literature. Bosman's 'Old Transvaal Story', which heads the collection, is redolent of old, rural South African life: it is a distillation in many ways of hundreds of years of oral culture, of tales doing the rounds by word of mouth from tribal kraal to farm stoep to village bar. In the way it treats its rustic material, however, it is quintessentially modern, and it therefore stands on the cusp of the modern era. By the time we come to Vladislavić's 'Journal of a Wall' and Isaacson's 'Holding Back Midnight', one cycle of South Africa's transition has been completed: not only has the tale been relocated to an urban milieu, it has also lost its capacity to evoke the very idea of community, the *sine qua non* of the oral tale. Paranoia and alienation lurk behind high suburban walls and this is reflected in the fragmented texture of the narratives themselves.

From the outset the idea was that this would be a small collection of stories and that it would be aimed principally at undergraduate university and college students. Given that South Africa is particularly rich in the genre of the short story, selecting a mere twelve stories called for very clear selection criteria. The decision was taken early on to cover only the period from after the Second World War to the present – roughly the past fifty years. How best, then, to represent nearly fifty years of short stories?

In the first instance, I limited myself to writers who have made a name for themselves as short story practitioners. Writers who have had isolated success with one or two stories, or established poets and novelists who have made sporadic forays into the field of the short story, were not considered. It was assumed that the intended reader would be wholly or largely unfamiliar with the South African short story, and the idea was that this reader should come away from this highly selective garnering having encountered some of the major exponents of the form. (Christopher Hope, better known as a novelist and poet, is the possible exception here. His one collection of stories was of sufficient moment, however, as to warrant his inclusion.)

Having decided which writers to include, the next challenge was to select a story to represent each of them. In many cases, four or five stories could readily have been chosen, and the choice became almost arbitrary. Here the notion of a representative sample again guided me, and well-known stories – stories that are deservedly famous – were chosen in many instances. This has meant that I have often made what might be seen as conservative choices; indeed, inveterate readers of the South African short story will meet with few surprises here. However, if the reader is likely to have only a brief encounter with the South African short story then it is as well that he or she encounters some of the best, and best-known, that the genre has to offer.

The hope, nonetheless, is that the reader will be encouraged to explore the South African short story further. To this end, a fairly extensive editorial apparatus has been appended to the text. In addition to the usual biographical notes on authors, some commentary on each of the stories is offered, and this includes extracts from the work of critics of South African literature. A survey essay on the historical development of the South African short story is also included so that readers can place the stories chosen here in a larger context.

The transitions that these stories explore are not complete – and never will be. In 1948 Bosman stood on the threshold of a dark era in South African history. Fifty years later we are again faced with fundamental societal change, this time of a more hopeful nature. Writers over the next fifty years will chart the future transitions; it is to be hoped that the wisdom, humour and perspicacity evident in the stories included in this anthology will assist all of us in making the right choices.

Craig MacKenzie
Johannesburg, 1999

OLD TRANSVAAL STORY

Herman Charles Bosman

A s Scully, I think, knew – have you ever chanced upon his 'Ukushwama'? – the Transvaal seems to have had only one ghost story. It is a story that I have heard often, told over and over again in voorkamer and by campfire, with the essential features always the same, and with only the details, in respect of characters and locale, differing with the mood and the personality – and the memory, perhaps – of each person that tells it.

The story of the Transvaal's only ghost goes something like this:

A solitary traveller on horseback enquires his way at a farmhouse after dark.

'That means you'll be going through the poort' (or the kloof or the drift, as the case may be) 'at full moon,' the farmer says to the traveller. 'Well, no man has ever been able to ride his horse through that poort at night when the moon is full.'

Actually, there is no need to tell the story any farther than that. In those few words the farmer has said everything . . . A certain place along the road is haunted, and even if the traveller should not happen to notice the ghost – because he is thinking of something else, likely – the horse certainly will see the ghost, and will rear up on his hind-legs. After that, neither whip nor spur, nor calling him by his first name, coaxingly, will get the horse past that spot where the spectre lurks.

Accordingly, the traveller turns back along the road he has come, riding quite fast, this time. And he arrives once more at the farmhouse where he received the unearthly warning in the first instance. The wise old farmer has known all along that the traveller would be back, of course, and after having persuaded him, without much difficulty, to spend the night there, proceeds to acquaint him in leisurely fashion over a jar of peach brandy with the circumstances that led to the poort becoming haunted.

This is a good story. I have heard it told – nearly always in the first person – by dozens of different people, always with only slight variations, and these of a strictly local character.

Indeed, I have heard this story so often, in different parts of the Transvaal, that it doesn't make my hair stand on end, any more. If the truth must be known, I've got somewhat blasé about the Transvaal's only ghost.

The result is that nowadays, when a man says, lowering his voice and trying to make his tones sound sepulchral, 'And so Oom Hannes Blignaut said to me that I would not be able to ride my horse through that poort in the full moon,' I short-circuit him by asking, 'But why didn't you go on a pushbike, instead?'

I have not, to date, found an answer to that one.

Similarly, as far as I have been able to discover, the Transvaal has got only one murder story – this, likewise, an amazingly good one. Only, through constant repetition, the gloss has for me been worn off this stirring old tale as well. I first heard it as a child; since then it has been related to me many times, as I am sure it has been to every South African who has spent some portion of his life on the Transvaal platteland. I suppose the story is based on historical fact: its salient features seem to relate to some murder that actually was committed long ago.

This story, I should like to add in parenthesis, has never been told to me in the first person. No man has ever said to me, 'And so after I hit my wife with the chopper I buried her under the mud floor of the voorkamer and later on the police came.'

For that, in rough outline, is the Transvaal's only murder story. It sounds bald, somehow, conveyed in those words. Put that way, it sounds more like a murder than like a murder story. But this old tale has a twist to it arising out of what happened in a certain period of time between the committing of the murder and the arrival of the police. The man has murdered his wife. – Good. – He has buried her under the floor of the voorkamer. – Right. – He proceeds to smooth over the broken portion of the floor with clay and moist cow-dung. – Yes, excellent. All that seems straightforward enough.

But it is at this very point that the totally unexpected happens. This is the sensational development in the plot that distinguishes the Transvaal's only murder story from almost any other murder story I have ever lighted upon. For it is not two plain-clothes policemen who come walking into the voorkamer, in the early evening, when the murderer is down on his hands and knees putting the final touches to the restoration of the damaged floor. The time for the landdrost's men to arrive is not yet. But a couple of men do enter: only, they carry in bottles. They are followed by a number of girls who carry in the fragrance of romance with a red veld-flower in their hair. Then more men come in with bottles. And then a man with a concertina. And there is much laughter. And more girls. Girls with names like Drieka and Tossie and Francina. It is a surprise party.

Of all things – yes, of all the nights in the year, this man's neighbours had to choose just that particular night for throwing a surprise party in his house.

As I have said, this is the Transvaal's oldest – and, as far as I know, only – murder story. I heard it first as a child. Since then I have heard it many times. So have you, too, I suppose.

Like the one about the ghost in the poort, this is also a very good tale, and where it is particularly admirable, from the narrator's point of view, is that it lends itself to the introduction of an infinite variety of graceful and delicate touches in the psychological unfolding of the later scenes. Here great play can be made of the murderer's character. If he is somebody without much refinement and just says straight out, 'I've buried my wife under the floor, there. This is no time for foolishness like dancing,' – then the story has got to end right there, of course. If he says, on the other hand, 'I'm sorry, my wife went unexpectedly to Potchefstroom,' and then allows the party to go on, trying to be as natural as possible, so as not to awaken unnecessary suspicions, then the subsequent developments offer charming possibilities.

To take, just at random, a single court-house scene.

'And so you danced,' the prosecutor would say to Kittie de Bruyn, one of the girls who was at that party. 'Did it not come as a shock to you afterwards, to think that you danced all night on the head of a dead woman?'

'But I danced lightly,' Kittie de Bruyn would answer, 'oh – lightly.'

It is a situation providing lots of blossomy openings for fragile irony and high drama.

Incidentally, I, too, have told that story before of the woman interred under the floor of the voorkamer. And I have always known that I would have to dig her up again, some time. She was too useful a character to be left lying there, buried under four lines of prose.

The lack of imagination – or, perhaps, meagreness of event – that has bestowed upon the Transvaal only one ghost story and one murder story, does not apply in respect of love stories. The Transvaal has hundreds of love stories, all opulently different. Woven on the common pattern of boy-meets-girl, one love story, in respect of its external shape, seems very much the same as another. And it is always at the very moment when you fancy that you have recognised the type of a love story, when you have pigeon-holed it in your mind as belonging to such-and-such a category – it is at that very moment that you are betrayed; for, lo, there is sudden witchery, and a wand is waved, and it is as though a line of African dancers comes running in suddenly, and you find that a whole number of people are laughing at you from behind the feathers and painted wood of their Congo masks.

One must be careful about classifying a love story, tabulating and cata-

3

loguing it as belonging to a certain sub-section of a particular group – index-
ing it and labelling it as conforming, in respect of characters and plot and
incident, to a well-known and clearly recognised pattern.

Take the love story of Gideon Welman and Alie du Plessis, for instance.
Superficially, it seems to conform to a pretty clearly defined type. A rustic
idyll. The course of true love not running entirely smoothly. A vague sugges-
tion of complications arising from the oldest geometrical symbol used in
romance – the triangle, which is also the shape of the human heart. On the
face of it, this is a simple kind of a tale that you would be able to classify very
easily. And yet, until almost the very end, Gideon Welman himself did not
know what the pattern was into which his own love story fitted.

Gideon Welman and Alie du Plessis were seated under an ox-wagon. It was
evening. A number of Boer families were trekking back to the Bushveld from
the Nagmaal at Zeerust. Next time Gideon Welman and Alie du Plessis would
be on that road they would be travelling down to Zeerust to get married. In a
few months' time they would be spending their honeymoon on that same
road, inside the ox-wagon under which they were at the moment seated. Alie
du Plessis was now half reclining against Gideon Welman, whose arms were
about her. Her fingers were plucking at a tuft of smooth, strong grass. The light
of the campfire flickered on their young faces. They were oblivious of the
people around the fire, who were roasting mealies and telling stories. They
were not, however, oblivious of the Bushveld night.

And it had to happen at that moment, while they were seated under the
wagon, that Alie said something about Rooi Jan Venter.

'There you go again,' Gideon Welman exclaimed. 'Why have you got to
keep on mentioning his name, anyway?'

The point was that Alie du Plessis cared for Gideon Welman, her bride-
groom to be, deeply enough. It was not her fault that her feelings for him were
not on a plane of ecstasy – were not in the nature of a romantic passion. She
did not get a wild thrill at the name 'Welman' – no relation of Gideon's – on
the sign-board of a butcher-shop in Zeerust. She did not flush tremulously
when she saw, outspanned on the kerkplein, a mule-cart whose infirm wheels
proclaimed it to be Gideon's.

Not that Alie du Plessis did not have a very genuine affection for Gideon
Welman, of course. But there you were …

Gideon's face was very white and tense in the flickering gleams of the
campfire.

So Gideon Welman and Alie du Plessis were married in Zeerust. For a while

– as far as the outside world was concerned, at least – they lived together hap-
pily in their little house in the Bushveld, with the newly whitewashed walls
and the roof thatched with what was still that year's grass. And then events
slid into that afternoon on which Gideon Welman was working very fast, and
in a half-daze. He had the queer feeling that he was living in another life,
going through a thing that had happened before, to somebody else, long ago.
It was quite dark by the time a knock came at the door.

And when he got up from the floor quickly, dusting his knees, Gideon
Welman knew what that old Transvaal story was, into whose pattern his own
story had now fitted, also. For the door of the voorkamer opened. And out of
the night came the laughter of girls. And Rooi Jan Venter and another young
man entered the voorkamer, carrying bottles.

Back to the scene

SIX FEET OF THE COUNTRY
Nadine Gordimer

M y wife and I are not real farmers – not even Lerice, really. We bought
our place, ten miles out of Johannesburg on one of the main roads,
to change something in ourselves, I suppose; you seem to rattle about so
much within a marriage like ours. You long to hear nothing but a deep, satisfying silence when you sound a marriage. The farm hasn't managed that for
us, of course, but it has done other things, unexpected, illogical. Lerice, who
I thought would retire there in Chekhovian sadness for a month or two, and
then leave the place to the servants while she tried yet again to get a part she
wanted and become the actress she would like to be, has sunk into the business of running the farm with all the serious intensity with which she once
imbued the shadows in a playwright's mind. I should have given it up long
ago if it had not been for her. Her hands, once small and plain and well-kept
– she was not the sort of actress who wears red paint and diamond rings – are
hard as a dog's pads.

I, of course, am there only in the evenings and at week-ends. I am a part-
ner in a travel agency which is flourishing – needs to be, as I tell Lerice, in
order to carry the farm. Still, though I know we can't afford it, and though
the sweetish smell of the fowls Lerice breeds sickens me, so that I avoid
going past their runs, the farm is beautiful in a way I had almost forgotten –
especially on a Sunday morning when I get up and go out into the paddock
and see not the palm trees and fish pond and imitation-stone bird bath of the
suburbs but white ducks on the dam, the lucerne field brilliant as window-
dresser's grass, and the little, stocky, mean-eyed bull, lustful but bored, having
his face tenderly licked by one of his ladies. Lerice comes out with her hair
uncombed, in her hand a stick dripping with cattle-dip. She will stand and
look dreamily for a moment, the way she would pretend to look sometimes
in those plays. 'They'll mate tomorrow,' she will say. 'This is their second
day. Look how she loves him, my little Napoleon.' So that when people come
out to see us on Sunday afternoon, I am likely to hear myself saying, as I pour
out the drinks, 'When I drive back home from the city every day, past those
rows of suburban houses, I wonder how the devil we ever did stand it . . .
Would you care to look around?' And there I am, taking some pretty girl and
her young husband stumbling down to our river-bank, the girl catching her
stockings on the mealie-stooks and stepping over cow-turds humming with

jewel-green flies while she says, '. . . the *tensions* of the damned city. And you're near enough to get into town to a show, too! I think it's wonderful. Why, you've got it both ways!'

And for a moment I accept the triumph as if I *had* managed it – the impossibility that I've been trying for all my life – just as if the truth was that you could get it 'both ways', instead of finding yourself with not even one way or the other but a third, one you had not provided for at all.

But even in our saner moments, when I find Lerice's earthy enthusiasms just as irritating as I once found her histrionical ones, and she finds what she calls my 'jealousy' of her capacity for enthusiasm as big a proof of my inadequacy for her as a mate as ever it was, we do believe that we have at least honestly escaped those tensions peculiar to the city about which our visitors speak. When Johannesburg people speak of 'tension' they don't mean hurrying people in crowded streets, the struggle for money, or the general competitive character of city life. They mean the guns under the white men's pillows and the burglar bars on the white men's windows. They mean those strange moments on city pavements when a black man won't stand aside for a white man.

Out in the country, even ten miles out, life is better than that. In the country, there is a lingering remnant of the pre-transitional stage; our relationship with the blacks is almost feudal. Wrong, I suppose, obsolete, but more comfortable all round. We have no burglar bars, no gun. Lerice's farm-boys have their wives and their piccanins living with them on the land. They brew their sour beer without the fear of police raids. In fact, we've always rather prided ourselves that the poor devils have nothing much to fear, being with us; Lerice even keeps an eye on their children, with all the competence of a woman who has never had a child of her own, and she certainly doctors them all – children and adults – like babies whenever they happen to be sick.

It was because of this that we were not particularly startled one night last winter when the boy Albert came knocking at our window long after we had gone to bed. I wasn't in our bed but sleeping in the little dressing-room-cum-linen-room next door, because Lerice had annoyed me, and I didn't want to find myself softening towards her simply because of the sweet smell of the talcum powder on her flesh after her bath. She came and woke me up. 'Albert says one of the boys is very sick,' she said. 'I think you'd better go down and see. He wouldn't get us up at this hour for nothing.'

'What time is it?'

'What does it matter?' Lerice is maddeningly logical.

I got up awkwardly as she watched me – how is it I always feel a fool when

I have deserted her bed? After all, I know from the way she never looks at me when she talks to me at breakfast the next day that she is hurt and humiliated at my not wanting her – and I went out, clumsy with sleep.

'Which of the boys is it?' I asked Albert as we followed the dance of my torch.

'He's too sick. Very sick, baas,' he said.

'But who? Franz?' I remembered Franz had had a bad cough for the past week.

Albert did not answer; he had given me the path, and was walking along beside me in the tall dead grass. When the light of the torch caught his face, I saw that he looked acutely embarrassed. 'What's this all about?' I said.

He lowered his head under the glance of the light. 'It's not me, baas. I don't know. Petrus he send me.'

Irritated, I hurried him along to the huts. And there, on Petrus's iron bed-stead, with its brick stilts, was a young man, dead. On his forehead there was still a light, cold sweat; his body was warm. The boys stood around as they do in the kitchen when it is discovered that someone has broken a dish – unco-operative, silent. Somebody's wife hung about in the shadows, her hands wrung together under her apron.

I had not seen a dead man since the war. This was very different. I felt like the others – extraneous, useless.

'What was the matter?' I asked.

The woman patted at her chest and shook her head to indicate the painful impossibility of breathing.

He must have died of pneumonia.

I turned to Petrus. 'Who was this boy? What was he doing here?' The light of a candle on the floor showed that Petrus was weeping. He followed me out the door.

When we were outside, in the dark, I waited for him to speak. But he didn't. 'Now come on, Petrus, you must tell me who this boy was. Was he a friend of yours?'

'He's my brother, baas. He come from Rhodesia to look for work.'

The story startled Lerice and me a little. The young boy had walked down from Rhodesia to look for work in Johannesburg, had caught a chill from sleeping out along the way, and had lain ill in his brother Petrus's hut since his arrival three days before. Our boys had been frightened to ask us for help for him because we had not been intended ever to know of his presence. Rhodesian natives are barred from entering the Union unless they have a permit; the young man was an illegal immigrant. No doubt our boys had managed the whole thing successfully several times before; a number of relatives must have walked the seven or eight hundred miles from poverty to the paradise of zoot suits, police raids, and black slum townships that is their *Egoli*, City of Gold – the African name for Johannesburg. It was merely a matter of getting such a man to lie low on our farm until a job could be found with someone who would be glad to take the risk of prosecution for employing an illegal immigrant in exchange for the services of someone as yet untainted by the city.

Well, this was one who would never get up again.

'You would think they would have felt they could tell *us*,' said Lerice next morning. 'Once the man was ill. You would have thought at least–' When she is getting intense over something, she has a way of standing in the middle of a room as people do when they are shortly to leave on a journey, looking searchingly about her at the most familiar objects as if she had never seen them before. I had noticed that in Petrus's presence in the kitchen, earlier, she had had the air of being almost offended with him, almost hurt.

In any case, I really haven't the time or inclination any more to go into everything in our life that I know Lerice, from those alarmed and pressing eyes of hers, would like us to go into. She is the kind of woman who doesn't mind if she looks plain, or odd; I don't suppose she would even care if she knew how strange she looks when her whole face is out of proportion with urgent uncertainty. I said, 'Now I'm the one who'll have to do all the dirty work, I suppose.'

She was still staring at me, trying me out with those eyes – wasting her time, if she only knew.

'I'll have to notify the health authorities,' I said calmly. 'They can't just cart him off and bury him. After all, we don't really know what he died of.'

She simply stood there, as if she had given up – simply ceased to see me at all.

I don't know when I've been so irritated. 'It might have been something contagious,' I said. 'God knows.' There was no answer.

I am not enamoured of holding conversations with myself. I went out to shout to one of the boys to open the garage and get the car ready for my morning drive to town.

As I had expected, it turned out to be quite a business. I had to notify the police as well as the health authorities, and answer a lot of tedious questions: How was it I was ignorant of the boy's presence? If I did not supervise my native quarters, how did I know that that sort of thing didn't go on all the time? Et cetera, et cetera. And when I flared up and told them that so long as

9

my natives did their work, I didn't think it my right or concern to poke my nose into their private lives, I got from the coarse, dull-witted police sergeant one of those looks that come not from any thinking process going on in the brain but from that faculty common to all who are possessed by the master-race theory – a look of insanely inane certainty. He grinned at me with a mixture of scorn and delight at my stupidity.

Then I had to explain to Petrus why the health authorities had to take away the body for a post-mortem – and, in fact, what a post-mortem was. When I telephoned the health department some days later to find out the result, I was told that the cause of death was, as we had thought, pneumonia, and that the body had been suitably disposed of. I went out to where Petrus was mixing a mash for the fowls and told him that it was all right, there would be no trouble; his brother had died from that pain in his chest. Petrus put down the paraffin tin and said, 'When can we go fetch him, baas?'

'To fetch him?'

'Will the baas please ask them when we must come?'

I went back inside and called Lerice, all over the house. She came down the stairs from the spare bedrooms, and I said, '*Now* what am I going to do? When I told Petrus, he just asked calmly when they could go and fetch the body. They think they're going to bury him themselves.'

'Well, go back and tell him,' said Lerice. 'You must tell him. Why didn't you tell him then?'

When I found Petrus again, he looked up politely. 'Look, Petrus,' I said. 'You can't go to fetch your brother. They've done it already – they've *buried* him, you understand?'

'Where?' he said, slowly, dully, as if he thought that perhaps he was getting this wrong.

'You see, he was a stranger. They knew he wasn't from here, and they didn't know he had some of his people here, so they thought they must bury him.' It was difficult to make a pauper's grave sound like a privilege.

'Please, baas, the baas must ask them.' But he did not mean that he wanted to know the burial-place. He simply ignored the incomprehensible machinery I told him had set to work on his dead brother; he wanted the brother back.

'But Petrus,' I said, 'how can I? Your brother is buried already. I can't ask them now.'

'Oh baas!' he said. He stood with his bran-smeared hands uncurled at his sides, one corner of his mouth twitching.

'Good God, Petrus, they won't listen to me! They can't, anyway. I'm sorry, but I can't do it. You understand?'

He just kept on looking at me, out of his knowledge that white men have everything, can do anything; if they don't, it is because they won't.

And then, at dinner, Lerice started. 'You could at least phone,' she said.

'*Christ*, what d'you think I am? Am I supposed to bring the dead back to life?'

But I could not exaggerate my way out of this ridiculous responsibility that had been thrust on me. 'Phone them up,' she went on. 'And at least you'll be able to tell him you've done it and they've explained that it's impossible.'

She disappeared somewhere into the kitchen quarters after coffee. A little later she came back to tell me, 'The old father's coming down from Rhodesia to be at the funeral. He's got a permit and he's already on his way.'

Unfortunately, it was not impossible to get the body back. The authorities said that it was somewhat irregular, but that since the hygiene conditions had been fulfilled, they could not refuse permission for exhumation. I found out that, with the undertaker's charges, it would cost twenty pounds. Ah, I thought, that settles it. On five pounds a month, Petrus won't have twenty pounds – and just as well, since it couldn't do the dead any good. Certainly I should not offer it to him myself. Twenty pounds – or anything else within reason, for that matter – I would have spent without grudging it on doctors or medicines that might have helped the boy when he was alive. Once he was dead, I had no intention of encouraging Petrus to throw away, on a gesture, more than he spent to clothe his whole family in a year.

When I told him, in the kitchen that night, he said 'Twenty pounds?'

I said, 'Yes, that's right, twenty pounds.'

For a moment, I had the feeling, from the look on his face, that he was calculating. But when he spoke again I thought I must have imagined it. 'We must pay twenty pounds!' he said in the faraway voice in which a person speaks of something so unattainable that it does not bear thinking about.

'All right, Petrus,' I said in dismissal, and went back to the living-room.

The next morning before I went to town, Petrus asked to see me. 'Please baas,' he said, awkwardly handing me a bundle of notes. They're so seldom on the giving rather than the receiving side, poor devils, that they don't really know how to hand money to a white man. There it was, the twenty pounds, in ones and halves, some creased and folded until they were soft as dirty rags, others smooth and fairly new – Franz's money, I suppose, and Albert's, and Dora the cook's, and Jacob the gardener's, and God knows who else's besides, from all the farms and small holdings round about. I took it in irritation more than in astonishment, really – irritation at the waste, the uselessness of this sacrifice by people so poor. Just like the poor everywhere, I

11

thought, who stint themselves the decencies of life in order to insure themselves the decencies of death. So incomprehensible to people like Lerice and me, who regard life as something to be spent extravagantly and, if we think about death at all, regard it as the final bankruptcy.

The farm-hands don't work on Saturday afternoon anyway, so it was a good day for the funeral. Petrus and his father had borrowed our donkey-cart to fetch the coffin from the city, where, Petrus told Lerice on their return, everything was 'nice' – the coffin waiting for them, already sealed up to save them from what must have been a rather unpleasant sight after two weeks' interment. (It had taken all that time for the authorities and the undertaker to make the final arrangements for moving the body.) All morning, the coffin lay in Petrus's hut, awaiting the trip to the little old burial ground, just outside the eastern boundary of our farm, that was a relic of the days when this was a real farming district rather than a fashionable rural estate. It was pure chance that I happened to be down there near the fence when the procession came past; once again Lerice had forgotten her promise to me and had made the house uninhabitable on a Saturday afternoon. I had come home and been infuriated to find her in a pair of filthy old slacks and with her hair uncombed since the night before, having all the varnish scraped from the living-room floor, if you please. So I had taken my No. 8 iron and gone off to practise my approach shots. In my annoyance, I had forgotten about the funeral, and was reminded only when I saw the procession coming up the path along the outside of the fence towards me; from where I was standing, you can see the graves quite clearly, and that day the sun glinted on bits of broken pottery, a lopsided homemade cross, and jam-jars brown with rainwater and dead flowers.

I felt a little awkward, and did not know whether to go on hitting my golf ball or stop at least until the whole gathering was decently past. The donkey-cart creaks and screeches with every revolution of the wheels and it came along in a slow, halting fashion somehow peculiarly suited to the two donkeys who drew it, their little potbellies rubbed and rough, their heads sunk between the shafts, and their ears flattened back with an air submissive and downcast; peculiarly suited, too, to the group of men and women who came along slowly behind. The patient ass. Watching, I thought, you can see now why the creature became a Biblical symbol. Then the procession drew level with me and stopped, so I had to put down my club. The coffin was taken down off the cart – it was a shiny, yellow-varnished wood, like cheap furniture – and the donkeys twitched their ears against the flies. Petrus, Franz, Albert and the old father from Rhodesia hoisted it on their shoulders and the procession moved on, on foot. It was really a very awkward moment. I stood there rather foolishly at the fence, quite still, and slowly they filed past, not looking up, the four men bent beneath the shiny wooden box, and the straggling troop of mourners. All of them were servants or neighbours' servants whom I knew as casual, easygoing gossipers about our lands or kitchen. I heard the old man's breathing.

I had just bent to pick up my club again when there was a sort of jar in the flowing solemnity of their processional mood; I felt it at once, like a wave of heat along the air, or one of those sudden currents of cold catching at your legs in a placid stream. The old man's voice was muttering something; the people had stopped, confused, and they bumped into one another, some pressing to go on, others hissing at them to be still. I could see that they were embarrassed, but they could not ignore the voice; it was much the way that the mumblings of a prophet, though not clear at first, arrest the mind. The corner of the coffin the old man carried was sagging at an angle; he seemed to be trying to get out from under the weight of it. Now Petrus expostulated with him.

The little boy who had been left to watch the donkeys dropped the reins and ran to see. I don't know why – unless it was for the same reason people crowd round someone who has fainted in a cinema – but I parted the wires of the fence and went through, after him.

Petrus lifted his eyes to me – to anybody – with distress and horror. The old man from Rhodesia had let go of the coffin entirely, and the three others, unable to support it on their own, had laid it on the ground, in the pathway. Already there was a film of dust lightly wavering up its shiny sides. I did not understand what the old man was saying; I hesitated to interfere. But now the whole seething group turned on my silence. The old man himself came over to me, with his hands outspread and shaking, and spoke directly to me, saying something that I could tell from the tone, without understanding the words, was shocking and extraordinary.

'What is it, Petrus? What's wrong?' I appealed.

Petrus threw up his hands, bowed his head in a series of hysterical shakes, then thrust his face up at me suddenly.

'He says, "My son was not so heavy".'

Silence. I could hear the old man breathing; he kept his mouth a little open, as old people do.

'My son was young and thin,' he said, at last, in English.

Again silence. Then babble broke out. The old man thundered against everybody; his teeth were yellowed and few, and he had one of those fine, grizzled, sweeping moustaches that one doesn't often see nowadays, which

13

must have been grown in emulation of early Empire-builders. It seemed to frame all his utterances with a special validity, perhaps merely because it was the symbol of the traditional wisdom of age – an idea so fearfully rooted that it carries still something awesome beyond reason. He shocked them; they thought he was mad, but they had to listen to him. With his own hands he began to prise the lid off the coffin and three of the men came forward to help him. Then he sat down on the ground; very old, very weak, and unable to speak, he merely lifted a trembling hand toward what was there. He abdicated, he handed it over to them; he was no good any more.

They crowded round to look (and so did I), and now they forgot the nature of this surprise and the occasion of grief to which it belonged, and for a few minutes were carried up in the astonishment of the surprise itself. They gasped and flared noisily with excitement. I even noticed the little boy who had held the donkeys jumping up and down, almost weeping with rage because the backs of the grown-ups crowded him out of his view.

In the coffin was someone no one had ever seen before: a heavily built, rather light-skinned native with a neatly stitched scar on his forehead – perhaps from a blow in a brawl that had also dealt him some other, slower-working injury which had killed him.

I wrangled with the authorities for a week over that body. I had the feeling that they were shocked, in a laconic fashion, by their own mistake, but that in the confusion of their anonymous dead they were helpless to put it right. They said to me, 'We are trying to find out,' and 'We are still making enquiries.' It was as if at any moment they might conduct me into their mortuary and say, 'There! Lift up the sheets; look for him – your poultry boy's brother. There are so many black faces – surely one will do?'

And every evening when I got home Petrus was waiting in the kitchen. 'Well, they're trying. They're still looking. The baas is seeing to it for you, Petrus,' I would tell him. 'God, half the time I should be in the office I'm driving around the back end of town chasing after this affair,' I added aside, to Lerice, one night.

She and Petrus both kept their eyes turned on me as I spoke, and, oddly, for those moments they looked exactly alike, though it sounds impossible: my wife, with her high, white forehead and her attenuated Englishwoman's body, and the poultry boy, with his horny bare feet below khaki trousers tied at the knee with string and the peculiar rankness of his nervous sweat coming from his skin.

'What makes you so indignant, so determined about this now?' said Lerice suddenly.

14

I stared at her. 'It's a matter of principle. Why should they get away with a swindle? It's time these officials had a jolt from someone who'll bother to take the trouble.'

She said, 'Oh.' And as Petrus slowly opened the kitchen door to leave, sensing that the talk had gone beyond him, she turned away, too.

I continued to pass on assurances to Petrus every evening, but although what I said was the same, and the voice in which I said it was the same, every evening it sounded weaker. At last, it became clear that we would never get Petrus's brother back, because nobody really knew where he was. Somewhere in a graveyard as uniform as a housing scheme, somewhere under a number that didn't belong to him, or in the medical school, perhaps, laboriously reduced to layers of muscles and strings of nerves? Goodness knows. He had no identity in this world anyway.

It was only then, and in a voice of shame, that Petrus asked me to try and get the money back.

'From the way he asks, you'd think he was robbing his dead brother,' I said to Lerice later. But as I've said, Lerice had got so intense about this business that she couldn't even appreciate a little ironic smile.

I tried to get the money; Lerice tried. We both telephoned and wrote and argued, but nothing came of it. It appeared that the main expense had been the undertaker, and, after all, he had done his job. So the whole thing was a complete waste, even more of a waste for the poor devils than I had thought it would be.

The old man from Rhodesia was about Lerice's father's size, so she gave him one of her father's old suits, and he went back home rather better off, for the winter, than he had come.

RAIN
Richard Rive

R ain pouring down and blotting out all sound with its sharp and vibrant tattoo. Dripping neon signs reflecting lurid reds and yellows in mirror-wet streets. Swollen gutters. Water overflowing and squelching onto pavements. Gurgling and sucking at storm-water drains. Table Mountain cut off by a grey film of mist and rain. A lost City Hall clock trying manfully to chime nine over an indifferent Cape Town. Baleful reverberations through a spluttering all-consuming drizzle.

Yellow light filtering through from Solly's 'Grand Fish and Chips Palace'. Door tightshut against the weather. Inside stuffy with heat, hot bodies, steaming clothes, and the nauseating smell of stale fish oil. Misty patterns on the plate-glass windows and a messy pool where rain has filtered beneath the door and mixed with the sawdust.

Solly himself in shirt sleeves and apron, sweating, vulgar and moody. Bellowing at a dripping woman who has just come in.

'Shut 'e damn door. You live in a tent?'

'Ag, Solly.'

'Don't ag me. You coloured people never shut blarry doors.'

'Don't you bloomingwell swear at me!'

'I bloomingwell swear at you, yes.'

'Come. Gimme two pieces o' fish. Tail cut.'

'Two pieces o' fish.'

'Raining like hell outside,' the woman said to no one.

'Mmmmmm. Raining like hell,' a thin befezzed Muslim cut in.

'One an' six. Thank you. An' close 'e door behin' you.'

'Thanks. Think you got 'e on'y door in Hanover Street?'

'Go to hell!' Solly cut the interchange short and turned to another customer.

The north-wester sobbed heavy rain squalls against the windowpanes. The Hanover Street bus screeched to a slithery stop and passengers darted for shelter in a cinema entrance. The street lamps shone blurredly.

Solly sweated as he wrapped parcels of fish and chips in a newspaper. Fish and chips. Vinegar? Wrap. One an' six please. Thank you! Next. Fish an' chips. No? Two fish. No chips? Salt? Vinegar? One an' six please. Thank you! Next. Fish an' chips?

'Close 'e blarry door!' Solly glared at a woman who had just come in. She half-smiled apologetically at him.

'You also live in a blarry tent?'

She struggled with the door and then stood dripping in a pool of wet sawdust. Solly left the counter to add two logs to the furnace. She moved out of the way. Another customer showed indignation at Solly's remarks.

'Fish an' chips. Vinegar? Salt? One an' six. Thank you. Yes, madam?'

'Could you tell me when the bioscope comes out?'

'Am I the blooming manager?'

'Please.'

'Half pas' ten, tonight,' the Muslim offered helpfully.

'Thank you. Can I stay here till then? It's raining outside.'

'I know it's blarrywell raining, but this is not a Salvation Army.'

'Please, baas!'

This caught Solly unaware. He had had his shop in that corner of Hanover Street since most could remember and had been called a great many unsavoury things in the years. Solly didn't mind. But this caught him unaware. Please, baas. This felt good. His imagination adjusted a black bow-tie to an evening suit. Please, baas.

'O.K. You stay for a short while. But when 'e rain stops you go!'

She nodded dumbly and tried to make out the blurred name of the cinema opposite, through the misted window.

'Waiting fer somebody?' Solly asked. No response.

'I ask if yer waiting fer somebody?' The figure continued to stare. 'Oh, go to hell,' said Solly, turning to another customer.

Through the rain blur Siena stared at nothing in particular. Dim visions of slippery wet cars. Honking and wheezing in the rain. Spluttering buses. Heavy, drowsy voices in the Grand Fish and Chips Palace. Her eyes travelled beyond the street and the water cascades of Table Mountain, beyond the winter of Cape Town to the summer of the Boland. Past the green grapelands of Stellenbosch and Paarl and the stuffy wheat district of Malmesbury to the lazy sun and laughter of Teslaarsdal.

Inside the gabled nineteenth-century mission church she had first met Joseph. The church is quiet and beautiful and the ivy climbs over it and makes it more beautiful. Huge silver oil lamps suspended from the roof, polished and shining. It was in the flicker of the lamps that she had first become aware of him. He was visiting from Cape Town. She sang that night as she had never sung before.

'Al ging ik ook in een dal der schaduw des doods . . .' Though I walk through the valley of the shadow of death . . . 'der schaduw des doods.'

And then he had looked at her. She felt as if everyone was looking at her. 'Ik zoude geen kwaad vreezen . . .' I will fear no evil. And she had not feared but loved. Had loved him. Had sung for him. For the wide eyes, the yellow skin, the high cheekbones. She had sung for a creator who could create a man like Joseph. 'Want gij zijt met mij; Uw stok en Uw staf, die vertroosten mij.'

Those were black-and-white polka-dot nights when the moon did a golliwog cakewalk across a banjo-strung sky. Nights of sweet remembrances when he had whispered love to her and told her of Cape Town. She had giggled coyly at his obscenities. It was fashionable, she hoped, to giggle coyly at obscenities. He lived in one of those streets off District Six, it sounded like Horsburg Lane, and was, he boasted, quite a one with the girls. She heard of Molly and Miena and Sophia and a sophisticated Charmaine who was almost a schoolteacher and always spoke English. But he told her that he had only found love in Teslaarsdal. She wasn't sure whether to believe him. And then he felt her richness, and the moon darted behind a cloud.

The loud screeching of the train to Cape Town. Screeching loud enough to,drown the protests of her family. The wrath of her father. The icy stares of Teslaarsdal matrons. Loud and confused screechings to drown her hysteria, her ecstasy. Drowned and confused in the roar of a thousand cars and a hundred thousand lights and a summer of carnival evenings that are Cape Town.

And the agony of the nights when he came home later and later and sometimes not at all. The waning of his passion and whispered names of others. Molly and Miena and Sophia, Charmaine. The helpless knowledge that he was slipping from her. Faster and faster. Gathering momentum.

Not that I'm saying so but I only heard. Why don't you go to bioscope one night and see for yourself? Marian's man is searching for Joseph. Searching for Joseph. Looking for Joseph. Knifing for Joseph. Joseph. Joseph! Joseph! Molly! Miena! Sophia! Names! Names! Names! Gossip. One-sided desire. Go to bioscope and see. See what? See why? When? Where?

And after he had been away a week she decided to see. Decided to go through the rain and stand in a sweating fish-and-chips shop owned by a blaspheming and vulgar man. And wait for the cinema to come out.

The rain had stopped sobbing against the plate-glass window. A skin-soaking drizzle now set in. Continuous. Unending. Filming everything with dark depression. A shivering, weeping neon sign flickering convulsively on and off. A tired Solly shooting a quick glance at a cheap alarm clock.

'Half pas' ten, bioscope out soon.'

Siena looked more intently through the misty screen. No movement whatsoever in the deserted cinema foyer.

'Time it was bloomingwell out.' Solly braced himself for the wave of after-show customers who would invade the Palace.

'Comin' out late tonight, missus.'

'Thank you, baas.'

Solly rubbed sweat out of his eyes and took in her neat and plain figure. Tired face but good legs. A few late stragglers catching colds in the streets. Wet and squally outside.

'Your man in bioscope?'

She was intent on a khaki-uniformed usher struggling to open the door.

'Man in bioscope, missus?'

The cinema had to come out some time or other. An usher opening the door. Adjusting the outside gate. Preparing for the crowds to pour out. To vomit and spill out.

'Man in bioscope?'

No response.

'Oh, go to hell!'

They would be out now. Joseph would be out. She rushed for the door, throwing words of thanks to Solly.

'Close 'e blarry door!'

She never heard him. The drizzle had stopped. An unnatural calm hung over the empty foyer, over the deserted street. She took up her stand on the bottom step. Expectantly. Her heart pounding.

Then they came. Pouring, laughing, pushing, jostling. She stared with fierce intensity, but faces passed too fast. Laughing, roaring, gay. Wide-eyed, yellow-skinned, high-cheekboned. Black, brown, ivory, yellow. Black-eyed, laughing-eyed, bouncing. No Joseph. Palpitating heart that felt like bursting into a thousand pieces. If she should miss him. She found herself searching for the wrong face. Solly's face. Ridiculously searching for hard blue eyes and a sharp white chin in a sea of ebony and brown. Solly's face. Missing half a hundred faces and then again searching for the familiar high cheekbones. Solly. Joseph. Molly. Miena. Charmaine.

The drizzle resumed. Studying overcoats instead of faces. Longing for the pale-blue shirt she had seen in the shop at Solitaire. A bargain for one pound five shillings. She had scraped and scrounged to buy it for him. A week's wages. Collecting her thoughts and continuing the search for Joseph. And then the thinning out of the crowd and the last few stragglers. The ushers shutting the iron gate. They might be shutting Joseph in. Herself out. Only ushers left.

'Please, is Joseph inside?'

'Who's Joseph?'

'Is Joseph still inside?'

'Joseph who?'

They were teasing her. Laughing behind her back. Preventing her from finding him.

'Joseph is inside!' she shouted frenziedly.

'Look, it's raining cats and dogs. Go home.'

Go home. To whom. To what? An empty room? An empty bed? And then she was aware of the crowd on the corner. Maybe he was there. Running and peering into every face. Joseph. The crowd in the drizzle. Two battling figures. Joseph. Figures locked in struggle slithering in the wet gutter. Muck streaking down clothes through which wet bodies were silhouetted. Joseph. A blue shirt. And then she wiped the rain out of her eyes and saw him. Fighting for his life. Desperately kicking in the gutter. Joseph. The blast of a police whistle. A pick-up van screeching to a stop.

'Please, sir, it wasn't him. They all ran away. Please, sir, he's Joseph. He done nothing. He done nothing, my baas. Please, sir, he's my Joseph. Please, baas!'

'Maak dat jy wegkom. Get away. Voetsak!'

'Please, sir, it wasn't him. They ran away!'

Solly's Grand Fish and Chips Palace crowded out. People milling inside. Rain once more squalling and sobbing against the door and windows. Swollen gutters unable to cope with the giddy rush of water. Solly sweating to deal with the after-cinema rush.

Fish an' chips. Vinegar? Salt? One an' six. Thank you. Sorry, no fish yet. Wait five minutes. Chips on'y. Vinegar? Ninepence. Tickey change. Thank you. Sorry, no fish. Five minutes time. Chips? Ninepence. Thank you. Solly paused for breath and stirred the fish.

'What's 'e trouble outside?'

'Real bioscope, Solly.'

'No man, outside!'

'I say, real bioscope.'

'What were 'e police doing? Sorry, no fish yet, sir. Five minutes time. What were 'e police doin'?'

'A fight in 'e blooming rain.'

'Jesus, in 'e rain.'

'Ja.'

'Who was fighting?'

'Joseph an' somebody.'

'Joseph?'

'Ja, fellow in Horsburg Lane.'

'Yes, I know Joseph. Always in trouble. Chucked him outta here a'reddy.'
'Well, that chap.'
'An' who?'
'Dinno.'
'Police got them?'
'Got Joseph.'
'Why were 'ey fighting? Fish in a minute sir.'
'Over a dame.'
'Who?'
'You know Marian who works by Patel? Now she. Her boyfriend caught 'em.'
'In bioscope?'
'Ja.'
Solly chuckled suggestively.
'See that woman an' 'e police.'
'What woman?' Solly asked.
'One crying to 'e police. They say it's Joseph's girl from 'e country.'
'Joseph always got plenty dames from 'e town an' country. F-I-S-H R-E-A-D-Y! Two pieces for you, sir? One an' six. Shilling change. Fish an' chips? One an' six. Thank you. Fish on'y? Vinegar? Salt? Ninepence. Tickey change. Thank you! What you say about 'e woman?'
'They say Joseph's girl was crying to 'e police.'
'Oh, he got plenty o' girls.'
'This one was living with him.'
'Oh, what she look like? Fish, sir?'
'Like 'e country. O.K. Nice legs.'
'Hmmmmm,' said Solly. 'Hey, close 'e damn door. Oh, you again.' Siena came in. A momentary silence. Then a buzzing and whispering.
'Oh,' said Solly, nodding as someone whispered over the counter to him. 'I see. She was waiting here. Musta been waiting for him.'
A young girl in jeans giggled.
'Fish an' chips costs one an' six, madam.'
'Wasn't it one an' three before?'
'Before the Boer War, madam. Price of fish go up. Potatoes go up an' you expect me to charge one an' three?'
'Why not?'
'Oh, go to hell! Next please!'
'Yes, that's 'e one, Solly.'
'Mmmmm. Excuse me, madam,' – turning to Siena – 'like some fish an' chips? Free of charge, never min' 'e money.'

'Thank you, my baas.'

The rain now sobbed wildly as the shop emptied, and Solly counted the cash in his till. Thousands of watery horses charging down the street. Rain drilling into cobbles and pavings. Miniature waterfalls down the sides of buildings. Blurred lights through unending streams. Siena listlessly holding the newspaper parcel of fish and chips.

'You can stay here till it clears up,' said Solly.

She looked up tearfully.

Solly grinned showing his yellow teeth. 'It's O.K.'

A smile flickered across her face for a second.

'It's quite O.K. by me.'

She looked down and hesitated for a moment. Then she struggled against the door. It yielded with a crash and the north-wester howled into Solly's Palace.

'Close 'e blarry door!' he said grinning.

'Thank you, my baas,' she said as she shivered out into the rain.

MRS PLUM
Es'kia Mphahlele

M y madam's name was Mrs Plum. She loved dogs and Africans and said that everyone must follow the law even if it hurt. These were three big things in Madam's life.

I came to work for Mrs Plum in Greenside, not very far from the centre of Johannesburg, after leaving two white families. The first white people I worked for as a cook and laundry woman were a man and his wife in Parktown North. They drank too much and always forgot to pay me. After five months I said to myself No. I am going to leave these drunks. So that was it. That day I was as angry as a red-hot iron when it meets water. The second house I cooked and washed for had five children who were badly brought up. This was in Belgravia. Many times they called me You Black Girl and I kept quiet. Because their mother heard them and said nothing. Also I was only new from Phokeng my home, far away near Rustenburg. I wanted to learn and know the white people before I knew how far to go with the others I would work for afterwards. The thing that drove me mad and made me pack and go was a man who came to visit them often. They said he was a cousin or something like that. He came to the kitchen many times and tried to make me laugh. He patted me on the buttocks. I told the master. The man did it again and I asked the madam that very day to give me my money and let me go.

These were the first nine months after I had left Phokeng to work in Johannesburg. There were many of us girls and young women from Phokeng, from Zeerust, from Shuping, from Kosten, and many other places who came to work in the cities. So the suburbs were full of blackness. Most of us had already passed Standard Six and so we learned more English where we worked. None of us liked to work for white farmers, because we know too much about them on the farms near our homes. They do not pay well and they are cruel people.

At Easter time so many of us went home for a long weekend to see our people and to eat chicken and sour milk and *morogo* – wild spinach. We also took home sugar and condensed milk and tea and coffee and sweets and custard powder and tinned foods.

It was a home-girl of mine, Chimane, who called me to take a job in Mrs Plum's house, just next door to where she worked. This is the third year now. I have been quite happy with Mrs Plum and her daughter Kate. By this I mean that my place as a servant in Greenside is not as bad as that of many others. Chimane too does not complain much. We are paid six pounds a month with free food and free servant's room. No one can ever say that they are well paid, so we go on complaining somehow. Whenever we meet on Thursday afternoons, which is time-off for all of us black women in the suburbs, we talk and talk and talk: about our people at home and their letters; about their illnesses; about bad crops; about a sister who wanted a school uniform and books and school fees; about some of our madams and masters who are good, or stingy with money or food, or stupid or full of nonsense, or who kill themselves and each other, or who are dirty – and so many things I cannot count them all.

Thursday afternoons we go to town to look at the shops, to attend a women's club, to see our boyfriends, to go to bioscope some of us. We turn up smart, to show others the clothes we bought from the black men who sell soft goods to servants in the suburbs. We take a number of things and they come round every month for a bit of money until we finish paying. Then we dress the way of many white madams and girls. I think we look really smart. Sometimes we catch the eyes of a white woman looking at us and we laugh and laugh and laugh until we nearly drop on the ground because we feel good inside ourselves.

II

What did the girl next door call you? Mrs Plum asked me the first day I came to her. Jane, I replied. Was there not an African name? I said yes, Karabo. All right, Madam said. We'll call you Karabo, she said. She spoke as if she knew a name is a big thing. I knew so many whites who did not care what they called black people as long as it was all right for their tongue. This pleased me, I mean Mrs Plum's use of *Karabo*; because the only time I heard the name was when I was at home or when my friends spoke to me. Then she showed me what to do: meals, meal times, washing, and where all the things were that I was going to use.

My daughter will be here in the evening, Madam said. She is at school. When the daughter came, she added, she would tell me some of the things she wanted me to do for her every day.

Chimane, my friend next door, had told me about the daughter Kate, how wild she seemed to be, and about Mr Plum who had killed himself with a gun in a house down the street. They had left the house and come to this one.

Madam is a tall woman. Not slender, not fat. She moves slowly, and speaks slowly. Her face looks very wise, her forehead seems to tell me she has a strong liver: she is not afraid of anything. Her eyes are always swollen at the lower eyelids like a white person who has not slept for many many nights or like a large frog. Perhaps it is because she smokes too much, like wet wood that will not know whether to go up in flames or stop burning. She looks me straight in the eyes when she talks to me, and I know she does this with other people too. At first this made me fear her, now I am used to her. She is not a lazy woman, and she does many things outside, in the city and in the suburbs.

This was the first thing her daughter Kate told me when she came and we met. Don't mind Mother, Kate told me, she is sometimes mad with people for very small things. She will soon be all right and speak nicely to you again.

Kate, I like her very much, and she likes me too. She tells me many things a white woman does not tell a black servant. I mean things about what she likes and does not like, what her mother does or does not do, all these. At first I was unhappy and wanted to stop her, but now I do not mind.

Kate looks very much like her mother in the face. I think her shoulders will be just as round and strong-looking. She moves faster than Madam. I asked her why she was still at school when she was so big. She laughed Then she tried to tell me that the school where she went was for big people, who had finished with lower school. She was learning big things about cooking and food. She can explain better, me I cannot. She came home on weekends.

Since I came to work for Mrs Plum Kate has been teaching me plenty of cooking. I first learned from her and Madam the word *recipes*. When Kate was at the big school, Madam taught me how to read cookery books. I went on very slowly at first, slower than an ox-wagon. Now I know more. When Kate came home, she found I had read the recipe she left me. So we just cooked straightaway. Kate thinks I am fit to cook in a hotel. Madam thinks so too. Never never! I thought. Cooking in a hotel is like feeding oxen. No one can say thank you to you. After a few months I could cook the Sunday lunch and later I could cook specials for Madam's or Kate's guests.

Madam did not only teach me cooking. She taught me how to look after guests. She praised me when I did very well; not like the white people I had worked for before. I do not know what runs crooked in the heads of other people. Madam also had classes in the evenings for servants to teach them how to read and write. She and two other women in Greenside taught in a church hall.

As I say, Kate tells me plenty of things about Madam. She says to me she says, My mother goes to meetings many times. I ask her I say, What for? She says to me she says, For your people. I ask her I say, My people are in Phokeng far away. They have got mouths, I say. Why does she want to say something for them? Does she know what my mother and what my father want to say? They can speak when they want to. Kate raises her shoulders and drops them and says, How can I tell you, Karabo? I don't say your people – your family only. I mean all the black people in this country. I say, Oh! What do the black people want to say? Again she raises her shoulders and drops them, taking a deep breath.

I ask her I say, With whom is she in the meetings?

She says, With other people who think like her.

I ask her I say, Do you say there are people in the world who think the same things?

She nods her head.

I ask, What things?

So that a few of your people should one day be among those who rule this country, get more money for what they do for the white man, and – what did Kate say again? Yes, that Madam and those who think like her also wanted my people who have been to school to choose those who must speak for them in the – I think she said it looks like a *kgotla* at home who rule the villages.

I say to Kate I say, Oh I see now. I say, Tell me Kate why is Madam always writing on the machine, all the time everyday nearly?

She replies she says, Oh my mother is writing books.

I ask, You mean a book like those? – pointing at the books on the shelves.

Yes, Kate says.

And she told me how Madam wrote books and other things for newspapers and she wrote for the newspapers and magazines to say things for the black people who should be treated well, be paid more money, for the black people who can read and write many things to choose those who want to speak for them.

Kate also told me she said, My mother and other women who think like her put on black belts over their shoulders when they are sad and they want to show the white government they do not like the things being done by whites to blacks. My mother and the others go and stand where the people in government are going to enter or go out of a building.

I ask her I say, Does the government and the white people listen and stop their sins? She says, No, but my mother is in another group of white people.

I ask, Do the people of the government give the women tea and cakes? Kate says, Karabo, how stupid! Oh!

I say to her I say, Among my people if someone comes and stands in front of my house I tell him to come in and I give him food. You white people are wonderful. But they keep standing there and the government people do not give them anything.

She replies, You mean strange. How many times have I taught you not to say *wonderful* when you mean *strange*! Well, Kate says with a short heart and looking cross and she shouts, Well they do not stand there the whole day to ask for tea and cakes, stupid. Oh dear!

Always when Madam finished to read her newspapers she gave them to me to read to help me speak and write better English. When I had read she asked me to tell her some of the things in it. In this way, I did better and better and my mind was opening and opening and I was learning and learning many things about the black people inside and outside the towns which I did not know in the least. When I found words that were too difficult or I did not understand some of the things I asked Madam. She always told me, You see this, you see that, eh? with a heart that can carry on a long way. Yes, Madam writes many letters to the papers. She is always sore about the way the white police beat up black people; about the way black people who work for whites are made to sit at the Zoo Lake with their hearts hanging, because the white people say our people are making noise on Sunday afternoon when they want to rest in their houses and gardens; about many ugly things that happen when some white people meet a black man on the pavement or street. So Madam writes to the papers to let others know, to ask the government to be kind to us.

In the first year Mrs Plum wanted me to eat at table with her. It was very hard, one because I was not used to eating at table with a fork and knife, two because I heard of no other kitchen worker who was handled like this. I was afraid. Afraid of everybody, of Madam's guests if they found me doing this. Madam said I must not be silly. I must show that African servants can also eat at table. Number three, I could not eat some of the things I loved very much: mealie-meal porridge with sour milk or *morogo*, stamped mealies mixed with butter beans, sour porridge for breakfast and other things. Also, except for morning porridge, our food is nice when you eat with the hand. So nice that it does not stop in the mouth or the throat to greet anyone before it passes smoothly down.

We often had lunch together with Chimane next door and our garden boy – Ha! I must remember never to say *boy* again when I talk about a man. This makes me think of a day during the first few weeks in Mrs Plum's house. I was talking about Dick her garden man and I said 'garden boy'. And she says to me she says, Stop talking about a 'boy', Karabo. Now listen here, she says, You Africans must learn to speak properly about each other. And she says, White people won't talk kindly about you if you look down upon each other.

I say to her I say, Madam, I learned the word from the white people I worked for, and all the kitchen maids say 'boy'.

She replies she says to me, Those are white people who know nothing, just low-class whites. I say to her I say, I thought white people know everything.

She said, You'll learn my girl and you must start in this house, hear? She left me thinking, my mind mixed up.

I learned. I grew up.

III

If any woman or girl does not know the Black Crow Club in Bree Street, she does not know anything. I think nearly everything takes place inside and outside that house. It is just where the dirty part of the city begins, with factories and the market. After the market is the place where Indians and Coloured people live. It is also at the Black Crow that the buses turn round and go back to the black townships. Noise, noise, noise all the time. There are women who sell hot sweet potatoes and fruit and monkey nuts and boiled eggs in the winter, boiled mealies and the other things in the summer, all these on the pavements. The streets are always full of potato and fruit skins and monkey nut shells. There is always a strong smell of roast pork. I think it is because of Piel's cold storage down Bree Street.

Madam said she knew the black people who work in the Black Crow. She was happy that I was spending my afternoon on Thursdays in such a club. You will learn sewing, knitting, she said, and other things that you like. Do you like to dance? I told her I said, Yes, I want to learn. She paid the two shillings fee for me each month.

We waited on the first floor, we the ones who were learning sewing; waiting for the teacher. We talked and laughed about madams and masters, and their children and their dogs and birds and whispered about our boyfriends.

Sies! My madam you do not know – *mojuta oa'nete* – a real miser ...

Jo – jo – jo! you should see our new dog. A big thing like this. People! Big in a foolish way ...

What! Me, I take a master's bitch by the leg, me, and throw it away so that it keeps howling, *tjwe – tjwe*! *ngo – wu ngo – wu*! I don't play about with them, me ...

Shame, poor thing! God sees you, true ...!

They wanted me to take their dog out for a walk every afternoon and I told them I said, It is not my work in other houses the garden man does it. I just said to myself I said, They can go to the chickens. Let them bite their elbow before I take out a dog, I am not so mad yet ...

Hei! It is not like the child of my white people who keeps a big white rat and you know what? He puts it on his bed when he goes to school. And let the blankets just begin to smell of urine and all the nonsense and they tell me to wash them. *Hei*, people!

Did you hear about Rebone, people? Her madam put her out because her master was always tapping her buttocks with his fingers. And yesterday the madam saw the master press Rebone against himself ...

Jo – jo – jo! people ...!

Dirty white man!

No, not dirty. The madam smells too old for him.

Hei! Go and wash your mouth with soap, this girl's mouth is dirty ...

Jo, Rebone, daughter of the people! We must help her to find a job before she thinks of going back home.

The teacher came. A woman with strong legs, a strong face, and kind eyes. She had short hair and dressed in a simple but lovely floral frock. She stood well on her legs and hips. She had a black mark between the two top front teeth. She smiled as if we were her children. Our group began with games, and then Lilian Ngoyi took us for sewing. After this she gave a brief talk to all of us from the different classes.

I can never forget the things this woman said and how she put them to us. She told us that the time had passed for black girls and women in the suburbs to be satisfied with working, sending money to our people and going to see them once a year. We were to learn, she said, that the world would never be safe for black people until they were in the government with the power to make laws. The power should be given by the Africans who were more than the whites.

We asked her questions and she answered them with wisdom. I shall put some of them down in my own words as I remember them.

Shall we take the place of the white people in the government?

Some yes. But we shall be more than they as we are more in the country. But also the people of all colours will come together and there are good white men we can choose and there are Africans some white people will choose to be in the government.

There are good madams and masters and bad ones. Should we take the good ones for friends?

A master and a servant can never be friends. Never, so put that out of your head, will you. You are not even sure if the ones you say are good are not like that because they cannot breathe or live without the work of your hands. As long as you need their money, face them with respect. But you must know that many sad things are happening in our country and you, all of you, must always be learning, adding to what you already know, and obey us when we ask you to help us.

29

At other times Lilian Ngoyi told us she said, Remember your poor people at home and the way in which the whites are moving them from place to place like sheep and cattle. And at other times again she told us she said, Remember that a hand cannot wash itself, it needs another to do it.

I always thought of Madam when Lilian Ngoyi spoke. I asked myself, What would she say if she knew that I was listening to such words. Words like: A white man is looked after by his black nanny and his mother when he is a baby. When he grows up the white government looks after him, sends him to school, makes it impossible for him to suffer from the great hunger, keeps a job ready and open for him as soon as he wants to leave school. Now Lilian Ngoyi asked she said, How many white people can be born in a white hospital, grow up in white streets, be clothed in lovely cotton, lie on white cushions; how many whites can live all their lives in a fenced place away from people of other colours and then, as men and women learn quickly the correct ways of thinking, learn quickly to ask questions in their minds, big questions that will throw over all the nice things of a white man's life? How many? Very very few! For those whites who have not begun to ask, it is too late. For those who have begun and are joining us with both feet in our house, we can only say, Welcome!

I was learning. I was growing up. Every time I thought of Madam, she became more and more like a dark forest which one fears to enter, and which one will never know. But there were several times when I thought, This woman is easy to understand, she is like all other white women.

What else are they teaching you at the Black Crow, Karabo?

I tell her I say, Nothing, Madam. I ask her I say, Why does Madam ask?

You are changing.

What does Madam mean?

Well, you are changing.

But we are always changing, Madam.

And she left me standing in the kitchen. This was a few days after I had told her that I did not want to read more than one white paper a day. The only magazines I wanted to read, I said to her, were those from overseas, if she had them. I told her that white papers had pictures of white people most of the time. They talked mostly about white people and their gardens, dogs, weddings and parties. I asked her if she could buy me a Sunday paper that spoke about my people. Madam bought it for me. I did not think she would do it.

There were mornings when, after hanging the white people's washing on the line, Chimane and I stole a little time to stand at the fence and talk. We always stood where we could be hidden by our rooms.

Hei, Karabo, you know what? That was Chimane.

No – what? Before you start, tell me, has Timi come back to you?

Ag, I do not care. He is still angry. But boys are fools, they always come back dragging themselves on their empty bellies. *Hei,* you know what?

Yes?

The Thursday past I saw Moruti K. K. I laughed until I dropped on the ground. He is standing in front of the Black Crow. I believe his big stomach was crying from hunger. Now he has a small dog in his armpit, and is standing before a woman selling boiled eggs and – *hei* home-girl! – tripe and intestines are boiling in a pot – oh, – the smell, you could fill a hungry belly with it, the way it was good. I think Moruti K. K. is waiting for the woman to buy a boiled egg. I do not know what the woman was still doing. I am standing nearby. The dog keeps wriggling and pushing out its nose, looking at the boiling tripe. Moruti keeps patting it with his free hand, not so? Again the dog wants to spill out of Moruti's hand and it gives a few sounds through the nose. *Hei* man, home-girl! One two three the dog spills out to catch some of the good meat! It misses falling into the hot gravy in which the tripe is swimming I do not know how. Moruti K. K. tries to chase it. It has tumbled on to the woman's eggs and potatoes and all are in the dust. She stands up and goes after K. K. She is shouting to him to pay, not so? Where am I at that time? I am nearly dead with laughter the tears are coming down so far.

I was myself holding tight on the fence so as not to fall through laughing. I held my stomach to keep back a pain in the side.

I ask her I say, Did Moruti K. K. come back to pay for the wasted food?

Yes, he paid.

The dog?

He caught it. That is a good African dog. A dog must look for its own food when it is not time for meals. Not these stupid spoiled angels the whites keep giving tea and biscuits.

Hmm.

Dick our garden man joined us, as he often did. When the story was repeated to him the man nearly rolled on the ground laughing.

He asks who is Reverend K. K.?

I say he is the owner of the Black Crow.

Oh!

We reminded each other, Chimane and I, of the round minister. He would come into the club, look at us with a smooth smile on his smooth round face. He would look at each one of us, with that smile on all the time, as if he had forgotten that it was there. Perhaps he had, because as he looked at us, almost stripping us naked with his watery shining eyes – funny – he could have been a farmer looking at his ripe corn, thinking many things.

K. K. often spoke without shame about what he called ripe girls – *matjitjana* – with good firm breasts. He said such girls were pure without any nonsense in their heads and bodies. Everybody talked a great deal about him and what they thought he must be doing in his office whenever he called in so-and-so.

The Reverend K. K. did not belong to any church. He baptised, married, and buried, for a fee, people who had no church to do such things for them. They said he had been driven out of the Presbyterian Church. He had formed his own, but it did not go far. Later, he came and opened the Black Crow. He knew just how far to go with Lilian Ngoyi. She said although she used his club to teach us things that would help us in life, she could not go on if he was doing any wicked things with the girls in his office. Moruti K. K. feared her, and kept his place.

IV

When I began to tell my story I thought I was going to tell you mostly about Mrs Plum's two dogs. But I have been talking about people. I think Dick is right when he says, What is a dog! And there are so many dogs, cats and parrots in Greenside and other places that Mrs Plum's dogs do not look special. But there was something special in the dog business in Madam's house. The way in which she loved them, maybe.

Monty is a tiny animal with long hair and small black eyes and a face nearly like that of an old woman. The other, Malan, is a bit bigger, with brown and white colours. It has small hair and looks naked by the side of the friend. They sleep in two separate baskets which stay in Madam's bedroom. They are to be washed often and brushed and sprayed and they sleep on pink linen. Monty has a pink ribbon which stays on his neck most of the time. They both carry a cover on their backs. They make me fed up when I see them in their baskets, looking fat, and as if they knew all that was going on everywhere.

It was Dick's work to look after Monty and Malan, to feed them, and to do everything for them. He did this together with the garden work and cleaning of the house. He came at the beginning of this year. He just came, as if from nowhere, and Madam gave him the job as she had chased away two before him, she told me. In both those cases, she said that they could not look after Monty and Malan.

Dick had a long heart, even although he told me and Chimane that European dogs were stupid, spoiled. He said, One day those white people wil put earrings and toe rings and bangles on their dogs. That would be the day he would leave Mrs Plum. For, he said, he was sure that she would want him to polish the rings and bangles with Brasso.

Although he had a long heart, Madam was still not sure of him. She often went to the dogs after a meal or after a cleaning and said to them, Did Dick give you food, sweethearts? Or, Did Dick wash you, sweethearts? Let me see. And I could see that Dick was blowing up like a balloon with anger. These things called white people! he said to me. Talking to dogs!

I say to him I say, People talk to oxen at home do I not say so?

Yes, he says, but at home do you not know that a man speaks to an ox because he wants to make it pull the plough or the wagon or to stop or to stand still for a person to inspan it? No one simply goes to an ox looking at him with eyes far apart and speaks to it. Let me ask you, do you ever see a person where we come from take a cow and press it to his stomach or his cheek? Tell me!

And I say to Dick I say, We were talking about an ox, not a cow.

He laughed with his broad mouth until tears came out of his eyes. At a certain point I laughed aloud too.

One day when you have time, Dick says to me, he says, you should look into Madam's bedroom when she has put a notice outside her door.

Dick, what are you saying? I ask.

I do not talk, me. I know deep inside me.

Dick was about our age, I and Chimane. So we always said *moshiman'o* when we spoke about his tricks. Because he was not too big to be a boy to us. He also said to us, *Hei, lona banyana kelona* – Hey, you girls, you! His large mouth always seemed to be making ready to laugh. I think Madam did not like this. Many times she would say, What is there to make you laugh here? Or in the garden she would say, This is a flower and when it wants water that is not funny! Or again, If you did more work and stopped trying to water my plants with your smile you would be more useful. Even when Dick did not mean to smile. What Madam did not get tired of saying was, If I left you to look after my dogs without anyone to look after you at the same time you would drown the poor things.

Dick smiled at Mrs Plum. Dick hurt Mrs Plum's dogs? Then cows can fly. He was really – really afraid of white people, Dick. I think he tried very hard not to feel afraid. For he was always showing me and Chimane in private how Mrs Plum walked, and spoke. He took two bowls and pressed them to his chest, speaking softly to them as Madam speaks to Monty and Malan. Or he sat at Madam's table and acted the way she sits when writing. Now and again he looked back over his shoulder, pulled his face long like a horse's making as if he were looking over his glasses while telling me something to do. Then he would sit on one of the armchairs, cross his legs and act the way Madam drank her tea; he held the cup he was thinking about between his thumb and the pointing finger, only letting their nails meet. And he laughed after every act. He did these things, of course, when Madam was not home. And where was I at such times? Almost flat on my stomach, laughing.

But oh how Dick trembled when Mrs Plum scolded him! He did his house-cleaning very well. Whatever mistake he made, it was mostly with the dogs; their linen, their food. One white man came into the house one afternoon to tell Madam that Dick had been very careless when taking the dogs out for a walk. His own dog was waiting on Madam's stoep. He repeated that he had been driving down our street and Dick had let loose Monty and Malan to cross the street. The white man made plenty of noise about this and I think wanted to let Madam know how useful he had been. He kept on saying, Just one inch, *just* one inch. It was lucky I put on my brakes quick enough ... But your boy kept on smiling – Why? Strange. My boy would only do it twice and only twice and then ...! His pass. The man moved his hand like one writing, to mean that he would sign his servant's pass for him to go and never come back. When he left, the white man said, Come on Rusty, the boy is waiting to clean you. Dogs with names, men without, I thought.

Madam climbed on top of Dick for this, as we say.

Once one of the dogs, I don't know which – Malan or Monty – took my stocking – brand new, you hear – and tore it with its teeth and paws. When I told Madam about it, my anger as high as my throat, she gave me money to buy another pair. It happened again. This time she said she was not going to give me money because I must also keep my stockings where the two gentle-men would not reach them. Mrs Plum did not want us ever to say *Voetsek* when we wanted the dogs to go away. Me I said this when they came sniffing at my legs or fingers. I hate it.

In my third year in Mrs Plum's house, many things happened, most of them all bad for her. There was trouble with Kate; Chimane had big trouble; my heart was twisted by two loves; and Monty and Malan became real dogs for a few days.

Madam had a number of suppers and parties. She invited Africans to some of them. Kate told me the reasons for some of the parties. Like her mother's books were finished, a visitor from across the seas and so on. I did not like the black people who came here to drink and eat. They spoke such difficult English like people who were full of all the books in the world. They looked at me as if I were right down there whom they thought little of – me a black person like them.

One day I heard Kate speak to her mother. She says, I don't know why you ask so many Africans to the house. A few will do at a time. She said something about the government which I could not hear well. Madam replies she says to her, You know some of them do not meet white people often, so far away in their dark houses. And she says to Kate that they do not come because they want her as a friend but they just want a drink for nothing.

I simply felt that I could not be the servant of white people and of blacks at the same time. At my home or in my room I could serve them without a feeling of shame. And now, if they were only coming to drink!

But one of the black men and his sister always came to the kitchen to talk to me. I must have looked unfriendly the first time, for Kate talked to me about it afterwards as she was in the kitchen when they came. I know that at that time I was not easy at all. I was ashamed and I felt that a white person's house was not the place for me to look happy in front of other black people while the white man looked on.

Another time it was easier. The man was alone. I shall never forget that night, as long as I live. He spoke kind words and I felt my heart grow big inside me. It caused me to tremble. There were several other visits. I knew that I loved him, I could never know what he really thought of me, I mean as a woman and he as a man. But I loved him, and I still think of him with a sore heart. Slowly I came to know the pain of it. Because he was a doctor and so full of knowledge and English I could not reach him. So I knew he could not stoop down to see me as someone who wanted him to love me.

Kate turned very wild. Mrs Plum was very much worried. Suddenly it looked as if she were a new person, with new ways and new everything. I do not know what was wrong or right. She began to play the big gramophone loud, as if the music were for the whole of Greenside. The music was wild and she twisted her waist all the time, with her mouth half open. She did the same things in her room. She left the big school and every Saturday night now she went out. When I looked at her face, there was something deep and wild there on it, and when I thought she looked young she looked old, and when I thought she looked old she was young. We were both twenty-two years of age. I think that I could see the reason why her mother was so worried, why she was suffering.

Worse was to come.

They were now openly screaming at each other. They began in the sitting room and went upstairs together, speaking fast hot biting words, some of which I did not grasp. One day Madam comes to me and says, You know Kate loves an African, you know the doctor who comes to supper here often. She says he loves her too and they will leave the country and marry outside. Tell me, Karabo, what do your people think of this kind of thing between a white woman and a black man? It *cannot* be right, can it?

I reply and I say to her, We have never seen it happen before where I come from.

That's right, Karabo, it is just madness.

Madam left. She looked like a hunted person.

These white women, I say to myself I say, these white women, why do not they love their own men and leave us to love ours!

From that minute I knew that I would never want to speak to Kate. She appeared to me as a thief, as a fox that falls upon a flock of sheep at night. I hated her. To make it worse, he would never be allowed to come to the house again.

Whenever she was home there was silence between us. I no longer wanted to know anything about what she was doing, where or how.

I lay awake for hours on my bed. Lying like that, I seemed to feel parts of my body beat and throb inside me, the way I have seen big machines doing, pounding and pounding and pushing and pulling and pouring some water into one hole which came out at another end. I stretched myself so many times so as to feel tired and sleepy.

When I did sleep, my dreams were full of painful things.

One evening I made up my mind, after putting it off many times. I told my boyfriend that I did not want him any longer. He looked hurt, and that hurt me too. He left.

The thought of the African doctor was still with me and it pained me to know that I should never see him again; unless I met him in the street on a Thursday afternoon. But he had a car. Even if I did meet him by luck, how could I make him see that I loved him? *Ag*, I do not believe he would even stop to think what kind of woman I am. Part of that winter was a time of longing and burning for me. I say part because there are always things to keep servants busy whose white people go to the sea for the winter.

To tell the truth, winter was the time for servants; not nannies, because they went with their madams so as to look after the children. Those like me stayed behind to look after the house and dogs. In winter so many families went away that the dogs remained the masters and madams. You could see them walk like white people in the streets. Silent but with plenty of power. And when you saw them you knew that they were full of more nonsense and fancies in the house.

There was so little work to do.

One week word was whispered round that a home-boy of ours was going to hold a party in his room on Saturday. I think we all took it for a joke. How could the man be so bold and stupid? The police were always driving about at night looking for black people; and if the whites next door heard the party noise – *oho!* But still, we were full of joy and wanted to go. As for Dick, he opened his big mouth and nearly fainted when he heard of it and that I was really going.

During the day on the big Saturday Kate came.

She seemed a little less wild. But I was not ready to talk to her. I was surprised to hear myself answer her when she said to me, Mother says you do not like a marriage between a white girl and a black man, Karabo.

Then she was silent.

She says, But I want to help him, Karabo.

I ask her I say, You want to help him to do what?

To go higher and higher, to the top.

I knew I wanted to say so much that was boiling in my chest. I could not say it. I thought of Lilian Ngoyi at the Black Crow, what she said to us. But I was mixed up in my head and in my blood.

You still agree with my mother?

All I could say was, I said to your mother I had never seen a black man and a white woman marrying, you hear me? What I think about it is my business.

I remembered that I wanted to iron my party dress and so I left her. My mind was full of the party again and I was glad because Kate and the doctor would not worry my peace that day. And the next day the sun would shine for all of us, Kate or no Kate, doctor or no doctor.

The house where our home-boy worked was hidden from the main road by a number of trees. But although we asked a number of questions and counted many fingers of bad luck until we had no more hands for fingers, we put on our best pay-while-you-wear dresses and suits and clothes bought from boys who had stolen them, and went to our home-boy's party. We whispered all the way while we climbed up to the house. Someone who knew told us that the white people next door were away for the winter. Oh, so that is the thing! we said.

We poured into the garden through the back and stood in front of his room laughing quietly. He came from the big house behind us, and were we not struck dumb when he told us to go into the white people's house! Was he mad? We walked in with slow footsteps that seemed to be sniffing at the floor, not sure of anything. Soon we were standing and sitting all over on the nice warm cushions and the heaters were on. Our home-boy turned the lights low. I counted fifteen people inside. We saw how we loved one another's evening dress. The boys were smart too.

Our home-boy's girlfriend Naomi was busy in the kitchen preparing food. He took out glasses and cold drinks – fruit juice, tomato juice, ginger beers,

and so many other kinds of soft drink. It was just too nice. The tarts, the biscuits, the snacks, the cakes, *woo*, that was a party, I tell you. I think I ate more
ginger cake than I had ever done in my life. Naomi had baked some of the
things. Our home-boy came to me and said, I do not want the police to come
here and have reason to arrest us, so I am not serving hot drinks, not even
beer. There is no law that we cannot have parties, is there? So we can feel free.
Our use of this house is the master's business. If I had asked him he would
have thought me mad.

I say to him I say, You have a strong liver to do such a thing.

He laughed.

He played pennywhistle music on gramophone records – Miriam Makeba,
Dorothy Masuka and other African singers and players. We danced and the
party became more and more noisy and more happy. *Hai*, those girls Miriam
and Dorothy, they can sing, I tell you! We ate more and laughed more and told
more stories. In the middle of the party, our home-boy called us to listen to
what he was going to say. Then he told us how he and a friend of his in
Orlando collected money to bet on a horse for the July Handicap in Durban.
They did this each year but lost. Now they had won two hundred pounds. We
all clapped hands and cheered. Two hundred pounds, *woo*!

You should go and sit at home and just eat time, I say to him. He laughs
and says, You have no understanding, not one little bit.

To all of us he says, Now my brothers and sisters enjoy yourselves. At home
I should slaughter a goat for us to feast and thank our ancestors. But this is
town life and we must thank them with tea and cake and all those sweet
things. I know some people think I must be so bold that I could be midwife
to a lion that is giving birth, but enjoy yourselves and have no fear.

Madam came back looking strong and fresh.

The very week she arrived the police had begun again to search servants'
rooms. They were looking for what they called loafers and men without
passes who they said were living with friends in the suburbs against the law.
Our dog's meat boys became scarce because of the police. A boy who had a
girlfriend in the kitchens, as we say, always told his friends that he was coming for dog's meat when he meant he was visiting his girl. This was because
we gave our boyfriends part of the meat the white people bought for the dogs
and us.

One night two policemen, one white and one black, entered Mrs Plum's
yard. They said they had come to search. She says, No, they cannot. They say,
Yes, they must do it. She answers, No. They forced their way to the back, to
Dick's room and mine. Mrs Plum took the hose that was running in the front

garden and quickly went round to the back. I cut across the floor to see what she was going to say to the men. They were talking to Dick, using dirty words. Mrs Plum did not wait, she just pointed the hose at the two policemen. This seemed to surprise them. They turned round and she pointed it into their faces. Without their seeing me I went to the tap at the corner of the house and opened it more. I could see Dick, like me, was trying to keep down his laughter. They shouted and tried to wave the water away, but she kept the hose pointing at them, now moving it up and down. They turned and ran through the back gate, swearing the while.

That fixes them, Mrs Plum said.

The next day the morning paper reported it.

They arrived in the afternoon – the two policemen – with another. They pointed out Mrs Plum and she was led to the police station. They took her away to answer for stopping the police while they were doing their work.

She came back and said she had paid bail.

At the magistrate's court, Madam was told that she had done a bad thing. She would have to pay a fine or else go to prison for fourteen days. She said she would go to jail to show that she felt she was not in the wrong.

Kate came and tried to tell her that she was doing something silly going to jail for a small thing like that. She tells Madam she says, This is not even a thing to take to the high court. Pay the money. What is £5?

Madam went to jail.

She looked very sad when she came out. I thought of what Lilian Ngoyi often said to us: You must be ready to go to jail for the things you believe are true and for which you are taken by the police. What did Mrs Plum really believe about me, Chimane, Dick and all the other black people? I asked myself. I did not know. But from all those things she was writing for the papers and all those meetings she was going to where white people talked about black people and the way they were treated by the government, from what those white women with black bands over their shoulders were doing standing where a white government man was going to pass, I said to myself I said, This woman, *hai*, I do not know, she seems to think very much of us black people. But why was she so sad?

Kate came back home to stay after this. She still played the big gramophone loud-loud-loud and twisted her body at her waist until I thought it was going to break. Then I saw a young white man come often to see her. I watched them through the opening near the hinges of the door between the kitchen and the sitting room where they sat. I saw them kiss each other for a long long time. I saw him lift up Kate's dress and her white-white legs begin to tremble, and – oh I am afraid to say more, my heart was beating hard. She called him Jim. I thought it was funny because white people in the shops call black men Jim.

Kate had begun to play with Jim when I met a boy who loved me and I loved. He was much stronger than the one I sent away and I loved him more, much more. The face of the doctor came to my mind often, but it did not hurt me so any more. I stopped looking at Kate and her Jim through openings. We spoke to each other, Kate and I, almost as freely as before but not quite. She and her mother were friends again.

Hallo, Karabo, I heard Chimane call me one morning as I was starching my apron. I answered. I went to the line to hang it. I saw she was standing at the fence, so I knew she had something to tell me. I went to her.

Hallo!

Hallo, Chimane!

O kae?

Ke teng. Wena?

At that moment a woman came out through the back door of the house where Chimane was working.

I have not seen that one before, I say, pointing with my head.

Chimane looked back. Oh, that one. *Hei*, daughter-of-the-people. *Hei*, you have not seen miracles. You know this is Madam's mother-in-law as you see her there. Did I never tell you about her?

No, never.

White people, nonsense. You know what? That poor woman is here now for two days. She has to cook for herself and I cook for the family.

On the same stove?

Yes, she comes after me when I have finished.

She has her own food to cook?

Yes, Karabo. White people have no heart, no sense.

What will eat them up if they share their food?

Ask me, just ask me. God! She clapped her hands to show that only God knew, and it was His business, not ours.

Chimane asks me she says, Have you heard from home?

I tell her I say, Oh daughter-of-the-people, more and more deaths. Something is finishing the people at home. My mother has written. She says they are all right, my father too and my sisters, except for the people who have died. Malebo, the one who lived alone in the house I showed you last year, a white house, he is gone. Then teacher Sedimo. He was very thin and looked sick all the time. He taught my sisters not me. His mother-in-law you remember I told you died last year – no, the year before. Mother says also there is a woman she does not think I remember because I last saw her when

I was a small girl she passed away in Zeerust she was my mother's greatest friend when they were girls. She would have gone to her burial if it was not because she has swollen feet.

How are the feet?

She says they are still giving her trouble. I ask Chimane, How are your people at Nokaneng? They have not written?

She shook her head.

I could see from her eyes that her mind was on another thing and not her people at that moment.

Wait for me Chimane eh, forgive me, I have scones in the oven, eh! I will just take them out and come back, eh!

When I came back to her Chimane was wiping her eyes. They were wet.

Karabo, you know what?

E – e. I shook my head.

I am heavy with child.

Hau!

There was a moment of silence.

Who is it, Chimane?

Timi. He came back only to give me this.

But he loves you. What does he say, have you told him?

I told him yesterday. We met in town.

I remembered I had not seen her at the Black Crow.

Are you sure, Chimane? You have missed a month?

She nodded her head.

Timi himself – he did not use the thing?

I only saw after he finished, that he had not.

Why? What does he say?

He tells me he says, I should not worry I can be his wife.

Timi is a good boy, Chimane. How many of these boys with town ways who know too much will even say, Yes it is my child?

Hai, Karabo, you are telling me other things now. Do you not see that I have not worked long enough for my people? If I marry now who will look after them when I am the only child?

Hm. I hear your words. It is true. I tried to think of something soothing to say.

Then I say, You can talk it over with Timi. You can go home and when the child is born you look after it for three months and when you are married you come to town to work and can put your money together to help the old people while they are looking after the child.

What shall we be eating all the time I am at home? It is not like those days gone past when we had land and our mother could go to the fields until the child was ready to arrive.

The light goes out in my mind and I cannot think of the right answer. How many times have I feared the same thing! Luck and the mercy of the gods that is all I live by. That is all we live by – all of us.

Listen, Karabo. I must be going to make tea for Madam. It will soon strike half-past ten.

I went back to the house. As Madam was not in yet, I threw myself on the divan in the sitting-room. Malan came sniffing at my legs. I put my foot under its fat belly and shoved it up and away from me so that it cried *tjunk – tjunk – tjunk* as it went out. I say to it I say, Go and tell your brother what I have done to you and tell him to try it and see what I will do. Tell your grandmother when she comes home too.

When I lifted my eyes he was standing in the kitchen door, Dick. He says to me he says, *Hau*! Now you have also begun to speak to dogs!

I did not reply. I just looked at him, his mouth ever stretched out like the mouth of a bag, and I passed to my room.

I sat on my bed and looked at my face in the mirror. Since the morning I had been feeling as if a black cloud were hanging over me, pressing on my head and shoulders. I do not know how long I sat there. Then I smelled Madam. What was it? Where was she? After a few moments I knew what it was. My perfume and scent. I used the same cosmetics as Mrs Plum's. I should have been used to it by now. But this morning – why did I smell Mrs Plum like this? Then, without knowing why, I asked myself I said, Why have I been using the same cosmetics as Madam? I wanted to throw them all out. I stopped. And then I took all the things and threw them into the dustbin. I was going to buy other kinds on Thursday; finished!

I could not sit down. I went out and into the white people's house. I walked through and the smell of the house made me sick and seemed to fill up my throat. I went to the bathroom without knowing why. It was full of the smell of Madam. Dick was cleaning the bath. I stood at the door and looked at him cleaning the dirt out of the bath, dirt from Madam's body. *Sies*! I said aloud. To myself I said, Why cannot people wash the dirt of their own bodies out of the bath? Before Dick knew I was near I went out. *Ag*, I said again to myself, why should I think about it now when I have been doing their washing for so long and cleaned the bath many times when Dick was ill? I had held worse things from her body times without number ...

I went out and stood midway between the house and my room, looking into the next yard. The three-legged grey cat next door came to the fence and our eyes met. I do not know how long we stood like that looking at each other. I was thinking, Why don't you go and look at your grandmother like that? when it turned away and mewed hopping on the three legs. Just like someone who feels pity for you.

In my room I looked into the mirror on the chest of drawers. I thought, Is this Karabo this?

Thursday came, and the afternoon off. At the Black Crow I did not see Chimane. I wondered about her. In the evening I found a note under my door. It told me if Chimane was not back that evening I should know that she was at 660 3rd Avenue, Alexandra Township. I was not to tell the white people.

I asked Dick if he could not go to Alexandra with me after I had washed the dishes. At first he was unwilling. But I said to him I said, Chimane will not believe that you refused to come with me when she sees me alone. He agreed.

On the bus Dick told me much about his younger sister whom he was help-ing with money to stay at school until she finished; so that she could become a nurse and a midwife. He was very fond of her, as far as I could find out. He said he prayed always that he should not lose his job, as he had done many times before, after staying a few weeks only at each job; because of this he had to borrow money from people to pay his sister's school fees, to buy her clothes and books. He spoke of her as if she were his sweetheart. She was clever at school, pretty (she was this in the photo Dick had shown me before). She was in Orlando Township. She looked after his old people, although she was only thirteen years of age. He said to me he said, Today I still owe many people because I keep losing my job. You must try to stay with Mrs Plum, I said.

I cannot say that I had all my mind on what Dick was telling me. I was thinking of Chimane: what could she be doing? Why that note?

We found her in bed. In that terrible township where night and day are full of knives and bicycle chains and guns and the barking of hungry dogs and of people in trouble. I held my heart in my hands. She was in pain and her face, even in the candlelight, was grey. She turned her eyes on me. A fat woman was sitting in a chair. One arm rested on the other and held her chin in its palm. She had hardly opened the door for us after we had shouted our names when she was on her bench again as if there were nothing else to do.

She snorted, as if to let us know that she was going to speak. She said, There is your friend. There she is my own-own niece who comes from the womb of my own sister, my sister who was made to spit out my mother's breast to give way for me. Why does she go and do such an evil thing. *Ao!* You young girls of today you do not know children die so fast these days that you have to thank God for sowing a seed in your womb to grow into a child. If she had let the child be born I should have looked after it or my sister would have been so happy to hold a grandchild on her lap, but what does it help? She has allowed a worm to cut the roots, I don't know.

Then I saw that Chimane's aunt was crying. Not once did she mention her niece by her name, so sore her heart must have been. Chimane only moaned.

Her aunt continued to talk, as if she was never going to stop for breath, until her voice seemed to move behind me, not one of the things I was thinking: trying to remember signs, however small, that could tell me more about this moment in a dim little room in a cruel township without street lights, near Chimane. Then I remembered the three-legged cat, its grey-green eyes, its *miau*. What was this shadow that seemed to walk about us but was not coming right in front of us?

I thanked the gods when Chimane came to work at the end of the week. She still looked weak, but that shadow was no longer there. I wondered Chimane had never told me about her aunt before. Even now I did not ask her.

I told her I told her white people that she was ill and had been fetched to Nokaneng by a brother. They would never try to find out. They seldom did, these people. Give them any lie, and it will do. For they seldom believe you whatever you say. And how can a black person work for white people and be afraid to tell them lies. They are always asking the questions, you are always the one to give the answers.

Chimane told me all about it. She had gone to a woman who did these things. Her way was to hold a sharp needle, cover the point with the finger, and guide it into the womb. She then fumbled in the womb until she found the egg and then pierced it. She gave you something to ease the bleeding. But the pain, spirits of our forefathers!

Mrs Plum and Kate were talking about dogs one evening at dinner. Every time I brought something to table I tried to catch their words. Kate seemed to find it funny, because she laughed aloud. There was a word I could not hear well which began with *sem*—: whatever it was, it was to be for dogs. This I understood by putting a few words together. Mrs Plum said it was something that was common in the big cities of America, like New York. It was also something Mrs Plum wanted and Kate laughed at the thought. Then later I was to hear that Monty and Malan could be sure of a nice burial.

Chimane's voice came up to me in my room the next morning, across the fence. When I come out she tells me she says, *Hei* child-of-my-father, here is something to tickle your ears. You know what? What? I say. She says, These white people can do things that make the gods angry. More godless people I have not seen. The madam of our house says the people of Greenside want to buy ground where they can bury their dogs. I heard them talk about it in the sitting room when I was giving them coffee last night. *Hei*, people, let our forefathers come and save us!

Yes, I say, I also heard the madam of our house talk about it with her daughter. I just heard it in pieces. By my mother, one day these dogs will sit at table and use knife and fork. These things are to be treated like people now, like children who are never going to grow up.

Chimane sighed and she says, *Hela batho*, why do they not give me some of that money they will spend on the ground and on gravestones to buy stockings! I have nothing to put on, by my mother.

Over her shoulder I saw the cat with three legs. I pointed with my head. When Chimane looked back and saw it she said, *Hm*, even *they* live like kings. The mother-in-law found it on a chair and the madam said the woman should not drive it away. And there was no other chair, so the woman went to her room.

Hela!

I was going to leave when I remembered what I wanted to tell Chimane. It was that five of us had collected £1 each to lend her so that she could pay the woman of Alexandra for having done that thing for her. When Chimane's time came to receive money we collected each month and which we took in turns, she would pay us back. We were ten women and each gave £2 at a time. So one waited ten months to receive £20. Chimane thanked us for helping her.

I went to wake up Mrs Plum as she had asked me. She was sleeping late this morning. I was going to knock at the door when I heard strange noises in the bedroom. What is the matter with Mrs Plum? I asked myself. Should I call her, in case she is ill? No, the noises were not those of a sick person. They were happy noises but like those a person makes in a dream, the voice full of sleep. I bent a little to peep through the keyhole. What is this? I kept asking myself. Mrs Plum! Malan! What is she doing this one? Her arm was round Malan's belly and pressing its back against her stomach at the navel, Mrs Plum's body in a nightdress moving in jerks like someone in fits ... her leg rising and falling ... Malan silent like a thing to be owned without any choice it can make to belong to another.

The gods save me! I heard myself saying, the words sounding like wind rushing out of my mouth. So this is what Dick said I would find out for myself!

No one could say where it all started; who talked about it first; whether the police wanted to make a reason for taking people without passes and people living with servants and working in town or not working at all. But the story rushed through Johannesburg that servants were going to poison the white people's dogs. Because they were too much work for us: that was the reason. We heard that letters were sent to the newspapers by white people asking the police to watch over the dogs to stop any wicked things. Some said that we the servants were not really bad, we were being made to think of doing these things by evil people in town and in the locations. Others said the police should watch out lest we poison madams and masters because black people did not know right from wrong when they were angry. We were still children at heart, others said. Mrs Plum said that she had also written to the papers.

Then it was the police came down on the suburbs like locusts on a cornfield. There were lines and lines of men who were arrested hour by hour in the day. They liked this very much, the police. Everybody they took, everybody who was working was asked, Where's the poison eh? Where did you hide it? Who told you to poison the dogs eh? If you tell us we'll leave you to go free, you hear? And so many other things.

Dick kept saying, It is wrong this thing they want to do to kill poor dogs. What have these things of God done to be killed for? Is it the dogs that make us carry passes? Is it dogs that make the laws that give us pain? People are just mad they do not know what they want, stupid! But when white policemen spoke to him, Dick trembled and lost his tongue and the things he thought. He just shook his head. A few moments after they had gone through his pockets he still held his arms stretched out, like the man of straw who frightens away birds in a field. Only when I hissed and gave him a sign did he drop his arms. He rushed to a corner of the garden to go on with his work.

Mrs Plum had put Monty and Malan in the sitting room, next to her. She looked very much worried. She called me. She asked me she said, Karabo, you think Dick is a boy we can trust? I did not know how to answer. I did not know whom she was talking about when she said we. Then I said, I do not know, Madam. You know! she said. I looked at her. I said, I do not know what Madam thinks. She said she did not think anything, that was why she asked. I nearly laughed because she was telling a lie this time and not I.

At another time I should have been angry if she lied to me, perhaps. She and I often told each other lies, as Kate and I also did. Like when she came back from jail, after that day when she turned a hosepipe on two policemen. She said life had been good in jail. And yet I could see she was ashamed to have been there. Not like our black people who are always being put in jail and only look at it as the white man's evil game. Lilian Ngoyi often told us this, and Mrs Plum showed me how true those words are. I am sure that we have kept to each other by lying to each other.

There was something in Mrs Plum's face as she was speaking which made me fear her and pity her at the same time. I had seen her when she had come from prison; I had seen her when she was shouting at Kate and the girl left the house; now there was this thing about dog poisoning. But never had I seen her face like this before. The eyes, the nostrils, the lips, the teeth seemed to be full of hate, tired, fixed on doing something bad; and yet there was something on that face that told me she wanted me on her side.

Dick is all right Madam, I found myself saying. She took Malan and Monty in her arms and pressed them to herself, running her hands over their heads. They looked so safe, like a child in a mother's arms.

Mrs Plum said, All right you may go. She said, Do not tell anybody what I have asked about Dick eh?

When I told Dick about it, he seemed worried.

It is nothing, I told him.

I had been thinking before that I did not stand with those who wanted to poison the dogs, Dick said. But the police have come out, I do not care what happens to the dumb things, now.

I asked him I said, Would you poison them if you were told by someone to do it?

No. But I do not care, he replied.

The police came again and again. They were having a good holiday, everyone could see that. A day later Mrs Plum told Dick to go because she would not need his work any more.

Dick was almost crying when he left. Is Madam so unsure of me? he asked. I never thought a white person could fear me! And he left.

Chimane shouted from the other yard. She said, *Hei ngoana'rona*, the boers are fire-hot eh!

Mrs Plum said she would hire a man after the trouble was over.

A letter came from my parents in Phokeng. In it they told me my uncle had passed away. He was my mother's brother. The letter also told me of other deaths. They said I would not remember some, I was sure to know the others. There were also names of sick people.

I went to Mrs Plum to ask her if I could go home. She asks she says, When did he die? I answer I say, It is three days, Madam. She says, So that they have buried him? I reply, Yes Madam. Why do you want to go home then? Because my uncle loved me very much Madam. But what are you going to do there? To take my tears and words of grief to his grave and to my old aunt, Madam. No you cannot go, Karabo. You are working for me you know? Yes, Madam. I, and not your people pay you. I must go Madam, that is how we do it among my people, Madam. She paused. She walked into the kitchen and came out again. If you want to go, Karabo, you must lose the money for the days you will be away. Lose my pay, Madam? Yes, Karabo.

The next day I went to Mrs Plum and told her I was leaving for Phokeng and was not coming back to her. Could she give me a letter to say that I worked for her. She did, with her lips shut tight. I could feel that something between us was burning like raw chillies. The letter simply said that I had worked for Mrs Plum for three years. Nothing more. The memory of Dick being sent away was still an open sore in my heart.

The night before the day I left, Chimane came to see me in my room. She had her own story to tell me. Timi, her boyfriend, had left her – for good. Why? Because I killed his baby. Had he not agreed that you should do it? No. Did he show he was worried when you told him you were heavy? He was worried, like me as you saw me, Karabo. Now he says if I kill one I shall eat all his children up when we are married. You think he means what he says? Yes, Karabo. He says his parents would have been very happy to know that the woman he was going to marry can make his seed grow.

Chimane was crying, softly.

I tried to speak to her, to tell her that if Timi left her just like that, he had not wanted to marry her in the first place. But I could not, no, I could not. All I could say was, Do not cry, my sister, do not cry. I gave her my handkerchief.

Kate came back the morning I was leaving, from somewhere very far I cannot remember where. Her mother took no notice of what Kate said asking her to keep me, and I was not interested either.

One hour later I was on the Railway bus to Phokeng. During the early part of the journey I did not feel anything about the Greenside house I had worked in. I was not really myself, my thoughts dancing between Mrs Plum, my uncle, my parents, and Phokeng, my home. I slept and woke up many times during the bus ride. Right through the ride I seemed to see, sometimes in sleep, sometimes between sleep and waking, a red car passing our bus, then running behind us. Each time I looked out it was not there.

Dreams came and passed. He tells me he says, You have killed my seed I wanted my mother to know you are a woman in whom my seed can grow ... Before you make the police take you to jail make sure that it is for something big you should go to jail for, otherwise you will come out with a heart and mind that will bleed inside you and poison you ...

The bus stopped for a short while, which made me wake up.

The Black Crow, the club women ... *Hei*, listen! I lie to the madam of our house and I say I had a telegram from my mother telling me she is very very sick. I show her a telegram my sister sent me as if Mother were writing. So I went home for a nice weekend ...

The laughter of the women woke me up, just in time for me to stop a line of saliva coming out over my lower lip. The bus was making plenty of dust now as it was running over part of the road they were digging up. I was sure the red car was just behind us, but it was not there when I woke.

Any one of you here who wants to be baptised or has a relative without a church who needs to be can come and see me in the office ... A round man with a fat tummy and sharp hungry eyes, a smile that goes a long, long way ...

The bus was going uphill, heavily and noisily.

I kick a white man's dog, me, or throw it there if it has not been told the black people's law ... This is Mister Monty and this is Mister Malan. Now get up you lazy boys and meet Mister Kate. Hold out your hands and say hallo to him ... Karabo, bring two glasses there ... Wait a bit – What will you chew boys while Mister Kate and I have a drink? Nothing? Sure?

We were now going nicely on a straight tarred road and the trees rushed back. Mister Kate. What nonsense, I thought.

Look Karabo, Madam's dogs are dead. What? Poison. I killed them. She drove me out of a job did she not? For nothing. Now I want her to feel she drove me out for something. I came back when you were in your room and took the things and poisoned them ... And you know what? She has buried them in clean pink sheets in the garden. *Ao,* clean clean good sheets. I am going to dig them out and take one sheet do you want the other one? Yes, give me the other one I will send it to my mother ... *Hei,* Karabo, see here they come. Monty and Malan. The bloody fools they do not want to stay in their hole. Go back you silly fools. Oh you do not want to move eh? Come here, now I am going to throw you in the big pool. No, Dick! No Dick! No, no! Dick! They cannot speak do not kill things that cannot speak. Madam can speak for them she always does. No! Dick ...!

I woke up with a jump after I had screamed Dick's name, almost hitting the window. My forehead was full of sweat. The red car also shot out of my sleep and was gone. I remembered a friend of ours who told us how she and the garden man had saved two white sheets in which their white master had buried their two dogs. They went to throw the dogs in a dam.

When I told my parents my story Father says to me he says, So long as you are in good health my child, it is good. The worker dies, work does not. There is always work. I know when I was a boy a strong sound body and a good mind were the biggest things in life. Work was always there, and the lazy man could never say there was no work. But today people see work as something bigger than everything else, bigger than health, because of money.

I reply I say, Those days are gone Papa. I must go back to the city after resting a little to look for work. I must look after you. Today people are too poor to be able to help you.

I knew when I left Greenside that I was going to return to Johannesburg to work. Money was little, but life was full and it was better than sitting in Phokeng and watching the sun rise and set. So I told Chimane to keep her eyes and ears open for a job.

I had been at Phokeng for one week when a red car arrived. Somebody was sitting in front with the driver, a white woman. At once I knew it to be Mrs Plum. The man sitting beside her was showing her the way, for he pointed towards our house in front of which I was sitting. My heart missed a few beats. Both came out of the car. The white woman said 'Thank you' to the man after he had spoken a few words to me.

I did not know what to do and how to look at her as she spoke to me. So I looked at the piece of cloth I was sewing pictures on. There was a tired but soft smile on her face. Then I remembered that she might want to sit. I went inside to fetch a low bench for her. When I remembered it afterwards, the thought came to me that there are things I never think white people can want to do at our homes when they visit for the first time: like sitting, drinking water or entering the house. This is how I thought when the white priest came to see us. One year at Easter Kate drove me home as she was going to the north. In the same way I was at a loss what to do for a few minutes.

Then Mrs Plum says, I have come to ask you to come back to me, Karabo. Would you like to?

I say I do not know, I must think about it first.

She says, Can you think about it today? I can sleep at the town hotel and come back tomorrow morning, and if you want to you can return with me.

I wanted her to say she was sorry to have sent me away, I did not know how to make her say it because I know white people find it too much for them to say sorry to a black person. As she was not saying it, I thought of two things to make it hard for her to get me back and maybe even lose me in the end.

I say, You must ask my father first, I do not know, should I call him?

Mrs Plum says, Yes.

I fetched both Father and Mother. They greeted her while I brought benches. Then I told them what she wanted.

Father asks Mother and Mother asks Father. Father asks me. I say if they agree, I will think about it and tell her the next day.

Father says, It goes by what you feel my child.

I tell Mrs Plum I say, If you want me to think about it I must know if you will want to put my wages up from £6 because it is too little.

She asks me, How much will you want?

Up by £4.

She looked down for a few moments.

And then I want two weeks at Easter and not just the weekend. I thought if she really wanted me she would want to pay for it. This would also show how sorry she was to lose me.

Mrs Plum says, I can give you one week. You see you already have something like a rest when I am in Durban in the winter.

I tell her I say, I shall think about it.

She left.

The next day she found me packed and ready to return with her. She was very pleased and looked kinder than I had ever know her. And me, I felt sure of myself, more than I had ever done.

Mrs Plum says to me, You will not find Monty and Malan.

Oh?

Yes, they were stolen the day after you left. The police have not found them yet. I think they are dead myself.

I thought of Dick ... my dream. Could he? And she ... did this woman come to ask me to return because she had lost two animals she loved?

Mrs Plum says to me she says, You know, I like your people, Karabo, the Africans.

And Dick and me? I wondered.

HEAVEN IS NOT CLOSED
Bessie Head

All her life Galethebege earnestly believed that her whole heart ought to be devoted to God, although one catastrophe after another occurred to deflect her from this path. It was only in the last five years of her life, after her husband, Ralokae, had died, that she was able to devote her whole mind to her calling. Then, all her pent-up and suppressed love for God burst forth and she talked only of Him, day and night – so her grandchildren, solemnly and with deep awe, informed the mourners at her funeral. All the mourners present at her hour of passing were utterly convinced that they had watched a profound and holy event. They talked about it for days afterwards.

Galethebege was well over ninety when she died and not at all afflicted by crippling ailments like most of the aged. In fact, only two days before her death had she complained to her grandchildren of a sudden fever and a lameness in her legs, and she had remained in bed. A quiet, thoughtful mood fell upon her. On the morning of the second day she had abruptly demanded that all the relatives be summoned.

'My hour has come,' she said, with lofty dignity.

No one quite believed it, because that whole morning she had sat bolt upright in bed and talked to all who had gathered, about God – whom she loved with her whole heart. Then, exactly at noon, she announced once more that her hour had indeed come and lay down peacefully like one about to take a short nap. Her last words were:

'I shall rest now because I believe in God.'

Then, a terrible silence filled the hut and seemed to paralyse the mourners for they all remained immobile for some time; each person present cried quietly because not one of them had ever witnessed such a magnificent death before. They only stirred when the old man, Modise, suddenly observed, with great practicality, that Galethebege was not in the correct position for death. She lay on her side with her right arm thrust out above her head. She ought to be turned over on her back, with her hands crossed over her chest, he said. A smile flickered over the old man's face as he said this, as though it was just like Galethebege to make such a miscalculation. Why, she knew the hour of her death and everything, then at the last minute forgot the correct sleeping posture for the coffin. Later that evening, as he sat with his children near the outdoor fire for the evening meal, a smile again flickered over his face.

'I am of a mind to think that Galethebege was praying for forgiveness for her sins this morning,' he said slowly. 'It must have been a sin to her to marry Ralokae. He was an unbeliever to the day of his death ... '

A gust of astonished laughter shook his family out of the solemn mood of mourning that had fallen upon them and they all turned eagerly towards their grandfather, sensing that he had a story to tell.

'As you all know,' the old man said wisely, 'Ralokae was my brother. But none of you present knows the story of Galethebege's life, but I know it ... '

As the flickering firelight lit up their faces, he told the following story: 'I was never like Ralokae, an unbeliever. But that man, my brother, draws out my heart. He liked to say that we as a tribe would fall into great difficulties if we forget our own customs and laws. Today, his words seem true. There is thieving and adultery going on such as was not possible under Setswana law.'

In the days when they were young, said the old man, Modise, it had become the fashion for all black people to embrace the Gospel. For some, it was the mark of whether they were 'civilised' or not. For some, like Galethebege, it was their whole life. Anyone with eyes to see would have known that Galethebege had been born good; under any custom, whether Setswana custom or Christian custom, she would still have been good. It was this natural goodness of heart that made her so eagerly pursue the word of the Gospel. There was a look on her face, absent, abstracted, as though she needed to share the final secret of life with God who could understand all things. So she was always on her way to church, and in her hours of leisure at home she could be found with her head buried in the Bible. And so her life would have gone on in this quiet and worshipful way, had not a sudden catastrophe occurred in the yard of Ralokae.

Ralokae had been married for nearly a year when his young wife died in childbirth. She died when the crops of the season were being harvested, and for a year Ralokae imposed on himself the traditional restraints and disciplines of boswagadi or mourning for the deceased. A year later, again at the harvest time, he underwent the cleansing ceremony demanded by custom and could once more resume the normal life of a man. It was the unexpectedness of the tragic event and the discipline it imposed on him, that made Ralokae take note of the life of Galethebege. She lived just three yards away from his own yard, and formerly he had barely taken note of her existence; it was too quiet and orderly. But during the year of mourning, it delighted him to hear that gentle and earnest voice of Galethebege informing him that such tragedies 'were the will of God'. As soon as he could, he began courting her. He was young and impatient to be married again and no one could bring back the dead. So a few days after the cleansing ceremony, he made his intentions very clear to her.

'Let us two get together,' he said. 'I am pleased by all your ways.'

Galethebege was all at the same time startled, pleased, and hesitant. She was hesitant because it was well known that Ralokae was an unbeliever; he had not once set foot in church. So she looked at him, begging an apology, and mentioned the matter which was foremost in her mind.

'Ralokae,' she said, uncertainly. 'I have set God always before me,' implying by that statement that perhaps he too was seeking a Christian life, like her own. But he only looked at her in a strange way, and said nothing. This matter was to stand like a fearful sword between them but he had set his mind on winning Galethebege as his wife. That was all he was certain of. He turned up in her yard day after day.

'Hullo girlfriend,' he would greet her, enchantingly.

He always wore a black beret perched at a jaunty angle on his head. His walk and manner were gay and jaunty too. He was so exciting as a man that he threw her whole life into turmoil. It was the first time love had come her way and it made the blood pound fiercely through her whole body till she could feel its very throbbing at the tips of her fingers. It turned her thoughts from God a bit, to this new magic life was offering her. The day she agreed to be his wife, that sword quivered like a fearful thing between them. Ralokae said very quietly and firmly: 'I took my first wife according to the old customs. I am going to take my second wife according to the old customs too.'

He could see the protest on her face. She wanted to be married in church according to Christian custom. However, he had his own protest to make. The God might be all right, he explained, but there was something wrong with the people who had brought the word of the Gospel to the land. Their love was enslaving black people and he could not stand it. That was why he was without belief. It was the people he did not trust. They were full of tricks. They were a people who, at the sight of a black man, pointed a finger in the air, looked away into the distance and said impatiently: 'Boy! Will you carry this! Boy! Will you fetch this!' They had brought a new order of things into the land and they made the people cry for love. One never had to cry for love in the customary way of life. Respect was just there for people all the time. That was why he rejected all things foreign.

What could a woman do with a man like that who knew his own mind? She either loved him or she was mad. From that day on, Galethebege knew what she would do. She would do all that Ralokae commanded as a good wife should. But her former life was like a drug. Her footsteps were too accustomed to wearing down the footpath to the church, and there they carried her to the missionary's house which stood just under the shadow of the church.

The missionary was a short, anonymous-looking man who wore glasses. He had been the resident missionary for some time, and like all his fellows he did not particularly like the people. He always complained to his own kind that they were terrible beggars and rather stupid. So when he opened the door and saw Galethebege there his expression, with its raised eyebrows said: 'Well, what do you want now?'

'I am to be married, sir,' Galethebege said politely, after the exchange of greetings.

The missionary smiled: 'Well come in my dear. Let us talk about the arrangements,' he said pleasantly.

He stared at her with polite, professional interest. She was a complete non-entity, a part of the vague black blur which was his congregation – oh, they noticed chiefs and people like that, but not the silent mass of humble and lowly who had an almost weird capacity to creep quietly through life. Her next words brought her sharply into focus.

'The man I am to marry, sir, does not wish to be married in the Christian way. He will only marry under Setswana custom,' she said softly.

They always knew the superficial stories about 'heathen customs' and an expression of disgust crept into his face – sexual malpractices were associated with the traditional marriage ceremony (and shudder!), they draped the stinking intestinal bag of the ox around their necks.

'That we cannot allow!' he said sharply. 'Tell him to come and marry in the Christian way.'

Galethebege started trembling all over. She looked at the missionary in alarm. Ralokae would never agree to this. Her intention in approaching the missionary was to acquire his blessing for the marriage, as though a compromise of tenderness could be made between two traditions opposed to each other. She trembled because it was beyond her station in life to be involved in controversy and protest. The missionary noted the trembling and alarm and his tone softened a bit, but his next words were devastating.

'My dear,' he said persuasively, 'heaven is closed to the unbeliever ... '

Galethebege stumbled home on shaking legs. It never occurred to her to question such a miserable religion which terrified people with the fate of eternal damnation in hell-fire if they were 'heathens' or sinners. Only Ralokae seemed quite unperturbed by the fate that awaited him. He smiled when Galethebege relayed the words of the missionary to him.

'Girlfriend,' he said, carelessly, 'you can choose what you like, Setswana custom or Christian custom. I have chosen to live my life by Setswana custom.'

Not once in her life had Galethebege's integrity been called into question. She wanted to make the point clear.

'What you mean, Ralokae,' she said firmly, 'is that I must choose you over my life with the church. I have a great love in my heart for you so I choose you. I shall tell the priest about this matter because his command is that I marry in church.'

Even Galethebege was astounded by the harshness of the missionary's attitude. The catastrophe she did not anticipate, was that he abruptly excommunicated her from the Church. She could no longer enter the village church if she married under Setswana custom. It was beyond her to reason that the missionary was the representative of both God and something evil, the mark of 'civilisation'. It was unthinkable that an illiterate and ignorant man could display such contempt for the missionary's civilisation. His rage and hatred were directed at Ralokae, and the only way in which he could inflict punishment was to banish Galethebege from the Church. If it hurt anyone at all, it was only Galethebege. The austere rituals of the Church, the mass, the sermons, the intimate communication in prayer with God – all this had thrilled her heart deeply. But Ralokae also was representative of an ancient stream of holiness that people had lived with before any white man had set foot in the land, and it only needed a small protest to stir up loyalty for the old customs.

The old man, Modise, paused at this point in the telling of his tale but his young listeners remained breathless and silent, eager for the conclusion.

'Today,' he continued, 'it is not a matter of debate because the young care neither way about religion. But in that day, the expulsion of Galethebege from the Church was a matter of debate. It made the people of our village ward think. There was great indignation because both Galethebege and Ralokae were much respected in the community. People then wanted to know how it was that Ralokae, who was an unbeliever, could have heaven closed to him? A number of people, including all the relatives who officiated at the wedding ceremony, then decided that if heaven was closed to Galethebege and Ralokae it might as well be closed to them too, so they all no longer attended church. On the day of their wedding, we had all our own things. Everyone knows the extent to which the cow was a part of the people's life and customs. We took our clothes from the cow and our food from the cow and it was the symbol of our wealth. So the cow was a holy thing in our lives. The elders then cut the intestinal bag of the cow in two and one portion was placed around the neck of Galethebege and one portion around the neck of Ralokae to indicate the wealth and good luck they would find together in married life. Then the porridge and meat were dished up in our mogopo bowls which we had used from old times. There was much capering and ululating that day because Ralokae had honoured the old customs . . . '

A tender smile once more flickered over the old man's face.

'Galethebege could never forsake the custom in which she had been brought up. All through her married life she would find a corner in which to pray. Sometimes Ralokae would find her so and ask: "What are you doing, Mother?" And she would reply: "I am praying to God." Ralokae would only smile. He did not even know how to pray to the Christian God.'

The old man leaned forward and stirred the dying fire with a partially burnt-out log of wood. His listeners sighed the way people do when they have heard a particularly good story. As they stared at the fire they found themselves debating the matter in their minds, as their elders had done some forty or fifty years ago. Was heaven really closed to the unbeliever, Ralokae? Or had Christian custom been so intolerant of Setswana custom that it could not hear the holiness of Setswana custom? Wasn't there a place in heaven too for Setswana custom? Then the gust of astonished laughter shook them again. Galethebege had been very well-known in the village ward over the past five years for the supreme authority with which she had talked about God. Perhaps her simple and good heart had been terrified that the doors of heaven were indeed closed on Ralokae and she had been trying to open them.

THE HAJJI
Ahmed Essop

W hen the telephone rang several times one evening and his wife did not attend to it as she usually did, Hajji Hassen, seated on a settee in the lounge, cross-legged and sipping tea, shouted: 'Salima, are you deaf?' And when he received no response from his wife and the jarring bell went on ringing, he shouted again: 'Salima, what's happened to you?'

The telephone stopped ringing. Hajji Hassen frowned in a contemplative manner, wondering where his wife was now. Since his return from Mecca after the pilgrimage, he had discovered novel inadequacies in her, or perhaps saw the old ones in a more revealing light. One of her salient inadequacies was never to be around when he wanted her. She was either across the road confabulating with her sister, or gossiping with the neighbours, or away on a shopping spree. And now, when the telephone had gone on assaulting his ears, she was not in the house. He took another sip of the strongly spiced tea to stifle the irritation within him.

When he heard the kitchen door open he knew that Salima had entered. The telephone burst out again in a metallic shrill and the Hajji shouted for his wife. She hurried to the phone.

'Hullo . . . Yes . . . Hassen . . . Speak to him? . . . Who speaking? . . . Caterine? . . . Who Caterine? . . . Au-right . . . I call him.'

She put the receiver down gingerly and informed her husband in Gujarati that a woman named 'Caterine' wanted to speak to him. The name evoked no immediate association in his memory. He descended from the settee and squeezing his feet into a pair of crimson sandals, went to the telephone.

'Hullo . . . Who? . . . Catherine? . . . No, I don't know you . . . Yes . . . Yes . . . Oh . . . now I remember . . . Yes . . . '

He listened intently to the voice, urgent, supplicating. Then he gave his answer:

'I am afraid I can't help him. Let the Christians bury him. His last wish means nothing to me . . . Madam, it's impossible . . . No . . . Let him die . . . Brother? Pig! Pig! Bastard!' He banged the receiver onto the telephone in explosive annoyance.

'O Allah!' Salima exclaimed. 'What words! What is this all about?'

He did not answer but returned to the settee, and she quietly went to the bedroom.

Salima went to bed and it was almost midnight when her husband came into the room. His earlier vexation had now given place to gloom. He told her of his brother Karim who lay dying in Hillbrow. Karim had cut himself off from his family and friends ten years ago; he had crossed the colour line (his fair complexion and grey eyes serving as passports) and gone to cohabit with a white woman. And now that he was on the verge of death he wished to return to the world he had forsaken and to be buried under Muslim funeral rites and in a Muslim cemetery.

Hajji Hassen had, of course, rejected the plea, and for good reason. When his brother had crossed the colour line, he had severed his family ties. The Hajji at that time had felt excoriating humiliation. By going over to the white Herrenvolk, his brother had trampled on something that was vitally part of him, his dignity and self-respect. But the rejection of his brother's plea involved a straining of the heartstrings and the Hajji did not feel happy. He had recently sought God's pardon for his sins in Mecca, and now this business of his brother's final earthly wish and his own intransigence was in some way staining his spirit.

The next day Hassen rose at five to go to the mosque. When he stepped out of his house in Newtown the street lights were beginning to pale and clusters of houses to assume definition. The atmosphere was fresh and heady, and he took a few deep breaths. The first trams were beginning to pass through Bree Street and were clanging along like decrepit yet burning spectres towards the Johannesburg City Hall. Here and there a figure moved along hurriedly. The Hindu fruit and vegetable hawkers were starting up their old trucks in the yards, preparing to go out for the day to sell to suburban housewives.

When he reached the mosque the Somali muezzin in the ivory-domed minaret began to intone the call for prayers. After prayers, he remained behind to read the Koran in the company of two other men. When he had done the sun was shining brilliantly in the courtyard onto the flowers and the fountain with its goldfish.

Outside the house he saw a car. Salima opened the door and whispered, 'Caterine'. For a moment he felt irritated, but realising that he might as well face her he stepped boldly into the lounge.

Catherine was a small woman with firm fleshy legs. She was seated cross-legged on the settee, smoking a cigarette. Her face was almost boyish, a look that partly originated in her auburn hair which was cut very short, and partly in the smallness of her head. Her eye-brows, firmly pencilled, accentuated the grey-green glitter of her eyes. She was dressed in a dark grey costume.

He nodded his head at her to signify that he knew who she was. Over the telephone he had spoken with aggressive authority. Now, in the presence of the woman herself, he felt a weakening of his masculine fibre.

'You must, Mr Hassen, come to see your brother.'

'I am afraid I am unable to help,' he said in a tentative tone. He felt uncomfortable; there was something so positive and intrepid about her appearance.

'He wants to see you. It's his final wish.'

'I have not seen him for ten years.'

'Time can't wipe out the fact that he's your brother.'

'He is a white. We live in different worlds.'

'But you must see him.'

There was a moment of strained silence.

'Please understand that he's not to blame for having broken with you. I am to blame. I got him to break with you. Really you must blame me, not Karim.'

Hassen found himself unable to say anything. The thought that she could in some way have been responsible for his brother's rejection of him had never occurred to him. He looked at his feet in awkward silence. He could only state in a lazily recalcitrant tone: 'It is not easy for me to see him.'

'Please come Mr Hassen, for my sake, please. I'll never be able to bear it if Karim dies unhappily. Can't you find it in your heart to forgive him, and to forgive me?'

He could not look at her. A sob escaped from her, and he heard her opening her handbag for a handkerchief.

'He's dying. He wants to see you for the last time.'

Hassen softened. He was overcome by the argument that she had been responsible for taking Karim away. He could hardly look on her responsibility as being in any way culpable. She was a woman.

'If you remember the days of your youth, the time you spent together with Karim before I came to separate him from you, it will be easier for you to pardon him.'

Hassen was silent.

'Please understand that I am not a racialist. You know the conditions in this country.'

He thought for a moment and then said: 'I will go with you.'

He excused himself and went to his room to change. After a while they set off for Hillbrow in her car.

He sat beside her. The closeness of her presence, the perfume she exuded stirred currents of feeling within him. He glanced at her several times, watched the deft movements of her hands and legs as she controlled the car. Her powdered profile, the outline taut with a resolute quality, aroused his imagination. There was something so businesslike in her attitude and bearing, so involved in reality (at the back of his mind there was Salima, flaccid, cowlike and inadequate) that he could hardly refrain from expressing his admiration.

'You must understand that I'm only going to see my brother because you have come to me. For no one else would I have changed my mind.'

'Yes, I understand. I'm very grateful.'

'My friends and relatives are going to accuse me of softness, of weakness.'

'Don't think of them now. You have decided to be kind to me.'

The realism and the commonsense of the woman's words! He was overwhelmed by her.

The car stopped at the entrance of a building in Hillbrow. They took the lift. On the second floor three white youths entered and were surprised at seeing Hassen. There was a separate lift for non-whites. They squeezed themselves into a corner, one actually turning his head away with a grunt of disgust. The lift reached the fifth floor too soon for Hassen to give a thought to the attitude of the three white boys. Catherine led him to apartment 65.

He stepped into the lounge. Everything seemed to be carefully arranged. There was her personal touch about the furniture, the ornaments, the paintings. She went to the bedroom, then returned and asked him in.

Karim lay in bed, pale, emaciated, his eyes closed. For a moment Hassen failed to recognize him: ten years divided them. Catherine placed a chair next to the bed for him. He looked at his brother and again saw, through ravages of illness, the familiar features. She sat on the bed and rubbed Karim's hands to wake him. After a while he began to show signs of consciousness. She called him tenderly by his name. When he opened his eyes he did not recognize the man beside him, but by degrees, after she had repeated Hassen's name several times, he seemed to understand. He stretched out a hand and Hassen took it, moist and repellent. Nausea swept over him but he could not withdraw his hand as his brother clutched it firmly.

'Brother Hassen, please take me away from here.'

Hassen's agreement brought a smile to his lips.

Catherine suggested that she drive Hassen back to Newtown where he could make preparations to transfer Karim to his home.

'No, you stay here. I will take a taxi.' And he left the apartment.

In the corridor he pressed the button for the lift. He watched the indicator numbers succeeding each other rapidly, then stop at five. The doors opened – and there they were again, the three white youths. He hesitated. The boys looked at him tauntingly. Then suddenly they burst into deliberately brutish laughter.

'Come into the parlour,' one of them said.

'Come into the Indian parlour,' another said in a cloyingly mocking voice.

Hassen looked at them, annoyed, hurt. Then something snapped within him and he stood there, transfixed. They laughed at him in a raucous chorus as the lift doors shut.

He remained immobile, his dignity clawed. Was there anything so vile in him that the youths found it necessary to maul that recess of self-respect within him? 'They are whites,' he said to himself in bitter justification of their attitude.

He would take the stairs and walk down the five floors. As he descended he thought of Karim. Because of him he had come there and because of him he had been insulted. The enormity of the insult bridged the gap of ten years when Karim had spurned him, and diminished his being. Now he was diminished again.

He was hardly aware that he had gone down five floors when he reached ground level. He stood still, expecting to see the three youths again. But the foyer was empty and he could see the reassuring activity of street life through the glass panels. He quickly walked out as though he would regain in the hubbub of the street something of his assaulted dignity.

He walked on, structures of concrete and glass on either side of him, and it did not even occur to him to take a taxi. It was in Hillbrow that Karim had lived with the white woman and forgotten the existence of his brother; and now that he was dying he had sent for him. For ten years Karim had lived without him. O Karim! The thought of the youth he had loved so much during the days they had been together at the Islamic Institute, a religious seminary though it was governed like a penitentiary, brought the tears to his eyes and he stopped against a shop window and wept. A few pedestrians looked at him. When the shopkeeper came outside to see the weeping man, Hassen, ashamed of himself, wiped his eyes and walked on.

He regretted his pliability in the presence of the white woman. She had come unexpectedly and had disarmed him with her presence and subtle talk. A painful lump rose in his throat as he set his heart against forgiving Karim. If his brother had had no personal dignity in sheltering behind his white skin, trying to be what he was not, he was not going to allow his own moral worth to be depreciated in any way.

When he reached central Johannesburg he went to the station and took the train. In the coach with the blacks he felt at ease and regained his self-possession. He was among familiar faces, among people who respected him. He felt as though he had been spirited away by a perfumed well-made wax doll, but had managed with a prodigious effort to shake her off.

When he reached home Salima asked him what had been decided and he answered curtly, 'Nothing.' But feeling elated after his escape from Hillbrow he added condescendingly, 'Karim left of his own accord. We should have nothing to do with him.'

Salima was puzzled, but she went on preparing supper.

Catherine received no word from Hassen and she phoned him. She was stunned when he said: 'I'm sorry but I am unable to offer any help.'

'But ... '

'I regret it. I made a mistake. Please make some other arrangements. Goodbye.'

With an effort of will he banished Karim from his mind. Finding his composure again he enjoyed his evening meal, read the paper and then retired to bed. Next morning he went to mosque as usual, but when he returned home he found Catherine there again. Angry that she should have come, he blurted out: 'Listen to me, Catherine. I can't forgive him. For ten years he didn't care about me, whether I was alive or dead. Karim means nothing to me now.'

'Why have you changed your mind? Do you find it so difficult to forgive him?'

'Don't talk to me of forgiveness. What forgiveness, when he threw me aside and chose to go with you? Let his white friends see to him, let Hillbrow see to him.'

'Please, please, Mr Hassen, I beg you ... '

'No, don't come here with your begging. Please go away.'

He opened the door and went out. Catherine burst into tears. Salima comforted her as best she could.

'Don't cry Caterine. All men hard. Dey don't understand.'

'What shall I do now?' Catherine said in a defeated tone. She was an alien in the world of the non-whites. 'Is there no one who can help me?'

'Yes, Mr Mia help you,' replied Salima.

In her eagerness to find some help, she hastily moved to the door. Salima followed her and from the porch of her home directed her to Mr Mia's. He lived in a flat on the first floor of an old building. She knocked and waited in trepidation.

Mr Mia opened the door, smiled affably and asked her in.

'Come inside, lady; sit down ... Fatima,' he called to his daughter, 'bring some tea.'

Mr Mia was a man in his fifties, his bronze complexion partly covered by a neatly trimmed beard. He was a well-known figure in the Indian community. Catherine told him of Karim and her abortive appeal to his brother. Mr

Mia asked one or two questions, pondered for a while and then said: 'Don't worry, my good woman. I'll speak to Hassen. I'll never allow a Muslim brother to be abandoned.'

Catherine began to weep.

'Here, drink some tea and you'll feel better.' He poured tea. Before Catherine left he promised that he would phone her that evening and told her to get in touch with him immediately should Karim's condition deteriorate.

Mr Mia, in the company of the priest of the Newtown mosque, went to Hassen's house that evening. They found several relatives of Hassen's seated in the lounge (Salima had spread the word of Karim's illness). But Hassen refused to listen to their pleas that Karim should be brought to Newtown.

'Listen to me Hajji,' Mr Mia said. 'Your brother can't be allowed to die among the Christians.'

'For ten years he has been among them.'

'That means nothing. He's still a Muslim.'

The priest now gave his opinion. Although Karim had left the community, he was still a Muslim. He had never rejected the religion and espoused Christianity, and in the absence of any evidence to the contrary it had to be accepted that he was a Muslim brother.

'But for ten years he has lived in sin in Hillbrow.'

'If he has lived in sin that is not for us to judge.'

'Hajji, what sort of a man are you? Have you no feeling for your brother?' Mr Mia asked.

'Don't talk to me about feeling. What feeling had he for me when he went to live among the whites, when he turned his back on me?'

'Hajji, can't you forgive him? You were recently in Mecca.'

This hurt Hassen and he winced. Salima came to his rescue with refreshments for the guests.

The ritual of tea-drinking established a mood of conviviality and Karim was forgotten for a while. After tea they again tried to press Hassen into forgiving his brother, but he remained adamant. He could not now face Catherine without looking ridiculous. Besides he felt integrated now; he would resist anything that negated him.

Mr Mia and the priest departed. They decided to raise the matter with the congregation in the mosque. But they failed to move Hassen. Actually his resistance grew in inverse ratio as more people came to learn of the dying Karim and Hassen's refusal to forgive him. By giving in he would be displaying mental dithering of the worst kind, as though he were a man without an inner fibre, decision and firmness of will.

Mr Mia next summoned a meeting of various religious dignitaries and received their mandate to transfer Karim to Newtown without his brother's consent. Karim's relatives would be asked to care for him, but if they refused Mr Mia would take charge.

The relatives, not wanting to offend Hassen and also feeling that Karim was not their responsibility, refused.

Mr Mia phoned Catherine and informed her of what had been decided. She agreed that it was best for Karim to be amongst his people during his last days. So Karim was brought to Newtown in an ambulance hired from a private nursing home and housed in a little room in a quiet yard behind the mosque.

The arrival of Karim placed Hassen in a difficult situation and he bitterly regretted his decision not to accept him into his own home. He first heard of his brother's arrival during the morning prayers when the priest offered a special prayer for the recovery of the sick man. Hassen found himself in the curious position of being forced to pray for his brother. After prayers several people went to see the sick man, others went up to Mr Mia to offer help. Hassen felt out of place and as soon as the opportunity presented itself he slipped out of the mosque.

In a mood of intense bitterness, scorn for himself, hatred of those who had decided to become his brother's keepers, infinite hatred for Karim, Hassen went home. Salima sensed her husband's mood and did not say a word to him.

In his room he debated with himself. In what way should he conduct himself so that his dignity remained intact? How was he to face the congregation, the people in the streets, his neighbours? Everyone would soon know of Karim and smile at him half sadly, half ironically, for having placed himself in such a ridiculous position. Should he now forgive the dying man and transfer him to his home? People would laugh at him, snigger at his cowardice, and Mr Mia perhaps even deny him the privilege: Karim was now *his* responsibility. And what would Catherine think of him? Should he go away somewhere (on the pretext of a holiday) to Cape Town, to Durban? But no, there was the stigma of being called a renegade. And besides, Karim might take months to die, he might not die at all.

'O Karim, why did you have to do this to me?' he said, moving towards the window and drumming at the pane nervously. It galled him that a weak, dying man could bring such pain to him. An adversary could be faced, one could either vanquish him or be vanquished, with one's dignity unravished, but with Karim what could he do?

He paced his room. He looked at his watch; the time for afternoon prayers was approaching. Should he expose himself to the congregation? 'O Karim! Karim!' he cried, holding on to the burglar-proof bar of his bedroom window.

Was it for this that he had made the pilgrimage – to cleanse his soul in order to return into the penumbra of sin? If only Karim would die he would be relieved of his agony. But what if he lingered on? What if he recovered? Were not prayers being said for him? He went to the door and shouted in a raucous voice: 'Salima!'

But Salima was not in the house. He shouted again and again, and his voice echoed hollowly in the rooms. He rushed into the lounge, into the kitchen, he flung the door open and looked into the yard.

He drew the curtains and lay on his bed in the dark. Then he heard the patter of feet in the house. He jumped up and shouted for his wife. She came hurriedly.

'Salima, Salima, go to Karim, he is in a room in the mosque yard. See how he is, see if he is getting better. Quickly!'

Salima went out. But instead of going to the mosque, she entered her neighbour's house. She had already spent several hours sitting beside Karim. Mr Mia had been there as well as Catherine – who had wept.

After a while she returned from her neighbour. When she opened the door her husband ran to her. 'How is he? Is he very ill? Tell me quickly!'

'He is very ill. Why don't you go and see him?'

Suddenly, involuntarily, Hassen struck his wife in the face.

'Tell me, is he dead? Is he dead?' he screamed.

Salima cowered in fear. She had never seen her husband in this raging temper. What had taken possession of the man? She retired quickly to the kitchen. Hassen locked himself in the bedroom.

During the evening he heard voices. Salima came to tell him that several people, led by Mr Mia, wanted to speak to him urgently. His first impulse was to tell them to leave immediately; he was not prepared to meet them. But he had been wrestling with himself for so many hours that he welcomed a moment when he could be in the company of others. He stepped boldly into the lounge.

'Hajji Hassen,' Mr Mia began, 'please listen to us. Your brother has not long to live. The doctor has seen him. He many not outlive the night.'

'I can do nothing about that,' Hassen replied, in an audacious matter-of-fact tone that surprised him and shocked the group of people.

'That is in Allah's hand,' said the merchant Gardee. 'In our hands lie forgiveness and love. Come with us now and see him for the last time.'

'I cannot see him.'

'And what will it cost you?' asked the priest who wore a long black cloak that fell about his sandalled feet.

'It will cost me my dignity and my manhood.'

'My dear Hajji, what dignity and what manhood? What can you lose by speaking a few kind words to him on his death-bed? He was only a young man when he left.'

'I will do anything, but going to Karim is impossible.'

'But Allah is pleased by forgiveness,' said the merchant.

'I am sorry, but in my case the circumstances are different. I am indifferent to him and therefore there is no necessity for me to forgive him.'

'Hajji,' said Mr Mia, 'you are only indulging in glib talk and you know it. Karim is your responsibility, whatever his crime.'

'Gentlemen, please leave me alone.'

And they left. Hassen locked himself in his bedroom and began to pace the narrow space between bed, cupboard and wall. Suddenly, uncontrollably, a surge of grief for his dying brother welled up within him.

'Brother! Brother!' he cried, kneeling on the carpet beside his bed and smothering his face in the quilt. His memory unfolded a time when Karim had been ill at the Islamic Institute and he had cared for him and nursed him back to health. How much he had loved the handsome youth!

At about four in the morning he heard an urgent rapping. He left his room to open the front door.

'Brother Karim dead,' said Mustapha, the Somali muezzin of the mosque, and he cupped his hands and said a prayer in Arabic. He wore a black cloak and a white skull-cap. When he had done he turned and walked away.

Hassen closed the door and went out into the street. For a moment his release into the street gave him a feeling of sinister jubilation, and he laughed hysterically as he turned the corner and stood next to Jamal's fruit-shop. Then he walked on. He wanted to get away as far as he could from Mr Mia and the priest who would be calling upon him to prepare for the funeral. That was no business of his. They had brought Karim to Newtown and they should see to him.

He went up Lovers' Walk and at the entrance of Orient House he saw the night-watchman sitting beside a brazier. He hastened up to him, warmed his hands by the fire, but he did this more as a gesture of fraternisation as it was not cold, and he said a few words facetiously. Then he walked on.

His morbid joy was ephemeral, for the problem of facing the congregation at the mosque began to trouble him. What opinion would they have of him when he returned? Would they not say: he hated his brother so much that he forsook his prayers, but now that his brother is no longer alive he returns. What a man! What a Muslim!

When he reached Vinod's Photographic Studio he pressed his forehead against the neon-lit glass showcase and began to weep.

A car passed by filling the air with nauseous gas. He wiped his eyes, and looked for a moment at the photographs in the showcase; the relaxed, happy, anonymous faces stared at him, faces whose momentary expressions were trapped in film. Then he walked on. He passed a few shops and then reached Broadway Cinema where he stopped to look at the lurid posters. There were heroes, lusty, intrepid, blasting it out with guns; women in various stages of undress; horrid monsters from another planet plundering a city; Dracula.

Then he was among the quiet houses and an avenue of trees rustled softly. He stopped under a tree and leaned against the trunk. He envied the slumbering people in the houses around him, their freedom from the emotions that jarred him. He would not return home until the funeral of his brother was over.

When he reached the Main Reef Road the east was brightening up. The lights along the road seemed to be part of the general haze. The buildings on either side of him were beginning to thin and on his left he saw the ghostly mountains of mine sand. Dawn broke over the city and when he looked back he saw the silhouettes of tall buildings bruising the sky. Cars and trucks were now rushing past him.

He walked for several miles and then branched off onto a gravel road and continued for a mile. When he reached a clump of blue-gum trees he sat down on a rock in the shade of the trees. From where he sat he could see a constant stream of traffic flowing along the highway. He had a stick in his hand which he had picked up along the road, and with it he prodded a crevice in the rock. The action, subtly, touched a chord in his memory and he was sitting on a rock with Karim beside him. The rock was near a river that flowed a mile away from the Islamic Institute. It was a Sunday. He had a stick in his hand and he prodded at a crevice and the weather-worn rock flaked off and Karim was gathering the flakes.

'Karim! Karim!' he cried, prostrating himself on the rock, pushing his fingers into the hard roughness, unable to bear the death of that beautiful youth.

He jumped off the rock and began to run. He would return to Karim. A fervent longing to embrace his brother came over him, to touch that dear form before the soil claimed him. He ran until he was tired, then walked at a rapid pace. His whole existence precipitated itself into one motive, one desire, to embrace his brother in a final act of love.

His heart beating wildly, his hair dishevelled, he reached the highway and walked on as fast as he could. He longed to ask for a lift from a passing motorist but could not find the courage to look back and signal. Cars flashed past him, trucks roared in pain.

When he reached the outskirts of Johannesburg it was nearing ten o'clock.

He hurried along, now and then breaking into a run. Once he tripped over a cable and fell. He tore his trousers in the fall and found his hands were bleeding. But he was hardly conscious of himself, wrapped up in his one purpose.

He reached Lovers' Walk, where cars growled around him angrily; he passed Broadway Cinema, rushed towards Orient House, turned the corner at Jamal's fruitshop. And stopped.

The green hearse, with the crescent moon and stars emblem, passed by; then several cars with mourners followed, bearded men, men with white skull-caps on their heads, looking rigidly ahead, like a procession of puppets, indifferent to his fate. No one saw him.

LEARNING TO FLY
Christopher Hope

innuendo

An African Fairy Tale

L ong ago, in the final days of the old regime, there was a colonel who held an important job in the State Security Police and his name was Rocco du Preez. Colonel du Preez was in charge of the interrogation of political suspects and because of his effect on the prisoners of the old regime he became widely known in the country as 'Window-jumpin'' du Preez. After mentioning his name it was customary to add 'thank God', because he was a strong man and in the dying days of the old regime everyone agreed that we needed a strong man. Now Colonel du Preez acquired his rather strange nickname not because he did any window jumping himself but rather because he had been the first to draw attention to this phenomenon which affected so many of the prisoners who were brought before him.

The offices of State Security were situated on the thirteenth floor of a handsome and tall modern block in the centre of town. Their high windows looked down on to a little dead end street far below. Once this street had been choked with traffic and bustling with thriving shops. Then one day the first jumper landed on the roof of a car parked in the street, and after that it was shut to traffic and turned into a pedestrian shopping mall. The street was filled in and covered over with crazy paving and one or two benches set up for weary shoppers. However, the jumpings increased and became a spate: sometimes one or two a week and several nasty accidents on the ground began to frighten off the shoppers.

Whenever a jump had taken place the whole area was cordoned off to allow in the emergency services; the police, the undertaker's men, the municipal workers brought in to hose down the area of impact which was often surprisingly large. The jumpings were bad for business and the shopkeepers grew desperate. The authorities were sympathetic and erected covered walk-ways running the length of the street leaving only the central area of crazy pavings and the benches, on which no one had ever been known to sit, exposed to the heavens; the walk-ways protected by their overhead concrete parapets were guaranteed safe against any and all flying objects. But still trade dwindled and one by one the shops closed and the street slowly died and came to be known by the locals, who gave it a wide berth, as the 'landing field'. — Metaphor

As everyone knows, window jumpings increased apace over the years and being well placed to study them probably led Colonel Rocco du Preez to his celebrated thesis afterwards included in the manual of psychology used by recruits at the Police College and known as Du Preez's Law. It states that all men, when brought to the brink, will contrive to find a way out if the least chance is afforded them and the choice of the means is always directly related to the racial characteristics of the individual in question. Some of Du Preez's remarks on the subject have come down to us, though these are almost certainly apocryphal, as are so many of the tales of the final days of the old regime. 'Considering your average white man,' Du Preez is supposed to have said, 'my experience is that he prefers hanging – whether by pyjama cord, belt, strips of blanket; providing he finds the handy protuberance, the cell bars, say, or up-ended bedstead he needs, you'll barely have turned your back and he'll be up there swinging from the light cord or other chosen noose. Your white man in his last throes has a wonderful sense of rhythm – believe me, whatever you may have heard to the contrary – I've seen several whites about to cough it and all of them have been wonderful dancers. Your Indian, now, he's something else, a slippery customer who prefers smooth surfaces. I've known Asians to slip and crack their skulls in a shower cubicle so narrow you'd have sworn a man couldn't turn in it. This innate slitheriness is probably what makes them good businessmen. Now, your Coloured, per contra, is more clumsy a character altogether. His hidden talent lies in his amazing lack of co-ordination. Even the most sober rogue can appear hopelessly drunk to the untrained eye. On the surface of things it might seem that you can do nothing with him; he has no taste for the knotted strip of blanket or the convenient boot-lace; a soapy bathroom floor leaves him unmoved – yet show him a short, steep flight of steps and he instinctively knows what to do. When it comes to Africans I have found that they, perverse as always, choose another way out. They are given to window jumping. This phenomenon has been very widespread in the past few years. Personally, I suspect its roots go back a long way, back to their superstitions – i.e. to their regard for black magic and witchcraft. Everyone knows that in extreme instances your average blackie will believe anything: that his witchdoctors will turn the white man's bullets to water; or, if he jumps out of a window thirteen storeys above terra firma he will miraculously find himself able to fly. Nothing will stop him once his mind's made up. I've seen up to six Bantu jump from a high window on one day. Though the first landed on his head and the others saw the result they were not deterred. It's as if despite the evidence of their senses they believed that if only they could practise enough they would one day manage to take off.'

'Window-jumpin'' du Preez worked in an office sparsely furnished with an old desk, a chair, a strip of green, government-issue carpet, a very large steel cabinet marked 'Secret' and a bare, fluorescent light in the ceiling. Poor though the furnishings were, the room was made light and cheerful by the large windows behind his desk and nobody remembers being aware of the meanness of the furnishings when Colonel du Preez was present in the room. When he sat down in his leather swivel chair behind his desk, witnesses reported that he seemed to fill up the room, to make it habitable, even genial. His reddish hair and green eyes were somehow enough to colour the room and make it complete. The eyes had a peculiarly steady glint to them. This was his one peculiarity. When thinking hard about something he had the nervous habit of twirling a lock of the reddish hair, a copper colour with gingery lights, in the words of a witness, around a finger. It was his only nervous habit. Since these were often the last words ever spoken by very brave men, we have to wonder at their ability to register details so sharply under terrible conditions; for it is these details that provide us with a glimpse of the man Du Preez, as no photographs have come down to us.

It was to this office that three plainclothes men one day brought a new prisoner. The charge-sheet was singularly bare: it read simply, Mphahlele . . . Jake. 'Possession of explosives.' Obviously they had got very little out of him. The men left closing the door softly, almost reverently, behind them.

The prisoner wore an old black coat, ragged grey flannels and a black beret tilted at an angle which gave him an odd, jaunty, rather continental look, made all the more incongruous by the fact that his hands were manacled behind him. Du Preez reached up with his desk ruler and knocked off the beret revealing a bald head gleaming in the overhead fluorescent light. It would have been shaved and polished Du Preez guessed, by one of the wandering barbers who traditionally gathered on Sundays down by the municipal lake, setting up three-legged stools and basins of water and hanging towels and leather strops for their cutthroat razors from the lower branches of a convenient tree and draping their customers in large red and white check cloths, giving them little hand mirrors so that they could look on while the barbers scraped, snipped, polished and gossiped away the sunny afternoon by the water's edge beneath the tall bluegums. Clearly Mphahlele belonged to the old school of whom there were fewer each year as the fashion for Afro-wigs and strange woollen bangs took increasing hold among younger Blacks. Du Preez couldn't help warming to this just a little. After all, he was one of the old school himself in the new age of trimmers and ameliorists. Mphahlele was tall, as tall as Du Preez and, he reckoned, about the same age – though it was always difficult to tell with Africans. A knife scar ran from his right eye down to his collar, the flesh fused in a livid welt as if a tiny mole had burrowed under the black skin pushing up a furrow behind it. His nose had been broken, too, probably as the result of the same township fracas, and had mended badly turning to the left and then sharply to the right as if unable to make up its mind. The man was obviously a brawler. Mphahlele's dark brown eyes were remarkably calm – almost to the point of arrogance Du Preez thought for an instant, before dismissing the absurd notion with a tiny smile. It shocked to see an answering smile on the prisoner's lips. However he was too old a hand to let this show.

'Where are the explosives?'

'I have no explosives,' Mphahlele answered. 'Also, I will tell you nothing.'

He spoke quietly but Du Preez thought he detected a most unjustifiable calm amounting to confidence, or worse, to insolence, and he noted how he talked with special care. It was another insight. On his pad he wrote the letters M. K. The prisoner's diction and accent betrayed him: Mission Kaffir. Raised at one of the stations by a foolish clergy as though he was one day going to be a white man. Of course, the word 'kaffir' was not a word in official use any longer. Like other names at that time growing less acceptable as descriptions of Africans: 'native', 'coon' and even 'bantu', the word had given way to softer names in an attempt to respond to the disaffection springing up among people. But Du Preez, as he told himself, was too old a dog to learn new tricks. Besides, he was not interested in learning to be more 'responsive'. He did not belong to the ameliorists. His job was to control disaffection and where necessary to put it down with proper force. And anyway, his notes were strictly for his own reference, private reminders of his first impressions of a prisoner, useful when, and if, a second interview took place. The numbers of people he saw was growing daily and he could not expect to keep track of them all in his head.

Du Preez left his desk and slowly circled the prisoner. 'Your comrade who placed the bomb in the shopping centre was a bungler. There was great damage. Many people were killed. Women and children among them. But he wasn't quick enough, your friend. The blast caught him too. Before he died he gave us your name. The paraffin tests show you handled explosives recently. I want the location of the cache. I want the make-up of your cell with names and addresses as well as anything else you might want to tell me.'

'If the bomb did its business then the man was no bungler,' Mphahlele said.

'The murder of women and children – no bungle?'

Mphahlele shrugged. 'Casualties of war.'

Du Preez circled him and stopped beside his right ear. 'I don't call the death of children war. I call it barbarism.'

'Our children have been dying for years but we have never called it barbarism. Now we are learning. You and I know what we mean. I'm your prisoner of war. You will do whatever you can to get me to tell you things you want to know. Then you will get rid of me. But I will tell you nothing. So why don't you finish with me now? Save time.' His brown eyes rested briefly and calmly on Du Preez's empty chair, and then swept the room as if the man had said all he had to say and was now more interested in getting to know that terrible office.

A muscle in Du Preez's cheek rippled and it took him a moment longer than he would have liked to bring his face back to a decent composure. Then he crossed to the big steel cabinet and opened it. Inside was the terrible, tangled paraphernalia of persuasion, the electric generator, the leads and electrodes, the salt water for sharpening contact and the thick leather straps necessary for restraining the shocked and writhing victim. At the sight of this he scored a point; he thought he detected a momentary pause, a faltering in the steady brown eyes taking stock of this office, and he pressed home the advantage. 'It's very seldom that people fail to talk to me after this treatment.' He held up the electrodes, 'The pain is intense.'

In fact, as we know now, the apparatus in the cabinet was not that actually used on prisoners – indeed, one can see the same equipment on permanent exhibition in the National Museum of the Revolution. But Du Preez, in fact, kept it for effect. The real thing was administered by a special team in a soundproof room on one of the lower floors. But the mere sight of the equipment, whose reputation was huge among the townships and shanty towns, was often enough to have the effect of loosening stubborn tongues. However, Mphahlele looked at the tangle of wires and straps as if he wanted to include them in his inventory of the room and his expression suggested not fear but rather – and this Du Preez found positively alarming – a hint of approval. There was nothing more to be said. He went back to his desk, pressed the buzzer and the plainclothes men came in and took Mphahlele downstairs.

Over the next twenty-four hours 'Window-jumpin'' du Preez puzzled over his new prisoner. It was a long time before he put his finger on some of the qualities distinguishing this man from others he'd worked with under similar circumstances. Clearly, Mphahlele was not frightened. But then other men had been brave too – for a while. It was not only bravery, one had to add to it the strange fact that this man quite clearly did not hate him. That was quite alarming: Mphahlele had treated him as if they were truly equals. There was an effrontery about this he found maddening and the more he thought about it, the more he raged inside. He walked over to the windows behind his desk and looked down to the dead little square with its empty benches and its crazy paving which, with its haphazard joins where the stones were cemented one to the next into nonsensical, snaking patterns, looked from the height of the thirteenth storey as if a giant had brought his foot down hard and the earth had shivered into a thousand pieces. He was getting angry. Worse, he was letting his anger cloud his judgement. Worse still, he didn't care.

Mphahlele was in a bad way when they brought him back to Du Preez. His face was so bruised that the old knife scar was barely visible, his lower lip was bleeding copiously and he swayed when the policemen let him go and might have fallen had he not grabbed the edge of the desk and hung there swaying. In answer to Du Preez's silent question the interrogators shook their heads. 'Nothing. He never said *nothing*.'

Mphahlele had travelled far in the regions of pain and it had changed him greatly. It might have been another man who clung to Du Preez's desk with his breath coming in rusty pants; his throat was choked with phlegm or blood he did not have the strength to cough away. He was bent and old and clearly on his last legs. One eye was puffed up in a great swelling shot with green and purple bruises, but the other, he noticed with a renewed spurt of anger, though it had trouble focusing, showed the same old haughty gleam when he spoke to the man.

'Have you any more to tell me about your war?'

Mphahlele gathered himself with a great effort, his one good eye flickering wildly with the strain. He licked the blood off his lips and wiped it from his chin. 'We will win,' he said, 'soon.'

Du Preez dismissed the interrogators with a sharp nod and they left his presence by backing away to the door, full of awe at his control. When the door closed behind them he stood up and regarded the swaying figure with its flickering eye. 'You are like children,' he said bitterly, 'and there is nothing we can do for you.'

'Yes,' said Mphahlele, 'we are your children. We owe you everything.'

Du Preez stared at him. But there was not a trace of irony to be detected. The madman was quite plainly sincere in what he said and Du Preez found that insufferable. He moved to the windows and opened them. It was now that, so the stories go, he made his fateful remark. 'Well, if you won't talk, then I suppose you had better learn to fly.'

What happened next is not clear except in broad outline even today, the records of the old regime which were to have been made public have unaccountably been reclassified as secret, but we can make an informed guess. Legend then says that Du Preez recounted for his prisoner his 'theory of desperate solutions' and that, exhausted though he was, Mphahlele showed quickening interest in the way out chosen by white men – that is to say, dancing. We know this is true because Du Preez told the policemen waiting outside the door when he joined them in order to allow Mphahlele to do what he had to do. After waiting a full minute, Du Preez entered his office again closing the door behind him, alone, as had become customary in such cases, his colleagues respecting his need for a few moments of privacy before moving on to the next case. Seconds later these colleagues heard a most terrible cry. When they rushed into the room they found it was empty.

Now we are out on a limb. We have no more facts to go on. All is buried in obscurity or say, rather, it is buried with Du Preez who plunged from his window down to the landing field at the most terrible speed, landing on his head. Jake Mphahlele has never spoken of his escape from Colonel 'Window-jumpin'' du Preez. All we have are the stories. Some firmly believe to this day that it was done by a special magic and Mphahlele had actually learnt to fly and that the Colonel on looking out of his window, was so jealous at seeing a black man swooping in the heavens that he had plunged after him on the supposition, regarded as axiomatic in the days of the old regime, that anything a black man could do, a white man could do ten times better. Others, more sceptical, said that the prisoner had hidden himself in the steel cabinet with the torture equipment and emerged to push Du Preez to hell and then escaped in the confusion you will get in a hive if you kill the queen bee. All that is known for sure is that Du Preez lay on the landing field like wet clothes fallen from a washing line, terribly twisted and leaking everywhere. And that in the early days of the new regime Jake Mphahlele was appointed chief investigating officer in charge of the interrogation of suspects and that his work with political prisoners, especially white prisoners, was soon so widely respected that he won rapid promotion to the rank of Colonel and became known throughout the country as Colonel Jake 'Dancin'' Mphahlele, and after his name it was customary to add 'thank God', because he was a strong man and in the early days of the new regime everyone agreed we needed a strong man.

THIS TIME OF YEAR
Sheila Roberts

S he stands near the fence at the harvested and churned section, once mealiefield. The earth is lumpy and brick red, rich as used oil, but there is no shine. There is no sun. The even, pale autumn sky, not so much white as eggshell grey, and the smell of rain somewhere, though there are no rain clouds, create a motionless clarity in which those still-standing tough stalks and the yellowing trees seem stark, nonliving pasteboard objects on a flattened landscape. Even the faded brown barn behind the unploughed mealies is showing up its lack of paint, and reposing isolated and unfounded as if suddenly placed there. She imagines that every pore of her face is like a dull freckle and that the grey streaks in her hair have singled themselves out for notice.

'You should marry me again,' Sam said last night.

She sees smoke coming from the Vosloo chimney at their place across the highway that for the moment is blessedly still. The reluctant billows hover; there is no breath of air to move them skywards. Why should the Vosloos want an open fire in this mild weather? she wonders. Perhaps the old woman, come to help out, is always cold.

A truck and a small Datsun neck-to-neck come sweeping by and she feels the earth rock underfoot. Can the solid dark earth rock, or is it only the noise translated by her ears into movement?

Last winter Mary Vosloo hanged herself in the back shed. Like Hannah, Mary had been thirty-nine then.

'Hannah, Mary Vosloo is dead,' her father told her. 'Died of heart failure, I hear.'

But of course it was not heart failure. Oh yes, the autopsy stated that death was caused by heart failure following strangulation. *Heart failure* was a comfortable, familiar phrase in the mouth of the community and in the elevated tones of the Dominee at the funeral. Nobody could bring himself to say *strangulation*, except Hannah who repeated it softly throughout the burial service and then aloud, suddenly, to her father in the kitchen afterwards. *Strangulation*, she said challengingly. He frowned, looked for a moment as if he knew something, then walked away. Hannah expected him of all people to have the courage to admit that Mary Vosloo's life had not been worth living.

The little tree next to the driveway is playing a painterly game. Some of its outer leaves are pale wilting yellow, others closer to the bole are a lively red, while those protected within the smaller branches boast a grim untimely green. She should photograph it, transfix it at this mutable stage. No, she shouldn't. The photograph would look flat while the tree is moving maliciously in circles of colour.

Tomorrow her father and Philamon will mow down the remaining mealies, then dig in the stalks, and the russet earth will fold over the rise and open up the far mottling koppie to their view.

'Why should I remarry you? I divorced you.'

'It's stupid for us not to be married after all this time.'

'My father won't have you here. You can't come to the house.'

'So what?'

'If I remarried you, I'd have to leave the farm.'

'We'll go 'n live in town.'

'I don't want to any more.'

'Marry me again, Hannah ... '

At the funeral, the Dominee spoke of the beauty of Mary Vosloo's life, of her service to her family and to her friends, of her excellence as a wife and mother. He spoke the fiction of someone's life: nothing about Jocko Vosloo beating Mary repeatedly and Mary hanging herself in the back shed. How did one look when strangulated? Black in the face, large purple tongue like a rotten fish protruding from cracked lips, eyes like mottled eggs ready to fall out of their casings?

A sports car blaring music from an opened window whizzes by

Her father made some money when the province ran the highway through the farm. And the noise had not become as bad as they had expected. Yet the earth certainly did tremble when the lorries thundered along. Thundered and whooshed like missiles. She thinks of the whole country shaking away as the streams of trucks, carrying food or soldiers, rocket interminably over every road, passing always the same things, road shoulders, turn-offs, bridges, farms, petrol stations, villages with cafés and Wimpy Bars. Yes, all the pathways above earth rumbling under the traffic and all the channels below earth flowing with the excreta from bread and steaks and chops and chips, and mealiemeal and tea, and beer and beer and beer ... horrible, horribly funny. But she can forget such absurd ideas when the highway is quiet, as now, and thousands of birds, high up and thick as locusts, escape northwards across the flat sky, and the smell from the churned earth makes her feel wealthy almost; momentarily makes her love the odour of her own body; convinces her that, unlike Mary Vosloo, she will never hang herself.

'Last time was the last time, Hannah,' her father said when she asked him to pay Sam's fine again. 'I never liked that fellow, and I like him even less now that someone else has been hurt because of his careless driving. I am paying nothing,' he emphasised, '*nothing*.'

Sam went to jail.

Once again she returned home to the farm, to a vacant kitchen, and a living-room starkly arranged by Philamon. She, Hannah, took over the chores of the farm-wife and was pleased to do it. And that winter, Mary Vosloo hanged herself.

The whole family disliked Sam from the beginning. Dislikes him, despises him his folly and his frequent binges. Or is some of their response nervousness because of this looks? He was and is ugly, Hannah admits, and wonders why people care about such things. She cares, she thinks, but only about herself, not about other people. Sam has dark straight hair, dead hair, and a face punctured by teeming acne scars that do sometimes seem to recede. Some forgotten Middle-Eastern ancestry has left him with blue circles under what appear to be brooding eyes (but are not, he is inveterately cheerful), circles that remain even after twelve hours' sleep. His nose is a bit distorted, pummelled too often during a mediocre school-days' boxing career, and he came back from the border a drunkard. The army is to blame, he says. But he stands well, and the black hair creeps like soft wires over his chest and into his groin. She loved it. She does not know if she does love it, or whether it matters if she does or she doesn't.

'He has the face of a murderer,' her mother said after a first meeting, her mother herself dying and afraid for her daughter.

'Murderer? What do you mean, Ma?'

'He looks like he could kill.'

'Rubbish!'

'Don't shout at me like that, Hannah!'

The sky is mauve and the Vosloos' lights go on. Hannah listens for a cricket but hears nothing. Too late. They are gone. Even the mosquitoes are going. Sam is out of jail now, waiting for her to return to him like every other time. His thin dark body. A dead-loss, a goddamned dead-loss, her father will say.

She hugs her large loose breasts to herself. She is thin but her breasts remain heavy and her stomach is round and soft, withered at the skin like a large overripe peach. Babies. She holds her body and hates it while loving her own presence in the autumn twilight that stirs her to want to keep living, to experience earthliness, earthiness, but in ways different from the past.

'Let me see you, let me *see* you!' he begged once, trying to force her knees apart and then, on succeeding, ejaculating immediately leaving him ashamed of his failure and her, strangely, of herself. She hated being looked at. She never knew why. She doesn't know why. Bodies were never spoken of at home. Nobody told her hers was ugly, repelling. It is ugly, repelling, she knows without having to be told.

She told her mother first that she was going to marry Sam and left it to her mother to tell her father.

'Jesus H. Christ, does she want to marry that ugly bastard of a loser? No, I say no!'

'But, dear, she is already thirty. Have you forgotten that she is already thirty?'

Hannah listened at the slightly-opened door, astonished, waiting for the silence to end. But her father had decided, it seemed, to say nothing further. Then she had known that she wanted his protest, his objections, so that she could counter them. Winning him over would have been her vindication.

A slight rain begins to fall, English rain one could say, and the leaves on the ground stand out like scraps of torn brown paper as a partial thinning of the smooth cloud-covering sends down a last light.

She wonders what it will be like, a second wedding ceremony. They will stand there, knowing all, linking hands, looking at the magistrate and into the collage of their past life together, and repeat words mechanically, sensing that the heartbeat and the hope are gone. Can she ever *not* be married to Sam? The divorce declared that they were apart. Truly they were apart, not simply because he was in jail.

Jail. She remembers old movies. Shadows of bars on sunlit floors, no not sunlit floors, neonlit floors, pyjama-clad men mopping wide expanses of tiled corridor, calls in the night, screams, lines at mealtimes, knives hidden in toothbrushes, rapes, nightmares, naked pin-ups. And Sam? What has he learnt?

She takes off her shoes and stands, sinking slightly, on the blackening earth, then she makes her way mulching towards the house, the rain wetting her temples and eyelids. Suddenly there is a smell of winter trying to overpower the ripe scent of scattering leaves and drying underbrush. Soon the colourlessness and the frozen air will fold them in, her father, herself, and the two boys.

At the garden tap she washes off her feet and treads to the kitchen where she stamps to dry them on the mat.

'What's for dinner, Ma?' says Sammie from the floor where he is brim-brimming a tiny car along imaginary byways.

'Food,' she says, 'food.'

'Always food,' says David from the table where he is doing homework. 'Poor us, Ma. We're too far from the shops and you never buy us sweets any more. We'll keep our teeth until we're very old, like Grandpa, and frighten people when we grin.'

'Don't be smarty-pants,' she says, smiling. He's getting big.

'Would you prefer to live in a town and eat a lot of junk?' she asks.

'Naa ... the farm's all right,' he says. He knows, she thinks.

'I want all my teef,' says Sammie from the floor.

Her father kept his mouth sullenly shut during the short, sparsely attended ceremony at the Magistrate's court. He didn't smile once as she and Sam were married, witnessed by Jocko and Mary Vosloo. He didn't want his teeth counted, she had thought, remembering the old family superstition. This was bad luck indeed; first a neighbour like Jocko, now a son-in-law like Sam.

'But if Cokes and potato crisps isn't junk, then tell me what is,' says David, mildly argumentative.

'I give you a decent lunch of meat sandwiches and fruit, and you can have milk too, if you let me know the night before ... ' says Hannah, not really listening to him as she bends to check the roast.

'Joey Vosloo eats potato crisps and dripping sammiches every day,' says Sammie. 'Joey Vosloo eats any ol' thing.' The little boy clutches at his throat and grimaces as if he is being choked. 'An' cold punkeen fritters ...'

'Stop that,' says Hannah, lifting her foot to jab him in the backside. Instead she bends and removes the twisted red leaf that has been caught in his fair hair that smells like puppy fur. 'Stop it,' she says, softer, 'and remind me to wash your hair tonight.'

The kitchen window is misting up so that only a deepening blue-grey can be seen beginning to disguise objects. A wind seems to have sprung up. She listens to the sound of dry leaves rubbing and falling. Or is it stronger rain? In this house surrounded as it is by trees, one never knows exactly whether the pattering and brushing comes from leaves or drops, or even from the birds that nest in the eaves this time of year.

Her husband found Mary Vosloo hanging. Thank God not Joey or ... she stops what she is doing, horrified, or the baby girl crawling into the shed and gurgling up at the dangling feet of her mother. Hanging. Conveying a clear message to her man and to her people. What message? It must be terribly clear, but what is it? I have more power to hurt myself than you have had or ever shall have again?

Perhaps she, Hannah, should have shut her trap about the arguments and the debts, and the repeated, minor car accidents always occurring when Sam was on the booze. She should have protected her parents. Instead, she used to turn up at the farm regularly to confide in her ailing mother, wanting perhaps to demonstrate that she too was suffering. How false of her, how undiscriminating. She was suffering life, after all, not its diminishment like her mother, or its distortion like Mary Vosloo. And she could rely on her mother to tell her father about Sam's goings-on, and her father would rage, she was sure. However, once he had grinned, showing his even strong teeth.

'So you cut up the three dresses with your garden shears, did you?'

'Yes, I cut them up. Ripped them up really,' she said, no longer so proud of herself. She had boasted the story to her sighing mother.

At the time she had felt up to her ribs in a squeezing quicksand of debt, her arms fluttering like trapped creatures, tearing at this bill and that final notice, phoning, pleading. Then Sam had come home one evening, merrily drunk, carrying a large gift for her, an oblong box covered in gift wrap. In it were three dresses he had bought for her on the one account she had managed to reduce. Smart dresses. She stared at them uncomprehendingly, then, running wildly to the workchest, she had grabbed a pair of shears and hacked at the garments, crying and crying and crying for hours, while he sat, elbows on knees, head dangling, in one of the easy chairs that was about to be repossessed.

It is rain and not leaves. The drops fall stronger now and throw streaks across the window-pane. She hears her father's footsteps upstairs, magnified heavily by the wooden boards. Yet it is right that they should sound so weighty. He is a big gaunt man with a strong jaw and a deep crease down each leathery cheek. When he opens his mouth to smile or grimace one is hard put to notice the difference. His protruding brown eyes always look the same. But he is an honest man, and just, and she realizes with shame that she was oblivious to what he was going through when he alone took care of her dying mother. She likes to think that he has smelled the food and is coming downstairs for it as millions of men in warm houses must be doing at that moment.

She ladles the food onto the plates, hammering the spoon slightly to get the mashed potatoes off it, and pouring gravy from the roasting pot. Sammie is moaning about not too many beans while David helps carry the plates through to the dining room. His grandfather is seated, pouring milk from the pitcher into the children's glasses. He pours a glass of wine from the demijohn and hands it carefully to David to pass to his mother.

You must remarry me Hannah.

How can I possibly?

She cuts up Sammie's meat into tiny pieces for him to manage.

'Jocko Vosloo is going to sell up,' says her father.

'Why?' she asks.

'He can't handle things any more.'

'But aren't you and Philamon going to help him plough the far end field?'

She knows that Jocko Vosloo can't keep his labourers because of his temper.

'It's also the house and the kids. His mother's too old to be of much help. He says he's going to sell up. He's going to leave the kids at his sister's place.'

'Is he ... very sad ... about it?' Hannah asks lamely.

Her father looks at her and fills his mouth with beef.

'Joey Vosloo won't ride in the school bus no more,' says Sammie.

'Shush!' says Hannah.

Was that Mary's message? Jocko, you lose me, you lose the kids, you lose the farm. My total loss equals almost, unfortunately *only* almost, your total loss.

While the boys splash in the bath and her father sits, pipe in mouth, studying a paint catalogue, Hannah stands at the sink stashing the plates for Philamon. She stares at the vague mirror the window has become.

Years ago she complained to Mary, her friend.

'All I do is drive and drive, Mary. He's lost his licence, so I have to drive him to the mine, drive the kids to school, pick up the kids, pick him up, drop him off at the bar, and then pick him up later. I don't know what's worse: being a chauffeur or worrying about him when he takes the car himself at night, even though he knows that if they catch him it's big trouble ... '

'At least you get out,' Mary said, her eyes curiously out of focus. 'At least he never lays a finger on you ... '

Just before the next accident, Hannah found under old documents and leaflets in the car's glove compartment an envelope of coloured photos, badly taken photos, poorly composed, amateurish. In all four shots the same woman with dyed hair standing up like a bonnet, posed, now with legs spread, now lying on a bed, now bending forward showing her arse and all else, now fingering the folds of her vagina. Hannah, cruel, showed them to her mother; Hannah wordless, shocked, her shy taciturn body stiff with an unlocatable disgust. Her mother shook her head, looked up at Hannah and said, 'Throw them away.'

'How could a woman degrade herself like that, Ma? How could Sam want to possess these things?'

'Throw them away,' said her mother.

Then came the accident in which a young pedestrian, one of the mine apprentices, was hurt. Sam went to jail and Hannah left the town and came back to the farm for the fourth time, in time to help her mother into the ambulance and to the hospital.

'You'll hate living out here permanently,' Mary said.

'I've always loved the farm,' said Hannah, feeling childish and ashamed.

A few stones of flicking hail crackle against the window. Hannah is astonished. Hail at this time of year? She peers and listens. One stone cracks, then another. Somebody is flinging pebbles at the window. She bends her head to see whether her father has heard. He is engrossed. Hannah wipes her hands and tiptoes to the back swingdoor and steps into the moist darkness.

'Hannah?'

'Why have you come here, Sam?'

'I had to see you. Talking on the phone like last night was no good.'

'How did you get here?'

'I borrowed a bike.'

Hannah bites back a laugh. The dicing king of Welkom has pedalled ten miles on a bicycle.

'Whose bike?'

'Never mind. Listen, there are jobs in Silverton and I'm shoving off in the morning. I want you and the kids to come . . .'

'No.'

'Remarry me, Hannah. Things'll be different.'

'No.'

'I'm warning you, this is your last chance with me, Hannah.'

'I'm staying on the farm, Sam.'

'I want to see the kids.'

'This is not your time. The magistrate gave you your times. And my father doesn't want you here . . . now.'

She feels a pang when he curses and turns the bike. She had expected more. But the rain is beginning to fall harder.

Back in the kitchen, Hannah begins to laugh into the dishcloth.

She laughs until the tears drip. The boys are beginning to fight, she can hear. The bath-water must be cold and the bathroom floor a swamp. Her father stomps into the kitchen, catalogue in hand, so Hannah wipes her face.

'Look here, Hannah. There's a new paint, good for outdoors, selling cheap. I think I'll repaint the barn in the spring.'

'Why not now?'

'Not this time of year. After the winter.'

'I'll help,' says Hannah.

'And David's old enough to help too. With Philamon, that makes four; we can get the job done quickly.' Rustling the catalogue, he moves away. Does he know that Sam has come and gone? Does he know that Hannah has been truly drawn back? Does he care?

The rain begins in earnest. At first Hannah thinks Sam is now throwing stones at the roof, then she tries to imagine him, head down, legs pumping the pedals like a schoolboy. She cannot. She tries to think of alternatives,

alternatives open to her, but can only think of life on a mine property with the tension of love (is it love?) and drunkenness, and the peace of life on the farm.

Actually, the house needs painting too. And in the spring she should enlarge the vegetable garden and plant more little trees like the spinning one in the driveway.

She hears Philamon at the back door, so heads for the bathroom to wash Sammie's hair.

THE TEST
Njabulo Ndebele

A s he felt the first drops of rain on his bare arms, Thoba wondered if he should run home quickly before there was a downpour. He shivered briefly, and his teeth chattered for a moment as a cold breeze blew and then stopped. How cold it had become, he thought. He watched the other boys who seemed completely absorbed in the game. They felt no rain, and no cold. He watched. The boys of Mayaba Street had divided themselves into two soccer teams. That was how they spent most days of their school vacations: playing soccer in the street. No, decided Thoba, he would play on. Besides, his team was winning. He looked up at the sky and sniffed, remembering that some grown-ups would say one can tell if it is going to rain by sniffing at the sky the way dogs do. He was not sure if he could smell anything other than the dust raised by the soccer players around him. He could tell, though, that the sky, having been overcast for some time, had grown darker.

Should I? he thought. Should I go home? But the ball decided for him when it came his way accidentally, and he was suddenly swept into the action as he dribbled his way past one fellow. But the next fellow took the ball away from him, and Thoba gave it up without a struggle. It had been a quick thrill. He had felt no rain, no cold. The trick is to keep playing and be involved, he thought. But he stopped, and looked at the swarm of boys chasing after the tennis ball in a swift chaotic movement away from him, like a whirlwind. They were all oblivious of the early warnings of rain. He did not follow them, feeling no inclination to do so. He felt uncertain whether he was tired or whether it was the fear of rain and cold that had taken his interest away from the game. He looked down at his arms. There they were: tiny drops of rain, some sitting on goose pimples, others between them. Fly's spit, he thought.

Soon there was a loud yell. Some boys were jumping into the air, others shaking their fists, others dancing in all sorts of ways. Some, with a determined look on their faces, trotted back to the centre, their small thumbs raised, to wait for the ball to be thrown in again. Someone had scored for Thoba's team. The scorer was raised into the air. It was Vusi. But Vusi's triumph was short-lived for it was just at that moment that the full might of the rain came. Vusi disappeared from the sky like a mole reversing into its hole. The boys of Mayaba Street scattered home, abandoning their match. The goal posts on either side disappeared when the owners of the shoes repossessed them. Thoba began to run home, hesitated, and changed direction to follow a little group of boys towards the shelter of the walled veranda of Simangele's home.

Thoba found only Simangele, Vusi, Mpiyakhe, and Nana on the veranda. He was disappointed. In the rush, it had seemed as if more boys had gone there. Perhaps he really should have run home, he thought. Too late, though. He was there now, at the veranda of Simangele's home, breathing hard like the others from the short impulsive sprint away from the rain. They were all trying to get the rain water off them: kicking it off their legs, or pushing it down their arms with their fingers, the way windscreen wipers do. Simangele wiped so hard that it looked as if he was rubbing the water into his skin. Only Vusi, who had scored the last goal, was not wiping off the water on him. There was an angry scowl on his face as he slowly massaged his buttocks, all the while cursing:

'The bastards,' he said. 'The bastards! They just dropped me. They let go of me like a bag of potatoes. I'll get them for that. One by one. I'll get them one by one.'

'What if you *are* a bag of potatoes?' said Simangele laughing. 'What do you think, fellows?' He was jumping up and down like a grown-up soccer player warming up just before the beginning of a game. He shadow-boxed briefly then jumped up and down again.

Simangele got no response from the others. It would have been risky for them to take sides. Thoba rubbed his arms vigorously, making it too obvious that he was shamming a preoccupation with keeping warm in order to avoid answering Simangele's question. But Vusi did not fear Simangele.

'This is no laughing matter,' he said.

'Then don't make me laugh,' replied Simangele, shadow-boxing with slow easy sweeps of his arms.

Vusi uttered a click of annoyance and looked away from Simangele. He continued to massage his buttocks.

Simangele looked at Vusi for a while, and then turned away to look at Nana.

'Are you warm?' he asked, suddenly looking gentle.

Nana, who was noticeably shivering, sniffed back mucus and nodded.

'Perhaps you should sit there at the corner,' said Simangele.

Thoba looked at Nana and felt vaguely jealous that Nana should receive such special attention from Simangele. But then Nana always received special attention. This thought made Thoba yearn for the security of his home. He began to feel anxious and guilty that he had not run home. Not only did he feel he did not matter to Simangele and Vusi, he also feared the possibility of a fight between these two. Quarrels made him uneasy. Always. What would his mother say if he was injured in a fight? Rather, wouldn't she be pleased to hear that he had run home as soon as the rain started? The rain. Yes, the rain. He looked at it, and it seemed ominous with its steady strength, as if it would go on raining for ever, making it impossible for him to get home before his mother. And how cold it was now! Should he? Should he run home? No. There was too much rain out there. Somewhat anxiously, he looked at the others, and tried to control his shivering.

The other three boys were looking at Nana huddling himself at the corner where the house and the veranda walls met. He looked frailer than ever, as if there were a disease eating at him all the time. Thoba wished he had a coat to put over Nana. But Nana seemed warm, for he had embraced his legs and buried his head between his raised knees. The only sound that came from him was a continuous sniff as he drew back watery mucus, occasionally swallowing it. Thoba wondered if Nana's grandmother was home. Or did the rain catch her far in the open fields away from the township, where it was said she dug all over for roots and herbs? She was always away looking for roots to heal people with. And when she was away, Nana was cared for by everyone in Mayaba Street. Thoba looked at Nana and wished that he himself was as lucky.

Just then, Mpiyakhe turned round like a dog wanting to sit, and sat down about a foot from Nana. He began to put his shoes on. Mpiyakhe's shoes had been one of the two pairs that had been used as goal posts. Thoba looked at Mpiyakhe's feet as Mpiyakhe slipped them into socks first, and noticed how smooth those feet were compared to Nana's which were deeply cracked. Then he looked at Vusi's and Simangele's feet. Theirs too were cracked. His were not. They were as smooth as Mpiyakhe's. Thoba remembered that he had three pairs of shoes, and his mother had always told him to count his blessings because most boys had only one pair, if any shoes at all, for both school and special occasions like going to church. Yet Thoba yearned to have cracked feet too. So whenever his mother and father were away from home, he would go out and play without his shoes. But Mpiyakhe never failed to wear his shoes. Perhaps that was why Mpiyakhe's shoes were always being used as goal posts. They were always available.

Soon, Thoba, Mpiyakhe, Vusi, and Simangele stood in a row along the low wall of the veranda, looking at the rain, and talking and laughing. The anxiety over a possible fight had disappeared, and Thoba felt contented as he nestled himself into the company of these daring ones who had not run home when the rain started. And it no longer mattered to him that his mother has always said to him: 'Always run home as soon as it begins to rain. I will not nurse a child who has said to illness "Come on, friend, let's hold hands and dance." Never!' And Thoba would always wonder how a boy could hold hands with a disease. He must ask his uncle next time he came to visit.

For the moment, Thoba was glad that there was nobody at home. His mother was on day duty at the Dunnotar Hospital, and, although it was the December vacation, his father still went to school saying there was too much preparation to be done.

'You ought to take a rest, Father,' Thoba's mother had said on the last Sunday of the school term. The two had been relaxing in the living room, reading the Sunday papers.

'Never!' Thoba's father had replied with offended conviction. 'Moulding these little ones requires much energy and self-sacrifice. I will not ever say "wait a minute" to duty. Don't you know me yet?'

'Oh, you teachers!' Thoba's mother had said with a sigh.

'Thoba!' called his father.

'*Baba!*' responded Thoba who had been in his bedroom memorising Psalm 23. He had to be ready for the scripture oral examination the following morning.

'Show yourself,' said his father. Thoba appeared timidly at the door and leaned against it.

'What,' his father asked, 'is the square root of three hundred and twenty-five?' Thoba looked up at the ceiling. After some silence his father looked up from his newspaper and cast a knowing glance at his wife.

'You see,' he said. 'It takes time.'

Thoba's mother rose from her chair, dropped her paper and walked towards Thoba, her arms stretched out before her in order to embrace him. Thoba allowed himself to be embraced, all the while wishing his mother had not done that. It made him too helpless.

'Only yesterday,' his father drove the point home, 'we were working on square roots, and he has already forgotten. What kind of exams he is going to write this coming week is anybody's guess. Son, there has got to be a difference between the son of a teacher and other boys. But never mind. Einstein, if you care to know .... Do you know him? Do you know Einstein?'

Thoba shook his head, brushing his forehead against his mother's breasts.

'Well, well,' his father said, 'you will know him in time. But that great mathematics genius was once your age; and then, he did not know his square roots.'

That was three weeks ago. And now, as Thoba looked at the other boys with him on the veranda, he felt glad that his father had gone to work, or else the man would certainly have turned the day into a tortuous tutorial. Instead, there was Thoba with Simangele and Vusi and Mpiyakhe, all by themselves, looking at the rain from the shelter of the famed veranda of Mayaba Street.

The veranda of Simangele's home was very popular with the boys of Mayaba Street. Simangele's parents had done all they could to chase the boys away. But then, it was the only veranda in the neighbourhood that was walled round. To most boys, its low front wall came up to their shoulders, so that anyone looking at them from the street would see many little heads just appearing above the wall. The boys loved to climb on that wall, run on it, chasing one another. There had been many broken teeth, broken arms, and slashed tongues. Yet the boys, with the memory of chickens, would be back not long after each accident.

Once, Simangele's parents decided to lock the gate leading into the yard. But the boys of Mayaba Street, led by none other than Simangele himself, simply scaled the fence. Then it became a game to race over it: either from the street into the yard, or from the yard into the street. The fence gave in. By the time it was decided to unlock the gate, it was too late. People either walked in through the gate, or walked over the flattened fence. Simangele's father then tried to surprise the boys by sneaking up on them with a whip. But it did not take long for them to enjoy being surprised and then chased down the street. He gave up.

Thoba, who was never allowed to play too long in the street, always felt honoured to be on that veranda. He was feeling exactly this way when, as he looked at the rain, he gave way to an inner glow of exultation.

'Oh!' he exclaimed, 'it's so nice during the holidays. We just play soccer all day.' He spoke to no one in particular. And nobody answered him. The others, with the exception of Mpiyakhe, really did not share Thoba's enthusiasm. They were always free, always playing in the street. Just whenever they wanted. Thoba envied these boys. They seemed not to have demanding mothers who issued endless orders, inspected chores given and done, and sent their children on endless errands. Thoba smiled, savouring the thrill of being with them, and the joy of having followed the moment's inclination to join them on the veranda.

'How many goals did we score?' asked Mpiyakhe.

'Seven,' replied Vusi.

'Naw!' protested Simangele. 'It was six.'

'Seven!' insisted Vusi.

'Six!' shouted Simangele.

The two boys glared at each other for the second time. Thoba noticed that Nana had raised his head and was looking fixedly at the brewing conflict.

The rain poured gently now; it registered without much intrusion in the boys' minds as a distant background to the brief but charged silence.

'It doesn't matter, anyway,' said Vusi with some finality. 'We beat you.'

'Naw!' retorted Simangele. 'You haven't beaten us yet. The game was stopped by the rain. We are carrying on after the rain.'

'Who said we'll want to play after the rain?' asked Vusi.

'That's how you are,' said Simangele. 'I've long seen what kind you are. You never want to lose.'

'Of course! Who likes to lose, anyway,' said Vusi triumphantly.

There followed a tense silence, longer this time. All the boys looked at the rain, and as it faded back into their consciousness, the tension seemed to dissolve away into its sound. They crossed their arms over their chests, clutching at their shoulders firmly against the cold. They seemed lost in thought as they listened to the sound of the rain on the corrugated roofs of the township houses. It was loudest on the roof of the A. M. E. church which stood some fifty yards away, at the corner of Mayaba and Thelejane Streets. The sound on this roof was a sustained, heavy patter which reverberated with the emptiness of a building that was made entirely of corrugated iron. Even when the rain was a light shower, the roar it made on the church roof gave the impression of hail. Occasionally, there would be a great gust of wind, and the noise of the rain on the roofs would increase, and a gust of sound would flow away in ripples from house to house in the direction of the wind, leaving behind the quiet, regular patter.

'If there was a service in there,' said Thoba breaking the silence, and pointing towards the church with his head, 'would the people hear the sermon?'

'Reverend Mkhabela has a big voice,' said Mpiyakhe, demonstrating the size of the voice with his hands and his blown up cheeks.

'No voice can be bigger than thunder,' said Vusi matter-of-factly.

'Who talked about thunder?' asked Simangele, and then declared emphatically, 'There's no thunder out there. It's only rain out there.'

'Well,' said Vusi who probably had not meant his observation to be scrutinised, 'it seems like thunder.'

'Either there is thunder, or there is no thunder,' declared Simangele.

'Exactly what do you want from me?' asked Vusi desperately. 'I wasn't even talking to you.'

'It's everybody's discussion,' said Simangele. 'So you don't have to be talking to me. But if I talk about what you have said, I will talk to you directly. So, I'm saying it again: either there is thunder there, or there is no thunder out there. And right now there is no thunder out there.'

Vusi stepped away from the wall and faced Simangele, who also stepped away from the wall, faced Vusi, and waited. There was only Thoba between them. A fight seemed inevitable, and Thoba trembled, out of fear, and then also from the cold, which he could now feel even more, because it again reasserted both itself and the rain as the reasons he should have gone home in order to avoid a silly fight. He should have gone home. His mother was right. Now, he could be caught in the middle. He felt responsible for the coming danger, because he had said something that had now gone out of control.

Mpiyakhe moved away from the wall and squatted next to Nana, who was also looking at the conflict. But a fight did not occur. Vusi stepped towards the wall, rested his hands on it, and looked out at the rain. Simangele made a click of annoyance and then turned towards the wall. Mpiyakhe sprang to his feet, and everybody looked at the rain once more. Thoba desperately tried to think of something pleasant to say; something harmless.

Then he saw two horses that were nibbling at the grass that loved to grow along the fence that surrounded the church. Horses loved to nibble at that grass, thought Thoba. And when they were not nibbling at the grass, they would be rubbing themselves against the fence. They loved that too. Horses were strange creatures. They just stood in the rain, eating grass as if there was no rain at all.

'Does a horse ever catch cold?' asked Thoba, again to no one in particular. It had been just an articulated thought. But Vusi took it up with some enthusiasm.

'Ho, boy! A horse?' exclaimed Vusi. 'A horse? It's got an iron skin. Hard. Tough.' He demonstrated with two black bony fists. 'They just don't get to coughing like people.'

'Now you want to tell us that a horse can cough,' said Simangele.

Nobody took that one up. The others looked at the two horses. Thoba considered Vusi's explanation, while at the same time frantically trying to find something to say before Simangele pressed his antagonism any further. An iron skin? thought Thoba, and then spoke again.

'What sound does the rain make when it falls on the back of a horse?' But Vusi ignored the question and made another contentious statement.

'Me,' said Vusi, 'I don't just catch cold. Not me!' he declared.

'Now you are telling us a lie,' said Simangele. 'And you know that very well.'

'Now, don't ever say I tell lies,' shouted Vusi.

'There's no person in this world who never gets ill,' insisted Simangele.

'I never said "never",' Vusi defended himself. 'I said, "don't just".'

Simangele did not pursue the matter. He had made his point. He was a year or two older than the other boys, and by far the tallest. The wall of the veranda came up to his chest. He had a lean but strong body. It was said he was like that because he was from the farms, and on the farms people are always running around and working hard all day, and they have no chance to get fat. So they become lean and strong. And when they get to the towns they become stubborn and arrogant because they don't understand things, and people laugh at them; and when people laugh at them they start fighting back. Then people say 'beware of those from the farms, they will stab with a broad smile on their faces.'

Simangele had lived in the township for two years now, but he was still known as the boy from the farms. And he could be deadly. Whenever there were street fights between the boys of Mayaba Street and those of Thipe Street, Simangele would be out there in front, leading the boys of Mayaba Street and throwing stones at the enemy with legendary accuracy. Sometimes Simangele would retreat during a fight, and then watch the boys of Mayaba Street being forced to retreat. Then he would run to the front again, and the enemy would retreat. And everybody would have seen the difference. Few boys ever took any chances with Simangele.

Vusi, on the other hand, was one of those boys who were good at many things. He was very inventive. He made the best bird traps, the best slings, the best wire cars; and four-three, and six-one, and five-two, always came his way in a game of dice. But it was in soccer that he was most famous. He was known to all the boys in the township, and everybody wanted to be on his side. He was nicknamed after Sandlane, Charterston Rovers' great dribbling wizard, who had a deformed right hand that was perpetually bent at the wrist, with the fingers stretched out firmly. And Vusi would always bend his wrist whenever the ball was in his possession. And his team mates would cheer 'Sandla-a-a-ne-e-e-!' And they would be looking at his deformed hand and its outstretched fingers, dry and dusty on the outside like the foot of a hen when it has raised its leg. And Vusi would go into a frenzy of dribbling, scoring goals with that sudden, unexpected shot.

Vusi was the only boy in Mayaba Street who could stand up to Simangele. The two had never actually fought, but they had been on the brink of fighting many times. The general speculation was that Simangele really did not want to take a chance; for who knew what would happen? Vusi was known to have outbraved many boys, even those acknowledged to be stronger than he. The problem with Vusi was that he fought to the death. All the boys knew he was a dangerous person to fight with, because you would be hitting and hitting him, but Vusi would keep coming and coming at you, and you would begin to lose hope. And then he might defeat you not because he was stronger, but because he kept coming at you, and you lost all hope. That is why it was thought Simangele never wanted to go all the way. In any case, there was really nothing awesome about Simangele's bravery. He had to be brave: he was older. But Vusi? He was a wonder.

It was for this reason that Thoba was busy considering Vusi's claim that he never got ill. It sounded familiar. Vusi was like Thoba's father. He was just that kind of person. Thoba's father was not the sick type; and Thoba's mother had always told visitors that her husband was a very strong man. And since Thoba felt instinctively on Vusi's side, he felt a pressing need to bear witness, if only to establish the truthfulness of Vusi's claim.

'My own father doesn't just get ill,' he declared. There was a brief silence after this and then the others began to laugh. And Thoba felt how terrible it was to be young and have no power. Whatever you said was laughed at. It was a deeply indulgent laugh that helped to blow away all the tension that had existed just before. They just laughed. It was always the case when you are not very strong, and you have to say something.

'What is he telling us, this one?' said Mpiyakhe in the middle of a guffaw. 'Your family gets knocked down with all kinds of diseases. Everybody knows that. Softies, all of you. You're too higher-up. That's your problem. Instead of eating *papa* and beans, you have too many sandwiches.'

'Now, that is a lot of shit you are saying,' said Thoba trying to work up anger to counter the laughter.

'Don't ever say that about what I'm saying,' threatened Mpiyakhe.

'And what if I say it?' retorted Thoba.

'Take him on, boy, take him on,' said Simangele nudging Mpiyakhe in the stomach with an elbow.

Thoba began to feel uneasy. It was strange how the conflict had suddenly shifted down to him and Mpiyakhe who were at the lower end of the pecking order among the boys of Mayaba Street. He had fought Mpiyakhe a few times, and it was never clear who was stronger. Today he would win, tomorrow he would lose. That was how it was among the weak; a constant, unresolved struggle. Why should a simple truth about one's father lead to ridicule and then to a fight? Thoba looked at Mpiyakhe and had the impulse to rush him. Should he? What would be the result of it? But the uncertainty of the outcome made Thoba look away towards the rain. He squeezed his shoulders, and felt deeply ashamed that he could not prove his worth before Vusi and Simangele. He had to find a way to deal with his rival.

Mpiyakhe's father was a prosperous man who ran a flourishing taxi service. His house, a famous landmark, was one of the biggest in the township. If a stranger was looking for some house in that neighbourhood, he was told: 'Go right down Mayaba Street until you see a big, green house. That will be Nzima's house. Once there, ask again ... '

Screwed on to the front gate of the big, green house was a wooden board on which was painted 'Love Your Wife' in white paint. And whenever a man got into Mpiyakhe's father's taxi, he was always asked: 'Do you love your wife?' Thus, Mpiyakhe's father was known throughout the township as 'Love Your Wife'. As a result, Mpiyakhe was always teased about his father by the boys of Mayaba Street. And whenever that happened, he would let out steam on Thoba, trying to transfer the ridicule. After all, both their families were 'higher-ups' and if one family was a laughing stock the same should be applied to the other.

Thoba and Mpiyakhe were prevented from fighting by Nana, who suddenly began to cough violently. They all turned towards him. The cough was a long one, and it shook his frail body until he seemed to be having convulsions. Thoba wondered if Nana was going to die. And what would Nana's grandmother do to them if Nana died in their presence? If she healed people, surely she could also kill them. Nana continued to cough. And the boys could see his head go up and down. They looked at each other anxiously as if wondering what to do. But the cough finally ceased; and when Nana looked up, there were tears in his eyes and much mucus flowing down in two lines over his lips. He swept his lower arm over his lips and nose and then rubbed it against the side of his shirt.

'You should go home,' said Vusi to Nana.

'How can he go home in this rain?' said Simangele, taking advantage of Nana's refusal. Vusi turned away indignantly. Thoba wondered if he should take off his shirt and give it to Nana. But he quickly decided against it. He himself could die. He turned away to look at the rain. He saw that Vusi was looking at the horses eating grass in the rain. He saw the concentration on Vusi's face. He watched as a sudden gleam came to Vusi's eye, and Vusi slowly turned his face away from the rain to fix an ominously excited gaze on Simangele. He looked at the rain again, and then his look took on a determined intensity. He turned to Simangele again.

'Simangele,' called Vusi. 'How would you like to be a horse in the rain?'

'A horse in the rain?' said Simangele tentatively. He looked at Thoba and Mpiyakhe, and seemed embarrassed, as if there was something he could not understand.

'Yes, a horse in the rain,' said Vusi. There was a look of triumph in his face. 'Look at the horses. They are in the rain. Yet they have nothing on them. I bet you can never go into the rain without your shirt.'

Simangele laughed. 'That is foolishness,' he said.

'No,' said Vusi. 'It is not foolishness.' And as he spoke, Vusi was slowly pulling out his shirt without loosening the belt that held it tightly round the waist where it was tucked into the trousers. All the while he was looking steadily at Simangele.

Simangele stopped laughing and began to look uneasy. Once more he looked at Vusi and Mpiyakhe. And then he looked at Nana on the floor. Their eyes met, and Simangele looked away quickly. Meanwhile, his jaws tightened, Vusi was unbuttoning his shirt from the rumpled bottom upwards. Then he took off his shirt slowly, exposing a thin, shining, black body, taut with strength. Thoba felt a tremor of iciness through his body as if it was his body that had been exposed. Vusi had thrust his chest out and arched his arms back so that his shirt dangled from his right hand. Soon his body was looking like a plucked chicken.

'I'm a horse now,' said Vusi. 'Let's see if you too can be a horse.' He did not wait for an answer. Dropping his shirt with a flourish, Vusi flung himself into the rain. He braced his head against the rain and ran up Thelejane Street, which was directly opposite Simangele's home and formed a T-junction with Mayaba Street. Thelejane Street went right up and disappeared in the distance. Vusi ran so fast, he seemed to have grown shorter. Soon he was a tiny black speck in the rain; and the far distance of the street seemed to swallow him up. Not once did he look back.

It had all happened so suddenly, Thoba thought. Just like the day a formation of military jets had suddenly come from nowhere and flown low round the township a number of times, deafening the place with noise. And then they were gone, leaving behind a petrifying, stunned silence which totally blocked thinking until many minutes later.

Simangele looked like someone who thought he had enough time, but when he got to the station found that the train was already pulling out, and that he had to suffer the indignity of running after it. He looked at Thoba and Mpiyakhe. They looked back. Then a wave of anger and frustration crossed his face.

'What are you doing here on my veranda?' he yelled at the two boys. They moved towards a corner away from him. There was silence. Then Simangele looked at Nana.

'I didn't mean you,' he said with a faint plea in his voice. Then he looked at the small figure in the rain. It was so far now that it did not even seem to be moving. He looked at the sky. It was grey, and the rain was grey. He looked at the two boys, again. Thoba cringed, and looked well into Simangele's eyes. And then suddenly Thoba did not feel afraid any more. As he looked into Simangele's eyes, he felt a strange sense of power over Simangele. Simangele did not want to go into the rain, but he would go, because Thoba was looking at him. Mpiyakhe was looking at him. Nana was looking at him with those large eyes. And they had all been there when Simangele was challenged. He would have to go.

Slowly, and seemingly with much pain, Simangele fingered the buttons of his shirt. He unbuttoned only the three upper buttons and pulled the shirt over his head. Just then, a gust of wind swept the rain, making it sound harder on the roofs of houses. Simangele shuddered. He threw his shirt on the floor and then stretched his leg out into the rain and watched his grey, dry skin turn brown and wet. Then he eased himself into the rain. He shivered, and that made him seem to decide he had better run. He was out there now, running in the street, following Vusi. But his strides were much less confident than Vusi's magnanimous strides. Simangele jumped over puddles where his challenger had just waded in and out of them like a galloping horse. Thoba and Mpiyakhe watched him in silence until he vanished into the distance.

Thoba and Mpiyakhe moved out of the corner at the same time, and went to stand before the low wall. They stood there looking out at the streets in silence. Thoba became aware that he was stealing glances at Mpiyakhe. Of course he was not afraid of him. Yes, indeed, Mpiyakhe was stealing glances at him too. But now that there were only the two of them, there really seemed no reason to quarrel. There was nobody else to entertain at the expense of each other. Nana? Thoba looked at him. Their eyes met. He looked away. Wouldn't questions be asked later? What did Thoba and Mpiyakhe do after Vusi and Simangele had run into the rain to settle scores? Weren't Thoba and Mpiyakhe known rivals? And then there was Nana to tell the story. There was the rain. There were the empty streets. It was cold out there. But there could be glory out there for a shirtless boy.

Thoba wondered if he should issue a challenge. That was certainly attractive. But less attractive was the ordeal of running in the rain. But there was no thunder. Only water. That's all. No lightning to fear. Only water falling from the sky. What was water? Only water. And the cold? Once he was out there he would forget about it, because he would be involved in the running. That's the trick. The horses went on eating wet grass. They were involved. How was the sound of the rain on the back of a horse? What sound would the rain make on a boy's body?

Thoba and Mpiyakhe looked at each other again, only to look away once more. Clearly there was something they could not confront. When Thoba stole a glance at Mpiyakhe through the corner of his eye, he noticed that Mpiyakhe was looking at him. When Mpiyakhe finally spoke, it was slowly and tentatively.

'Do you ... ' he asked, 'do you want to go into the rain?'

Thoba pretended he had not heard, and continued to look at the rain. But then he broke into a smile, and turned his face to look at Mpiyakhe. Mpiyakhe had not issued a challenge. He had not. He had merely asked a question. Here was an uneasy boy who was trying to persuade him into an intimate truce. Here was a boy who assumed there were mutual fears; who did not know for sure. Here was a boy asking his way into a compromise. This boy did not deserve an answer.

Slowly and deliberately, and with a gleam in his eye, Thoba unbuttoned his shirt, and as he pulled it over his head, he felt the warmth of his breath on his chest. And that gave him a momentary impression of dreaming, for he had a clear image of Vusi taking off his shirt. But the image did not last; it was shattered by the re-emergence of his head into the cold. He shivered as goose pimples literally sprang out on his skin before his eyes. But he would have to be reckless. That was bravery. Bravery meant forgetting about one's mother.

Thoba threw his shirt on to the floor where it joined Vusi's and Simangele's. And the last thing he did before he burst into the rain was look at Nana, as if pleading for approval. Their eyes met. Those were the eyes he would carry in his mind into the rain, as if the whole township was looking at him. Mpiyakhe? He did not even deserve a glance.

When the cold water of the rain hit him, Thoba had the impulse to run back on to the veranda. But when he got into the street, he felt nothing but exhilaration. There was something freeing in the tickling pressure of the soft needles of rain on his skin. And then he ran in spurts: running fast and slowing down, playing with the pressure of the rain on him. It was a pleasant sensation; a soft, pattering sensation. And the rain purred so delicately against his ears. And when he waded in and out of puddles, savouring the recklessness, it was so enchanting to split the water, creating his own little thunder from the numerous splashes. He was alone in the street with the rain. He was shirtless in the rain. How many people were watching him from the protective safety of their houses? How many? They were sitting round their kitchen stoves, taking no challenges. Mpiyakhe? Was he watching him? Of course. Mpiyakhe, the vanquished. Everybody would know. Vusi and Simangele would know that he, Thoba, had bravely followed them into the cold rain.

He passed the A. M. E. church and crossed Thipe Street. Where were the boys of that street? They would not come out to fight on such a day. Weaklings, the lot of them. Up he went, crossing Ndimande Street. Where were the boys of that street? Weaklings too. They were not in the rain.

He ran up towards the crèche now. He had been there as a child, when he was younger than he was now. Would he be recognised from the windows as the man who had been there as a child? Would the matron see him? Would she say, 'There is my little man'? Should he slow down and be seen? No. The man broke into a sprint. Wouldn't it be better for them to say, 'Doesn't that look like Thoba?' They wouldn't be sure. That way they would think about him a little longer, trying to be sure. He wished he were a blur. The wind and the water! He could not feel them any more, for they had dissipated into the sustained alacrity of speed.

Beyond the crèche was the Dutch Reformed Church, and beyond that, far out of the township, were the rugged, rocky hills where men and women always went in pairs, on Sunday afternoons. Thoba slowed down somewhat. If he ran further up the street, he would get nearer those hills, and one could never be sure about those hills. It was said there was a beast there which swallowed up little children, especially in bad weather. He wondered if Vusi and Simangele had gone further up. No, he would not go towards the hills. Thoba passed the church, but instead of going up, he turned left into Twala Street. Even though he could outrun the beast, it would be foolish to go nearer it first.

As he turned into Twala Street, he tried to increase his speed once more, but noted with faint anxiety that he was unable to. He was slowing down now, and that was not good. He was very far from home now. Did he reach the limits of his endurance so soon? And yet the surge of exhilaration was definitely beginning to fade away. But he would have to keep up the pace at least until the crèche was well out of sight. Why did people tire? Did Vusi tire, or did he run all the way? There was no sign of him. Maybe it was the Dutch Reformed Church; he shouldn't have looked at it. He should have closed his eyes when he passed it, for that was the church of ill luck. Everybody said so. But he would have to run, all the same. At least until the crèche was well out of sight. And as soon as he made that commitment, Thoba suddenly felt as he had the day his mother had beaten him with a wet dishcloth for cracking open an egg that had a half-formed chick in it.

Thoba had vowed that he would cry until his father came back home to deal with his mother. His father did not come. So long after the tears and the anger had gone, Thoba had continued to cry with his voice only. It had been painful in his throat and somewhere in his chest. And now, as he continued to run, Thoba realised that the fire was going out of him. There was left only the pain of tiring legs. Yet, he was too far from home to tire. He looked back briefly. The crèche was out of sight; and just then, the tiredness assailed him. He could feel the ache in his calves. He slowed down to an easy trot. If only he could reach Nala Street; that would take him back home.

Then he became conscious of the sound of water rushing down in two streams on the sides of the street, towards the Dutch Reformed Church. His eyes followed the direction of the water until he saw the church in the distance back there. He turned away quickly. What would happen if the water went into the church and flooded it? Would it float like Noah's ark?

When he turned left at Mosotwana Street, he saw Nala Street some five houses away. And only then did he realise why he had heard the sound of the rushing streams so clearly. It had stopped raining. There was a heavy stillness around him, for the roofs of houses had gone silent. And the sound of rushing water made the streams sound bigger than they actually were. He began to feel exposed. He broke his trot and walked, arms akimbo. He was tired, and the rain was as embarrassingly tired, for it was now falling in tiny droplets as weak as the sprays at the edge of a waterfall. There was no one else in the street, not even a stray dog. And then he began to feel cold.

He was about three houses from Nala Street when a familiar taxi turned into Mosotwana Street, forcing him to run towards the nearest fence away from danger. He wondered if Mpiyakhe's father had seen him. Thoba stopped, rested his arms on the fence, so that those in the taxi could see only his back. He enjoyed the wonderful sensation of stillness. But that was not to last very long. The taxi stopped only about ten yards away from Thoba. A man got off and ran into the next house as if he thought it was still raining. Thoba heard Mpiyakhe's father shout after the man: 'Love your wife!' In a few seconds, the taxi started up, but it did not go forward; instead it reversed and stopped about two yards from Thoba. Thoba froze. So the man had recognised him.

'Hey, boy!' shouted Mpiyakhe's father. 'Are you not teacher Mbele's son?'

Thoba turned his head and nodded. The passengers in the taxi were all looking at him. Why did Mpiyakhe's father not leave him alone?

'Yes, I thought so,' said Mpiyakhe's father. 'Do your parents know you are here?'

Thoba looked away and did not answer.

'Boy, I'm talking to you.'

Thoba looked at the man again. His head was sticking out of the driver's open window. What would happen if another car came and the head was still sticking out? Surely that head would be sliced off.

'Boy, I'm talking to you.'

First it was Mpiyakhe; now it was his father.

'Now get into this car, and let me take you home.'

It could not be. To be taken home like a drenched chicken! To be taken home in his enemy's car! It could not be. His own feet would carry him home.

'Come on. Get into the car.'

Thoba began to walk away.

'Boy, I will not let your parents accuse me of killing you!'

Thoba continued to trudge away.

'Boy, get into this car!'

Nothing would stop him.

'You all saw him defy me, didn't you!'

When Thoba heard the engine of the car revving up, he tried to run. But he needn't have: the car went on its way in the opposite direction. Thoba ran for only a few yards before he reached Nala Street.

When he looked down Nala Street in the far distance, Thoba saw something which discouraged him further. Two buses were lugging up slowly towards the township. They were the first afternoon buses bringing workers who knocked off early. If only he could reach the bus stop and pass it before the buses got there. If not it would be embarrassing. All those people! What would they say? What was a shirtless boy doing in the cold rain? But the pain in the calves. The pain in the thighs. He just wanted to stand still. Then he began to shiver violently. It always got colder after the rain. He must move on. But try as he might, he could not run. He knew then that he would never beat the buses to the bus stop. And by the time they got there, and the passengers were streaming out of them like ants, Thoba was still very far from the bus stop, and would surely meet the workers coming up.

And he saw them: the bulk of them. Women. They knocked off too early. That was their problem. They were coming up: a disordered column of women with shopping bags balanced on their heads. He would meet them somewhere in the middle of the street. If only he could run so fast that when he passed them, they would be a blur to him; and he would be a blur to them. He knew he wouldn't make it. He felt so exposed: shirtless; shoeless; a wet body in a dripping pair of pants that clung tightly and coldly to him. They would surely see the outline of his buttocks. And his penis? Would they see it too? That would be worse.

Indeed, there was mother Mofokeng, one of Thoba's mother's many friends. Everybody knew his mother. Mother Mofokeng would certainly recognise him. Then he stepped on to a pointed stone. At first the pain was dull, but once it cut through his almost iced foot, it tore up to his chest. He jerked to a stop, grimacing with pain, as he raised the hurt foot every so slightly as if he wanted to keep it on the ground at all costs. He felt like a sleeping horse when it lifts one hoof a fraction from the ground. He was far from home. And he felt tears forming in his eyes. But he fought them back by blinking repeatedly.

'Wonder of wonders!' exclaimed mother Mofokeng. 'What am I seeing? God in heaven what am I seeing? Curse me if this isn't the nurse's child!'

'Which nurse?' asked another mother.

'Staff nurse Mbele's son,' said mother Mofokeng.

'Is this the nurse's child? He looks so much like her!'

'Son,' inquired mother Mofokeng, 'what are you doing here in the cold?'

Thoba looked at her, and then looked at the battered leather shopping bag balanced on her head. It was bulging with vegetables. Some spinach and carrots were peeping from a hole on the side.

'Here's a child who will die of cold,' said a mother who had just joined the crowd.

'And you'd think his mother would know better,' said another.

'Where's your shirt, son?' asked mother Mofokeng.

'This is what I've always maintained about school holidays,' said another. 'You are busy working your heart out at the white man's, and your children are busy running wild. I don't know why they have these holidays.'

'And in this weather of all weathers in the world,' said another.

'Woman!' exclaimed another. 'I'm telling you, what else can you do with children?'

How could Thoba explain? Should he walk away or continue to listen? The questions were piling up; being as many as there were women returning from work. He would wait. Surely it would be disrespectful to walk away from elders. Yet the questions came; and the piercing cold; and the stinging pain of muscles. His teeth began to chatter.

'Whose child is this?'

'Shame! What happened to him?'

'Where's his shirt? Did anybody take your shirt, son?'

'Who has done this sin?'

'Leave the child alone! Run home, son!'

'It's so easy to die!'

'Exposure!'

'Sponge wet. Look how the trousers cling to him.'

'Women of the township! Why don't you leave this child alone?'

Thoba had crossed his arms across his chest as if that way he could create some heat. Better the rain than the cold which follows it. He was far from home, and the women had created a cordon of humiliation around him. Then he felt two thin lines of heat flowing down his cheeks. His tears had betrayed him. And the eyes grew painful. Instead of the speed he had desired, it was now his tears that had turned the women into a blur. He could not see them now. That was the time to leave.

'Here's my jersey, son,' said mother Mofokeng. 'Bring it back tomorrow.'

Thoba felt the warm wool settle on his shoulders. But he had begun to move. And he saw the forms before him part; and then came a grey emptiness. He limped away, wounded with sympathy. A few feet away from the women, he impulsively began to run. He did not see where he was going; as he picked up speed, the jersey slipped from his shoulders. And he heard the countless voices of women shouting: 'It has slipped! It has fallen! Pick it up! The jersey has fallen! Pick it up, son! Stop him! Stop him!' Thoba broke into a sprint. It was the most satisfying sprint, for it was so difficult, so painful. It had led him out of humiliation.

When he finally cleared his eyes with the back of his hand, Thoba realised that he was at the junction where Nala, Moshoeshoe, and Ndimande Streets met. Just across the street was the Police station. More buses were coming up. More women were coming. Thoba definitely felt no pain now. He flew past the Police station, the bus stop, Thipe Street . . . Mayaba Street was the next. Where were the boys of Mayaba Street? Would they be waiting for his return? As he took the corner into Mayaba Street, Thoba increased his speed; and, spreading his arms out like the wings of an aeroplane, he banked into Mayaba Street.

The street was as empty as he had left it at the other end. No Vusi, no Simangele, no Mpiyakhe, no Nana. No boys had come out yet to race little twigs on the streamlets in the street. Was anybody looking through the window? Was Mpiyakhe, the vanquished, still on the veranda? Or had his father rescued him? Thoba wondered if he should run on to the veranda to collect his shirt. No. Let it lie there on the floor of the veranda of Simangele's home. It would be tomorrow's testimony.

There was no one at home yet when Thoba arrived. He would have to make the fire before his mother came. But the stillness inside his home suddenly made him feel lonely, and all the pain came back again. No, he would not make the fire. Let his mother do whatever she liked with him. He would not make the fire. He passed on from the kitchen into his bedroom. There, he took off his trousers, and left them in a wet little heap on the floor close to his bed. He felt dry, but cold, as he slipped into the blankets. He felt warm, deep inside him. And as he turned over in bed, looking for the most comfortable position, he felt all the pain. But, strangely enough, he wished he could turn around as many times as possible. There was suddenly something deeply satisfying and pleasurable about the pain. And as he slid into a deep sleep, he smiled, feeling so much alive.

A TRIP TO THE GIFBERGE

Zoë Wicomb

Y ou've always loved your father better.
That will be her opening line.

The chair she sits in is a curious affair, crude like a crate with armrests. A crate for a large tough-skinned vegetable like hubbard squash which is of course not soft as its name suggests.

I move towards her to adjust the goatskin kaross around her shoulders. It has slipped in her attempt to rise out of the chair. I brace myself against the roar of distaste but no, perhaps her chest is too tight to give the words their necessary weight. No, she would rather remove herself from my viperous presence. But the chair is too low and the gnarled hands spread out on the armrests cannot provide enough leverage for the body to rise with dignity. ('She doesn't want to see you,' Aunt Cissie said, biting her lip.)

Her own words are a synchronic feat of syllables and exhalations to produce a halting hiss. 'Take it away. I'll suffocate with heat. You've tried to kill me enough times.' I drop the goatskin on to the ground before realising that it goes on the back of the chair.

I have never thought it unreasonable that she should not want to see me. It is my insistence which is unreasonable. But why, if she is hot, does she sit here in the last of the sun? Her chair stands a good twenty yards from the house, beyond the semi-circle of the grass broom's vigorous expressionistic strokes. From where I stand, having made the predicted entrance through the back gate, she is a painterly arrangement alone on the plain. Her house is on the very edge of the location. Behind her the Matsikamma Range is interrupted by two swollen peaks so that her head rests in the cleavage.

Her chair is uncomfortable without the kaross. The wood must cut into the small of her back and she is forced to lean forward, to wriggle. Our eyes meet for a second, accidentally, but she shuts hers instantly so that I hold in my vision the eyes of decades ago. Then they flashed coal-black, the surrounding skin taut across the high cheekbones. Narrow, narrow slits which she forced wide open and like a startled rabbit stared entranced into a mirror as she pushed a wave into the oiled black hair.

'If only,' she lamented, 'if only my eyes were wider I would be quite nice, really nice,' and with a snigger, 'a princess.'

Then she turned on me, 'Poor child. What can a girl do without good looks? Who'll marry you? We'll have to put a peg on your nose.'

And the pearled half moon of her brown fingertip flashed as she stroked appreciatively the curious high bridge of her own nose. Those were the days of the monthly hairwash in the old house. The kitchen humming with pots of water nudging each other on the stove, and afterwards the terrible torments of the comb as she hacked with explorer's determination the path through the tangled undergrowth, set on the discovery of silken tresses. Her own sleek black waves dried admirably, falling into place. Mother.

Now it is thin, scraped back into a limp plait pinned into a bun. Her shirt is the fashionable cut of this season's muttonleg sleeve and I remember that her favourite garments are saved in a mothballed box. Now and then she would bring something to light, just as fashion tiptoeing out of a dusty cupboard would crack her whip after bowing humbly to the original. How long has she been sitting here in her shirt and ill-matched skirt and the nimbus of anger?

She coughs. With her eyes still closed she says, 'There's Jantjie Bêrend in an enamel jug on the stove. Bring me a cup.'

Not a please and certainly no thank you to follow. The daughter must be reminded of her duty. This is her victory: speaking first, issuing a command.

I hold down the matted Jantjie Bêrend with a fork and pour out the yellowish brew. I do not anticipate the hand thrust out to take the drink so that I come too close and the liquid lurches into the saucer. The dry red earth laps up the offering of spilled infusion which turns into a patch of fresh blood.

'Clumsy like your father. He of course never learned to drink from a cup. Always poured it into a saucer, that's why the Shentons all have lower lips like spouts. From slurping their drinks from saucers. Boerjongens, all of them. My Oupa swore that the English potteries cast their cups with saucers attached so they didn't have to listen to Boers slurping their coffee. Oh, he knew a thing or two, my Oupa. Then your Oupa Shenton had the cheek to call me a Griqua meid.'

Her mouth purses as she hauls up the old grievances for which I have no new palliatives. Instead I pick up the bunch of proteas that I had dropped with my rucksack against the wall. I hand the flowers to her and wonder how I hid my revulsion when Aunt Cissie presented them to me at the airport.

'Welcome home to South Africa.' And in my arms the national blooms rested fondly while she turned to the others, the semi-circle of relatives moving closer. 'From all of us. You see everybody's here to meet the naughty girl.'

'And Eddie,' I exclaimed awkwardly as I recognised the youngest uncle now pot-bellied and grey.

'Ag no man, you didn't play marbles together. Don't come here with disrespectful foreign ways. It's your Uncle Eddie,' Aunt Cissie reprimanded. 'And Eddie,' she added, 'you must find all the children. They'll be running all over the place like chickens.'

'Can the new Auntie ride in our car?' asked a little girl tugging at Aunt Cissie's skirt.

'No man, don't be so stupid, she's riding with me and then we all come to my house for something nice to eat. Did your Mammie bring some roeties?' I rubbed the little girl's head but a tough protea had pierced the cellophane and scratched her cheek which she rubbed self-pityingly.

'Come get your baggage now', and as we waited Aunt Cissie explained. 'Your mother's a funny old girl, you know. She just wouldn't come to the airport and I explained to her the whole family must be there. Doesn't want to have anything to do with us now, don't ask me why, jus turned against us jus like that. Doesn't talk, not that she ever said much, but she said, right there at your father's funeral – pity you couldn't get here in time – well, she said, "Now you can all leave me alone", and when Boeta Danie said, "Ag man sister you mustn't talk so, we've all had grief and the Good Lord knows who to take and who to leave", well you wouldn't guess what she said' ... and Aunt Cissie's eyes roved incredulously about my person as if a good look would offer an explanation ... 'she said plainly, jus like that, "Danie", jus dropped the Boeta there and then in front of everybody, she said ... and I don't know how to say it because I've always had a tender place in my heart for your mother, such a lovely shy girl she was ...'

'Really?' I interrupted. I could not imagine her being described as shy.

'Oh yes, quite shy, a real lady. I remember when your father wrote home to ask for permission to marry, we were so worried. A Griqua girl, you know, and it was such a surprise when he brought your mother, such nice English she spoke and good features and a nice figure also.'

Again her eyes took in my figure so that she was moved to add in parenthesis, 'I'll get you a nice step-in. We get good ones here with the long leg, you know, gives you a nice firm hip-line. You must look after yourself man; you won't get a husband if you let yourself go like this.'

Distracted from her story she leaned over to examine the large ornate label of a bag bobbing by on the moving belt.

'That's not mine,' I said.

'I know. I can mos see it says Mev. H. J. Groenewald,' she retorted. Then, appreciatively as she allowed the bag to carry drunkenly along, 'But that's now something else hey. Very nice. There's nothing wrong in admiring something nice man. I'm not shy and there's no Apartheid at the airport. You spend all that time overseas and you still afraid of Boers.' She shock her head reproachfully.

'I must go to the lavatory,' I announced.

'O.K. I'll go with hey.'

And from the next closet her words rose above the sound of abundant pee gushing against the enamel of the bowl, drowning my own failure to produce even a trickle.

'I made a nice pot of beans and samp, not grand of course but something to remind you you're home. Stamp-en-stoot we used to call it on the farm', and her clear nostalgic laughter vibrated against the bowl.

'Yes,' I shouted, 'funny, but I could actually smell beans and samp hovering just above the petrol fumes in the streets of London.'

I thought of how you walk along worrying about being late, or early, or wondering where to have lunch, when your nose twitches with a teasing smell and you're transported to a place so specific and the power of the smell summons the light of that day when the folds of a dress draped the brick wall and your hands twisted anxiously, Is she my friend, truly my friend?

While Aunt Cissie chattered about how vile London was, a terrible place where people slept under the arches in newspapers and brushed the pigeon-shit off their brows in the mornings. Funny how Europeans could sink so low. And the Coloured people from the West Indies just fighting on the streets, killing each other and still wearing their doekies from back home. Really, as if there weren't hairdressers in London. She had seen it all on TV. Through the door I watched the patent-leather shoes shift under the heaving and struggling of flesh packed into corsets.

'Do they show the riots here in South Africa on TV?'

'Ag, don't you start with politics now,' she laughed, 'but I got a new TV you know.'

We opened our doors simultaneously and with the aid of flushing water she drew me back, 'Yes, your father's funeral was a business.'

'What did Mamma say?'

'Man, you mustn't take notice of what she says. I always say that half the time people don't know what they talking about and blood is thicker than water so you jus do your duty hey.'

'Of course Auntie. Doing my duty is precisely why I'm here.' It is not often that I can afford the luxury of telling my family the truth.

'But what did she say?' I persisted.

'She said she didn't want to see you. That you've caused her enough trouble and you shouldn't bother to go up to Namaqualand to see her. And I said, "Yes Hannah it's no way for a daughter to behave but her place is with you now."' Biting her lip she added, 'You mustn't take any notice. I wasn't going to say any of this to you, but seeing that you asked ... Don't worry man, I'm going with you. We'll drive up tomorrow.'

'I meant what did she say to Uncle Danie?'

'Oh, she said to him, "Danie", jus like that, dropped the Boeta right there in the graveyard in front of everyone, she said, "He's dead now and I'm not your sister so I hope you Shentons will leave me alone." Man, a person don't know what to do.'

Aunt Cissie frowned.

'She was always so nice with us you know, such a sweet person, I jus don't understand, unless ...' and she tapped her temple, 'unless your father's death jus went to her head. Yes,' she sighed, as I lifted my rucksack from the luggage belt, 'it never rains but pours; still, every cloud has a silver lining', and so she dipped liberally into her sack of homilies and sowed them across the arc of attentive relatives.

'It's in the ears of the young,' she concluded, 'that these thoughts must sprout.'

She has never seemed more in control than at this moment when she stares deep into the fluffy centres of the proteas on her lap. Then she takes the flowers still in their cellophane wrapping and leans them heads down like a broom against the chair. She allows her hand to fly to the small of her back where the wood cuts.

'Shall I get you a comfortable chair? There's a wicker one by the stove which won't cut into your back like this.'

Her eyes rest on the eaves of the house where a swallow circles anxiously.

'It won't of course look as good here in the red sand amongst the thornbushes,' I persist.

A curt 'No.' But then the loose skin around her eyes creases into lines of suppressed laughter and she levers herself expertly out of the chair.

'No, it won't, but it's getting cool and we should go inside. The chair goes on the stoep', and her overseer's finger points to the place next to a tub of geraniums. The chair is heavy. It is impossible to carry it without bruising the shins. I struggle along to the unpolished square of red stoep that clearly indicates the permanence of its place, and marvel at the extravagance of her gesture.

She moves busily about the kitchen, bringing from the pantry and out of the oven pots in advanced stages of preparation. Only the peas remain to be shelled but I am not allowed to help.

'So they were all at the airport hey?'

'Not all, I suppose; really I don't know who some of them are. Neighbours for all I know,' I reply guardedly.

'No you wouldn't after all these years. I don't suppose you know the young ones at all; but then they probably weren't there. Have better things to do than hang about airports. Your Aunt Cissie wouldn't have said anything about them ... Hetty and Cheryl and Willie's Clint. They'll be at the political meetings, all UDF people. Playing with fire, that's what they're doing. Don't care a damn about the expensive education their parents have sacrificed for.'

Her words are the ghostly echo of years ago when I stuffed my plaits into my ears and the sour guilt rose dyspeptically in my throat. I swallow, and pressing my back against the cupboard for support I sneer, 'Such a poor investment children are. No returns, no compound interest, not a cent's worth of gratitude. You'd think gratitude were inversely proportionate to the sacrifice of parents. I can't imagine why people have children.'

She turns from the stove, her hands gripping the handles of a pot, and says slowly, at one with the steam pumping out the truth, 'My mother said it was a mistake when I brought you up to speak English. Said people spoke English just to be disrespectful to their elders, to You and Your them about. And that is precisely what you do. Now you use the very language against me that I've stubbed my tongue on trying to teach you it. No respect! Use your English as a catapult!'

I fear for her wrists but she places the pot back on the stove and keeps her back turned. I will not be drawn into further battle. For years we have shunted between understanding and failure and I the Caliban will always be at fault. While she stirs ponderously, I say, 'My stories are going to be published next month. As a book I mean.'

She sinks into the wicker chair, her face red with steam and rage.

'Stories,' she shouts, 'you call them stories? I wouldn't spend a second gossiping about things like that. Dreary little things in which nothing happens, except ... except ...' and it is the unspeakable which makes her shut her eyes for a moment. Then more calmly, 'Cheryl sent me the magazine from Joburg, two, three of them. A disgrace. I'm only grateful that it's not a Cape Town book. Not that one could trust Cheryl to keep anything to herself.'

'But they're only stories. Made up. Everyone knows it's not real, not the truth.'

'But you've used the real. If I can recognise places and people, so can others, and if you want to play around like that why don't you have the courage to tell the whole truth? Ask me for stories with neat endings and you won't have to invent my death. What do you know about things, about people,

109

this place where you were born? About your ancestors who roamed these hills? You left. Remember?' She drops her head and her voice is barely audible.

'To write from under your mother's skirts, to shout at the world that it's all right to kill God's unborn child! You've killed me over and over so it was quite unnecessary to invent my death. Do people ever do anything decent with their education?'

Slumped in her chair she ignores the smell of burning food so that I rescue the potatoes and baste the meat.

'We must eat,' she sighs. 'Tomorrow will be exhausting. What did you have at Cissie's last night?'

'Bobotie and sweet potato and stamp-en-stoot. They were trying to watch the television at the same time so I had the watermelon virtually to myself.'

She jumps up to take the wooden spoon from me. We eat in silence the mutton and sousboontjies until she says that she managed to save some prickly pears. I cannot tell whether her voice is tinged with bitterness or pride at her resourcefulness. She has slowed down the ripening by shading the fruit with castor-oil leaves, floppy hats on the warts of great bristling blades. The flesh is nevertheless the colour of burnt earth, a searing sweetness that melts immediately so that the pips are left swirling like gravel in my mouth. I have forgotten how to peel the fruit without perforating my fingers with invisible thorns.

Mamma watches me eat, her own knife and fork long since resting sedately on the plate of opaque white glass. Her finger taps the posy of pink roses on the clean rim and I am reminded of the modesty of her portion.

'Tomorrow,' she announces, 'we'll go on a trip to the Gifberge.'

I swallow the mouthful of pips and she says anxiously, 'You can drive, can't you?' Her eyes are fixed on me, ready to counter the lie that will attempt to thwart her and I think wearily of the long flight, the terrible drive from Cape Town in the heat.

'Can't we go on Thursday? I'd like to spend a whole day in the house with the blinds drawn against the sun, reading the *Cape Times*.'

'Plenty of time for that. No, we must go tomorrow. Your father promised, for years he promised, but I suppose he was scared of the pass. Men can't admit that sort of thing, scared of driving in the mountains, but he wouldn't teach me to drive. Always said my chest wasn't good enough. As if you need good lungs to drive.'

'And in this heat?'

'Don't be silly, child, it's autumn and in the mountains it'll be cool. Come,' she says, taking my arm, and from the stoep traces with her finger the line along the Matsikamma Range until the first deep fold. 'Just there you see, where the mountains step back a bit, just there in that kloof the road goes up.'

Maskam's friendly slope stops halfway, then the flat top rises perpendicularly into a violet sky. I cannot imagine little men hanging pegged and roped to its sheer sides.

'They say there are proteas on the mountain.'

'No,' I counter, 'it's too dry. You only find proteas in the Cape Peninsula.'

'Nonsense,' she says scornfully, 'you don't know everything about this place.'

'Ag, I don't care about this country; I hate it.'

Sent to bed, I draw the curtains against huge stars burning into the night.

'Don't turn your light on, there'll be mosquitoes tonight,' she advises.

My dreams are of a wintry English garden where a sprinkling of snow lies like insecticide over the stubbles of dead shrub. I watch a flashing of red through the wooden fence as my neighbour moves along her washing line pegging out the nappies. I want to call to her that it's snowing, that she's wasting her time, but the slats of wood fit closely together and I cannot catch at the red of her skirt. I comfort myself with the thought that it might not be snowing in her garden.

Curtains rattle and part and I am lost, hopelessly tossed in a sharp first light that washes me across the bed to where the smell of coffee anchors me to the spectre of Mamma in a pale dressing gown from the past. Cream, once primrose seersucker, and I put out my hand to clutch at the fabric but fold it over a saucer-sized biscuit instead. Her voice prises open the sleep seal of my eyes.

'We'll go soon and have a late breakfast on the mountain. Have another biscuit,' she insists.

At Van Rhynsdorp we stop at the store and she exclaims appreciatively at the improved window dressing. The wooden shelves in the window have freshly been covered with various bits of patterned fablon on which oil lamps, toys and crockery are carefully arranged. On the floor of blue linoleum a huge doll with blonde curls and purple eyes grimaces through the faded yellow cellophane of her box. We are the only customers.

Old Mr Friedland appears not to know who she is. He leans back from the counter, his left thumb hooked in the broad braces while the right hand pats with inexplicable pride the large protruding stomach. His eyes land stealthily, repeatedly, on the wobbly topmost button of his trousers as if to catch the moment when the belly will burst into liberty.

She has filled her basket with muddy tomatoes and takes a cheese from the counter.

'Mr Friedland,' she says in someone else's voice, 'I've got the sheepskins for Mr Friedland in the bakkie. Do ... er ... does Mr Friedland want them?'

'Sheepskins?'

His right hand shoots up to fondle his glossy black plumage and at that moment, as anyone could have predicted, at that very moment of neglect, the trouser button twists off and shoots into a tower of tomato cans.

'Shenton's sheepskins.' She identifies herself under cover of the rattling button.

The corvine beak peck-pecks before the words tumble out hastily, 'Yes, yes, they say old Shenton's dead hey? Hardworking chap that!' And he shouts into a doorway, 'Tell the boy to get the skins from the blue bakkie outside.'

I beat the man in the white polystyrene hat to it and stumble in with the stiff salted skins which I dump at his fussy directions. The skin mingles with the blue mottled soap to produce an evil smell. Mr Friedland tots up the goods in exchange and I ask for a pencil to make up the outstanding six cents.

'Ugh,' I grunt, as she shuffles excitedly on the already hot plastic seat, her body straining forward to the lure of the mountain, 'How can you bear it?'

'What, what?' She resents being dragged away from her outing. 'Old Friedland you mean? There are some things you just have to do whether you like it or not. But those people have nothing to do with us. Nothing at all. It will be nice and cool in the mountains.'

As we leave the tarred road we roll up the windows against the dust. The road winds perilously as we ascend and I think sympathetically of Father's alleged fear. In an elbow of the road we look down on to a dwarfed home-stead on the plain with a small painted blue pond and a willow lurid against the grey of the veld. Here against the black rock the bushes grow tall, verdant, and we stop in the shadow of a cliff. She bends over the bright feathery foliage to check, yes it is ysterbos, an infallible remedy for kidney disorders, and for something else, but she can't remember other than that the old people treasured their bunches of dried ysterbos.

'So close to home,' she sighs, 'and it is quite another world, a darker, green-er world. Look water!' And we look up into the shaded slope. A fine thread of water trickles down its ancient worn path, down the layered rock. Towards the bottom it spreads and seeps and feeds woman-high reeds where strange red birds dart and rustle.

The road levels off for a mile or so but there are outcroppings of rock all around us.

'Here we must be closer to heaven,' she says. 'Father would've loved it here. What a pity he didn't make it.'

I fail to summon his face flushed with pleasure; it is the stern Sunday face of the deacon that passes before me. She laughs.

'Of course he would only think of the sheep, of how many he could keep on an acre of this green veld.'

We spread out our food on a ledge and rinse the tomatoes in a stone basin. The flask of coffee has been sweetened with condensed milk and the Van Rhynsdorp bread is crumbly with whole grains of wheat. Mamma apologises for no longer baking her own. I notice for the first time a slight limp as she walks, the hips working unevenly against a face of youthful eagerness as we wander off.

'And here,' I concede, 'are the proteas.'

Busy bushes, almost trees, that plump out from the base. We look at the familiar tall chalice of leathery pink and as we move around the bush, deciding, for we must decide now whether the chalice is more attractive than the clenched fist of the imbricated bud, a large whirring insect performs its aerobatics in the branches, distracting, so that we linger and don't know. Then the helicopter leads us further, to the next bush where another type beckons. These are white protea torches glowing out of their silver-leafed branches. The flowers are open, the petals separated to the mould of a cupped hand so that the feathery parts quiver to the light.

'I wonder why the Boers chose the protea as national flower,' I muse, and find myself humming mockingly:

Suikerbossie'k wil jou hê,
Wat sal jou Mamma daarvan sê ...

She harmonises in a quavering voice.

'Do you remember,' she says, 'how we sang? All the hymns and carols and songs on winter evenings. You never could harmonise.' Then generously she adds, 'Of course there was no one else to sing soprano.'

'I do, I do.'

We laugh at how we held concerts, the three of us practising for weeks as if there would be an audience. The mere idea of public performance turns the tugging condition of loneliness into an exquisite terror. One night at the power of her command the empty room would become a packed auditorium of rustles and whispers. And around the pan of glowing embers the terror thawed as I opened my mouth to sing. With a bow she would offer around the bowl of raisins and walnuts to an audience still sizzling with admiration.

'And now,' she says, 'I suppose you actually go to concerts and theatres?'

'Yes. Sometimes.'

'I can't imagine you in lace and feathers eating walnuts and raisins in the interval. And your hair? What do you do with that bush?'

'Some perfectly sensible people,' I reply, 'pay pounds to turn their sleek hair into precisely such a bushy tangle.'

'But you won't exchange your boskop for all the daisies in Namaqualand! Is that sensible too? And you say you're happy with your hair? Always? Are you really?'

'I think we ought to go. The sun's getting too hot for me.'

'Down there the earth is baking at ninety degrees. You won't find anywhere cooler than here in the mountains.'

We drive in silence along the last of the incline until we reach what must be the top of the Gifberge. The road is flanked by cultivated fields and a column of smoke betrays a hidden farmhouse.

'So they grow things on the mountain?'

'Hmm,' she says pensively, 'someone once told me it was fertile up here, but I had no idea of the farm!'

The bleached mealie stalks have been stripped of their cobs and in spite of the rows lean arthritically in the various directions that pickers have elbowed them. On the other side a crop of pumpkins lies scattered like stones, the foliage long since shrivelled to dust. But the fields stop abruptly where the veld resumes. Here the bushes are shorter and less green than in the pass. The road carries on for two miles until we reach a fence. The gate before us is extravagantly barred; I count thirteen padlocks.

'What a pity,' she says in a restrained voice, 'that we can't get to the edge. We should be able to look down on to the plain, at the strip of irrigated vines along the canal, and the white dorp and even our houses on the hill.'

I do not mind. It is mid-afternoon and the sun is fierce and I am not allowed to complain about the heat. But her face crumples. For her the trip is spoiled. Here, yards from the very edge, the place of her imagination has still not materialised. Nothing will do but the complete reversal of the image of herself in the wicker chair staring into the unattainable blue of the mountain. And now, for one brief moment, to look down from these very heights at the cars crawling along the dust roads, at the diminished people, at where her chair sits empty on the arid plain of Klein Namaqualand.

Oh, she ought to have known; at her age ought not to expect the unattainable ever to be anything other than itself. Her disappointment is unnerving. Like a tigress she paces along the cleared length of fence. She cannot believe its power when the bushes disregard it with such ease. Oblivious roots trespass with impunity and push up their stems on the other side. Branches weave decoratively through the diamond mesh of the wire.

'Why are you so impatient?' she complains. 'Let's have an apple then you won't feel you're wasting your time. You're on holiday, remember.'

I am ashamed of my irritation. In England I have learnt to cringe at the thought of wandering about, hanging about idly. Loitering even on this side of the fence makes me feel like a trespasser. If someone were to question my right to be here ... I shudder.

She examines the padlocks in turn, as if there were a possibility of picking the locks.

'You could climb over, easy,' she says.

'But I've no desire to.'

'Really? You don't?' She is genuinely surprised that our wishes do not coincide.

'I think I saw an old hut on our way up,' she says as we drive back through the valley. We go slow until she points, there, there, and we stop. It is further from the road than it seems and her steps are so slow that I take her arm. Her fluttering breath alarms me.

It is probably an abandoned shepherd's hut. The reed roof, now reclaimed by birds, has parted in place to let in shafts of light. On the outside the raw brick has been nibbled at by wind and rain so that the pattern of rectangles is no longer discernible. But the building does provide shelter from the sun. Inside, a bush flourishes in the earth floor.

'Is it ghanna?' I ask.

'No, but it's related, I think. Look, the branches are a paler grey, almost feathery. It's Hotnos-kooigoed.'

'You mean Khoi-Khoi-kooigoed.'

'Really, is that the educated name for them? It sounds right doesn't it?' And she repeats Khoi-Khoi-kooigoed, relishing the alliteration.

'No, it's just what they called themselves.'

'Let's try it,' she says, and stumbles out to where the bushes grow in abundance. They lift easily out of the ground and she packs the uprooted bushes with the one indoors to form a cushion. She lies down carefully and mutters about the heat, the fence, the long long day and I watch her slipping off to sleep. On the shaded side of the hut I pack a few of the bushes together and sink my head into the softness. The heat has drawn out the thymish balm that settles soothingly about my head. I drift into a drugged sleep.

Later I am woken by the sun creeping round on to my legs. Mamma starts out of her sleep when I enter the hut with the remaining coffee.

'You must take up a little white protea bush for my garden,' she says as we walk back to the bakkie.

'If you must,' I retort. 'And then you can hoist the South African flag and sing "Die Stem".'

'Don't be silly; it's not the same thing at all. You who're so clever ought to know that proteas belong to the veld. Only fools and cowards would hand them over to the Boers. Those who put their stamp on things may see in it their own histories and hopes. But a bush is a bush; it doesn't become what people think they inject into it. We know who lived in these mountains when the Europeans were still shivering in their own country. What they think of the veld and its flowers is of no interest to me.'

As we drive back we watch an orange sun plummet behind the hills. Mamma's limp is pronounced as she gets out of the bakkie and hobbles in to put on the kettle. We are hungry. We had not expected to be out all day. The journey has tired her more than she will admit.

I watch the stars in an ink-blue sky. The Milky Way is a smudged white on the dark canvas; the Three Kings flicker, but the Southern Cross drills her four points into the night. I find the long axis and extend it two and a half times, then drop a perpendicular, down on to the tip of the Gifberge, down on to the lights of the Soeterus Winery. Due South.

When I take Mamma a cup of cocoa, I say, 'I wouldn't be surprised if I came back to live in Cape Town again.'

'Is it?' Her eyes nevertheless glow with interest.

'Oh, you won't approve of me here either. Wasted education, playing with dynamite and all that.'

'Ag man, I'm too old to worry about you. But with something to do here at home perhaps you won't need to make up those terrible stories hey?'

JOURNAL OF A WALL
Ivan Vladislavić

31 May

I have a feeling that I am starting this too late.

It is hardly three weeks since he started the wall – but already he has laid the foundations. That is not too much to catch up, perhaps. But it would have been pleasantly symmetrical to have begun on the same day, to have taken up my pen as he took up his trowel.

I should have foreseen it all. I had a sense, when they delivered the bricks, that something in which I would have a part was beginning. If I had not been watching from behind the curtains in my lounge, like a spy, perhaps it would have been clear to me that I was meant to be more than an observer.

They brought the bricks almost three weeks ago. Saturday 11 May, as I look at my calendar. I was watching the cricket on television when I heard the truck stop across the road. The engine revved for several minutes – I suppose the driver had gone in to check whether he was at the right address – and that's why I went to investigate.

When I looked out through the curtains he was crossing the lawn with a man wearing blue overalls. His wife was watching from the verandah.

The bricks were packed incongruously in huge plastic bags. very strong plastic, I suppose. He went straight up to the truck, put one foot on the rear wheel and hoisted himself up. He took out a pocket-knife and cut a slit in the plastic, put his finger in to touch the bricks. He held his hand there for a minute, as if he was taking a pulse. Then he put his eye to the slit. It took a long time before he was satisfied. I had an inkling then that something important was beginning. I should have fetched a pen and started recording immediately. I would have had the details now, those all-important beginning moments. Already the memories are fading: I can't remember when she went back inside, for instance, but I don't think that she watched the unloading.

He supervised that task himself. It didn't take long. I wished that the bricks weren't wrapped in plastic; then they could have been passed along a chain of sure hands from the back of the truck to a corner of the garden. Instead the driver of the truck operated a small crane mounted just behind the cab, and the man directed him to pile the bags of bricks one on top of the other on the pavement. I remember at least that there were nine bags. When that was over he went inside – it was probably then that I noticed she was gone – and returned with a pen to sign the delivery papers.

After the truck had gone he went straight back into the house. I was surprised. I expected him to examine the bricks again. But apparently he was satisfied.

I returned to the television set. The game was over. I watched for a while, hoping to get the final score. But I was restless. The news came on. It was Michael de Morgan. He told us there was unrest in the townships again. He showed us a funeral crowd being dispersed with tear-gas. A bus burned in the background. Then a camera in a moving car tracking along the naked faces of houses, and children peeling away from the vehicle like buck in the game reserve. A cloud of black smoke from a supermarket. Soldiers. Some people hurling bricks into the burning bus.

The following scenes may upset some viewers, Michael de Morgan said gently.

I switched off the set. I was upset enough.

I went back to the window. It was almost dark outside, the house across the road a blue shadow. But the front door was open, and in the glow from the lounge I could see him reclining in an easy chair on the verandah, with his feet up on a table, drinking a beer.

The pile of bricks was another dark shape in the twilight. From the way in which he was sitting, with his legs swung to one side, I would say that he was watching over them. He looked as if he was going to stay there all night. Or perhaps he was trying to decide what to build. Or had already decided and could see the final product, with each brick in place.

I was restless that evening, and upset and depressed. I drank too much. The room wanted to spin. That impulse came to me through the bed-springs, just a gentle tremor at first, but the walls of the house held fast. I put one foot on the floor, trying to weigh it down. Then it came again, the room trying to twist itself free from the rest of the house, rip up its tap-root and ascend into the sky. Plaster powder rained down on me as cracks chased through the walls and ran themselves into corners. Then the rafters cracked like ribs and the room began to turn. The whole place rattled and groaned, spun faster and faster, and then rose slowly like an ancient flying-machine, ripping roof-tiles like finger-nails, tearing the sinews of electrical wiring, bursting the veins of waterpipes, up into the night sky.

I went to look through the bedroom window. The city was spread out below me like a map, but I couldn't get my bearings. There was my house, with its gaping wound. I felt a wind on my neck, and when I looked up

I saw the ceiling drift away. The night, effervescent with stars, poured in.

I sat down on the end of my bed. The bricks began to peel away from the walls in squadrons and they flew down to my neighbour's house and assembled themselves into barbecues and watchtowers and gazebos and rondawels and bomb shelters. When all the walls had unravelled completely I was left floating on the raft of the floor, dragged by the currents of the sky this way and that, until the boards all rotted away below me and I sank down into my bathroom and got sick.

I woke up very late on Sunday morning, feeling terrible. It was several hours before I could bring myself to get up and take a shower. The room had fitted itself back into the house imperfectly, with the doors and windows in the wrong places, and the floors were awash with books, broken glass, clockwork, clothing, kindling. I decided to put off tidying up until after breakfast – which was lunch, actually.

While I was eating I suddenly remembered my neighbour's bricks, and rushed to the lounge window. I was surprised and hurt to discover that he had already started work without me. He was digging a trench along the boundary of his property, where the fence used to be. The fence posts were still there, but the wire itself lay in a huge buckled roll on the front lawn. A wall! Of course.

After some minutes of watching him I hit on a plan for getting a closer view of the building operations. I strolled to the shop, bought the Sunday paper, and then took a slightly longer route which would take me past his house on my way home. It worked perfectly. I stopped to tie my shoelaces, which I had cunningly loosened before I rounded the corner, so that I could get a good look at the trench and, indeed, at him. Fortunately, he was working with his back to me.

The trench seemed to me inordinately deep – although I must say that I have never actually built a wall myself – eighteen inches or more. And at least two foot across. It was possible that he was planning to build an extremely thick, high wall of the kind that is fairly common in our suburb, in which case the foundations would have to be secure. But I was more inclined to think that he was simply an amateur. He didn't look as if he had built a wall before either.

Frankly, he was a disappointment to me. It was the first time I had really seen him from close range. Indeed, until the day before it would be true to say that I had never seen him. He was simply the driver of a car or the pusher of a lawnmower. My first real glimpse of him, swinging up onto the truck, had convinced me that he was strong, seasoned, capable. Now I saw how wrong I was. He had taken off his shirt (it hung limply on one of the fence posts) and his back was pale and flabby. His neck was burnt slightly red. He was wearing long pants, which looked clean and ironed, not at all like work pants. What bothered me most was the way in which he swung the pick; there was no conviction in it at all. I wished that I could get a look at his hands.

Of course, I probably didn't think all this in the time it takes to tie a shoelace: it is more likely that I simply observed and then thought about it all later, as I read my newspaper in a deckchair in the front garden.

I spent the better part of the afternoon watching him from behind the paper. He never looked my way once. He worked very slowly, but steadily, and by five o'clock, when it had become quite cool and almost time for me to go in, he had finished the trench. He put on his shirt and fetched her out of the house to review the day's achievements. He seemed very pleased with himself: he even sprang into the hole and did a little jig for her, and that made me like him more. And she put her arm around his shoulders when they went back in, and that made me proud of her too.

I waited for a few minutes, thinking that they would perhaps come out onto the verandah for sundowners, but the door remained closed, and eventually I also had to go in.

Nothing happened for a week. I had hoped that he would not do any more building while I was away at work. I noted with relief that he was waiting for the following weekend. The week dragged.

Once or twice during the week I saw him inspecting the trench after work, probably checking for subsidence; and once or twice when my evening strolls took me past the trench I too was able to make a quick examination. It seemed to be holding up well. On those occasions I also managed to get a closer look at the bricks. He seemed to have forgotten about them. I admired that in him – his patience, his faith. It is possible, of course, that he inspected the bricks late at night after I had gone to sleep, but I doubt it.

Their habits seemed to be fairly steady. He usually came in at about five thirty and put the car straight in the garage. They didn't go out much. They would watch television every night until about ten thirty and then retire to bed. The television was on from about six, and so I presumed that either they ate as soon as he came in from work or they took their meals in front of the set.

I speculated about the programmes they watched. Did the news upset them? I for one was finding the news depressing – full of death and destruction. Who would build amid these ruins? I used to stand behind my curtain and look across at their lounge window, flickering blue as a screen. What on earth were they shoring up?

On the following Saturday (this would have been the 18th of May) I was up early, early enough to see the building sand delivered. Would that I had been ready with pen and paper to describe how that mountain of fine white sand slid from the back of the tip-truck, and the great cloud of dust that boiled up and hung over the houses.

I knew when I saw that perfect dune, white as flour, spilling over the kerb and the pavement, that the foundations would be laid that day. He materialized out of the dust-storm, wearing a blue T-shirt this time but the same pants (fortunately starting to look a little grubby and crumpled) and carrying a spade and a bucket of water. He stood for a while staring into the dust as if waiting for instructions. Then he set to, separating a pile of the sand and shovelling it onto a sheet of corrugated iron. He seemed a little more lively this morning. I was pleased. There was quite a spring in his step as he went off to the garage.

The combined haze of the dust-cloud and the net curtain behind which I was standing was making it very difficult for me to see what was going on. By this time a sense was growing in me that it was very important to catch every detail, although I was still blind to the fact that I should have been writing it all down as it happened.

There he was returning with a bag of cement on his shoulder. I could see him quite clearly for a while but then he was back in the haze.

I paced my lounge, searching for an excuse to get closer to him. The one I finally found was a little obvious perhaps, but he generally seemed to take no notice of me, so I decided to chance it. I pulled my car out of the garage, fetched a bucket of water, and started to wash the windscreen. By now the dust had settled somewhat, and I was surprised to see her coming into view. She was sitting on a kitchen chair, and wearing a pale-pink dressing-gown. She was holding a book, and at first I thought she was reading. Then it seemed to me that she was reading out instructions. As I watched he measured out a quantity of cement in a tin and sprinkled it over the sand. He looked at her. She spoke again. He mixed the sand and the cement with the spade and shaped it into a dam.

Jesus! I said to myself, they're following a recipe.

Then I realized with a start that I was staring. I quickly dipped my sponge in the water and sloshed it over the roof of the car. Schooled my arm to keep rubbing as I watched.

When he had finished the mixing he put the cement in a wheelbarrow and carried it to the beginning of the trench. She walked with him, reading all the way, and watched over him as he tipped the cement into the trench and smoothed it with a length of wood.

And so it went. After the third trip she went inside – presumably he had memorized the procedure – and I did not see her again that day. When he broke for lunch so did I. When I heard the spade clattering on the corrugated iron again a half-hour later I went back to washing the car.

He worked as doggedly laying the foundations as he had done digging the trench, and I found my admiration for him growing. After a whole day of washing my car I was exhausted; he neither slackened nor speeded up as he approached the end of the trench, just worked on at the same relentlessly steady pace. He seemed to me to be a remarkable example of soldiering on. I needed to take a leaf out of his book. I thanked him silently as he set to cleaning the wheelbarrow and the spade with meticulous care.

I resolved to try and follow his example in the week ahead. It would be at least a week before the building proper could begin; the foundations would have to settle. He would be patient, and so would I.

On the Monday evening after he had laid the foundations I saw him come home from work. After he had put the car in the garage and closed the door I expected him to walk down to the building-site for some kind of inspection. But he went straight inside. It made me feel a little foolish, as if I was letting the side down. I put the whole thing out of my mind. Yet I was waiting for the weekend with a growing sense of anticipation.

So I was immediately uneasy when he parked the car in the driveway on Friday evening, instead of putting it in the garage as usual. He hurried inside. Surely they weren't planning to go out? I had specifically decided to get an early night so that I would be fresh for the next day's building, and I expected him to do the same.

I was alarmed when he came out just a few minutes later carrying a suitcase. He put it in the boot and went back inside. Could it be true? Would they go away on such an important weekend? It was inconceivable. I brought a bottle over to the window and poured myself a large Scotch. There he was, coming out again. He went to the car and started cleaning the windscreen. Then I knew it was true. I finished the drink, poured another one. Perhaps they were going to the drive-in? With a suitcase? No ... He went back inside. The lights in the house went out one by one. Then they both came out of the front door. She was wearing a nightie and large pink slippers and carrying a suitcase, a smaller version of the one he had put in the boot. They left the hallway light burning. He took the case from her and they walked to the car. How could they do this to me!

I quickly opened the curtains, switched the light on, and stood in the centre of the window, one hand holding the bottle of Scotch and the other pressed against the glass. I stared hard at them, took a long swig from the bottle. The car still hadn't moved. Then she got out and went back inside. Going to check that the taps are off, I thought. The swines. She was back very quickly, carrying a book and something in a brown paper bag. She got in and he switched the interior light on. They both looked at the book. Now the car started, the tail-lights glowed red in the dusk, the car was reversing, they were driving away.

The inside of the car was a warm, light bubble. I saw his profile, and beyond it her face, as soft and ripe as a fruit. She was looking at him, or perhaps at me, and I wondered what she thought of me, weeping at my post, holding my pickled tongue in one cupped palm and the bloodied bayonet in the other.

I finished the Scotch and went for a walk. Oh, I walked all over the place, staring into the blank faces of walls, peering into the blind eyes of windows, shouting obscenities into the leafy ears of hedges. I made the dogs bark. I rattled gates and banged on doors. I put the fear of the devil into the whole suburb. Those sleeping houses, their gigantic gasping and snoring, their tossing and turning. I waded through drifts of dry leaves in the culverts. I left my footprints in flowerbeds. I beat their welcome mats against their front doors until their gardens choked on the dust of ten thousand five o'clock feet. The breeze smelt of formalin. Everything was covered in wax and powdered and pinned. I brought back a newspaper billboard that said THREE MORE DIE IN UNREST and it was easy to believe in unrest and death with the rattle of leaves in the throats of the drains, the letterboxes choked with pamphlets, the bottles of milk souring on the doorsteps.

I forgave them.

I went over just after midnight, in an overcoat, in a balaclava. I shone my torch along the length of the trench: it was looking good. In a few places the earth had subsided, and I cleared it with my hands, and swept up a few dry leaves.

I brought back with me a brick.

I put it on my desk, on an embroidered cloth, and turned the fluorescent lamp on it. It was an extraordinary brick. It looked so heavy, as if it had been hewn from solid rock in the quarries of some not yet discovered planet. It was reddish brown, with a cracked, cratered surface, and it was still warm to the touch. It looked as if it would plummet through the desk, the floor, sink down into the earth as if it were water.

Yet the more I looked at it, the more it looked like a familiar object. After a long time of watching it, it began to look like a loaf of bread, hot from the oven, steaming, fermenting inside.

I could hardly sleep that night with its hard presence in the house, its bubbling and hissing. But I eventually sank into the mottled depths of a dreamless sleep.

In the morning the brick had cooled. Its surface had hardened to a stiff crust.

I was tempted to keep it as some sort of memento. But by late afternoon I had begun to resent its stony silence, its impenetrable skin, and I resolved to return it to the pile as soon as it grew dark. I wanted to maintain some connection with it, however, so I marked each of its impassive faces with a small dot of white paint, and put it in the oven to dry.

When it was dark I took the brick over concealed in a folded newspaper which I carried under my arm. On the pavement I was suddenly tempted to explore the house and the back garden. The front lawn lay spread like a huge welcome mat, inviting me into the nooks and crannies of their private spaces. But I was afraid: someone could see me and mistake me for a burglar. So I returned the brick to its pile and carefully folded the plastic wrapper over it.

I was just turning back towards my own house when I spotted the letters, jutting like a tongue from the letterbox. I looked around quickly. There was no one in sight. I was bold enough to take the letters onto their verandah and skim through them in the light from behind the frosted panes of the front door. There were three letters. One was addressed to The Householder. The other two were addressed to Mr G. B. Groenewald. I returned the letters to the box and scurried home with my discovery.

Mr and Mrs Groenewald returned from their outing on Sunday evening. I was overjoyed to see them. I wanted them to know that I had taken good care of everything in their absence, so I flashed my lounge light in a cryptic morse of welcome and affection. No answering signal came. I suspect that they were tired from their journey and went straight to bed.

The week that followed was uneventful: we were all waiting for the weekend. Then today – yes, it is the 31st of May today – I finally realized what I had to do: I had to write it all down. I have laid my own foundations, and from now on it will be brick for word, word for brick. Tomorrow the building begins. I must have a good night's sleep.

1 June

7.15 a.m.

I have made my arrangements; I have pen and paper, I have a chair in front of the window. I set it all up last night. This morning I was up at six. Showered, shaved, put on my work clothes. Now I am waiting for us to begin.

8.30 a.m.

Here he comes. He is wearing the blue check and the trousers. He pauses on the top step of the verandah, looks out over his kingdom. Ah, if he knew that I was watching he wouldn't stretch in that bone-cracking way. He goes to the garage. He looks quite energetic, although a shadow of sleep drags across the lawn behind him. He opens the garage door, goes into the twilight. Comes out pushing the wheelbarrow loaded with a bag of cement, a spade, a box of tools. Goes to the beginning of the trench. Drags the piece of corrugated iron over, shovels sand into it.

Let me leave him to mix while I describe briefly the sky behind him: it is a flat sky, like faded blue canvas. It could be dangling from the top of my window frame. At the bottom the canvas is notched raggedly by the roofs of the houses. A slight breeze comes up and the canvas sways: a black edge opens up between it and the houses, closes again as the breeze drops.

He has mixed the cement. He leaves it to set, pushes the barrow to the pile of bricks. He slits the plastic with one long, sure pass of the pocket-knife. There are beads of moisture on the plastic and they run to rivers as he peels it back from the wound. His hand goes in. Comes out with a brick. He weighs it in his hand, turns it to look at it from all angles, puts it in the wheelbarrow. Reaches for another. If I had binoculars perhaps I would be able to tell, even at this distance, which brick is mine.

The wheelbarrow is full. He pushes it to the beginning of the trench. He takes a ball of string from the tool-box, stretches a length between the first fence post and the second, checks it with a spirit-level. When he stands the string cuts him just below the knee. Surely that is too low? He kneads the cement with the back of the spade. He takes up his trowel. He goes down on his knees in the trench. He reaches for a brick. Weighs it. His hands go down into the earth. Damn! I can't see what he's doing. I've missed the laying of the first brick!

10.30 a.m.

He works incredibly slowly. As if there were only one place in the whole bloody wall where any particular brick will fit.

He has laid three courses so far, and has just started the fourth. This is the first course I can see clearly. He weighs each brick in his hand. Then he settles it on its dollop of cement, shuffles it in, taps it with the handle of the trowel, slices off the oozing cement, taps it again. Sometimes he starts over, scraping the surface clean, putting the brick aside and choosing another. I cannot see why. They look the same to me.

I wonder where she is? I expected her to be there for the first brick.

I should go over and speak to him. It would be simple. Perhaps he would welcome some discussion. I would suggest, for example, that he make the wall slightly higher: what good is a wall if one can see over it? I would also advise him to wear a hat – I could offer to lend him one of mine. He's not used to the sun.

I could tell him how interested I am in his project. That would surprise him. If I told him about my own plan to document the whole process and showed him the work I have done so far, perhaps he would let me bring a chair over and sit right there, where I could record smells, noises; perhaps he would answer a few questions about his motivations, and even listen to some constructive criticism.

On the other hand my interest could affect him badly. Perhaps I should let him carry on unhindered for a while, until we have a clearer picture of the road ahead.

12.30 p.m.
I am pleased to note that he has moved the string to shoulder height. But now he is going inside, probably for lunch.

2.45 p.m.
I don't know whether I will be able to keep this up. He loves this wall, every brick of it, but he loves it so passionlessly, with a love so methodical and dis-ciplined, that it might as well be loathing.

He has loved his wall up to shoulder height, brick by careful brick, and now he fetches a step-ladder and the wall goes higher. He checks each course with the spirit-level, and then stands back to look at his work.

It is very boring to watch.

5.00 p.m.
He has finished work for the day. The wall is about two metres high. He has filled in the panel between the first two fence posts. Unless he speeds up con-siderably, I estimate that it will be several months before the wall is completed.

They are sitting now on the verandah. She came out a few minutes ago and put two beers on the table. Came down to inspect the wall. I couldn't see her response, because she looked at it from the inside, as if that was the more important side. But she seemed to say something to him, because he spoke and listened and then smiled. Then she went back to the verandah and sat in the other chair. They raised their glasses to one another and I raised mine too and clinked it against the window-pane.

2 June

It is Sunday evening. He has finished another panel. This morning he up-rooted the second fence post and strung the marker between the wall and the third post.

I think that I have caught up with him only to become bored.

He is a machine. His hands repeat themselves – brick after brick after brick they open and shut like pliers. His flabby muscles contract and relax in a pre-dictable rhythm.

I think I dislike him. Why must he weigh each brick and toss it over in his hand? Why must he tap each brick with the handle of the trowel, twice on one side, three times on the other, and once solidly in the middle, before he is satisfied? The man has no imagination. I can see already that his wall will be just another wall. An ordinary coincidence of bricks and mortar, pre-sentably imperfect. It won't fall down, but then it won't fly either. He'll prob-ably put plaster over his careful bricks and paint it green and people will think it was bought in a shop.

29 June

Today the wall finally passed the half-way mark. For the first time I can no longer see them as they drink their customary beer. I have resolved to speak to them before they disappear entirely.

30 June

I am writing this from the Café Zurich. I simply had to get out. I had to get away from them. I have delayed recording the events of yesterday evening because I needed time to calm down. I was so angry – and it will become clear that I had every reason to be – that I was sure my observations would seem spiteful and unfair.

But I think that I now have sufficient emotional distance from the incident to put it down objectively, as it happened.

During the course of yesterday afternoon, watching another panel of bricks edging up into the air, obscuring the house, I had become worried about the Groenewalds. More specifically, I had become worried about our relationship. There they were, celebrating the crossing of the half-way line, but hidden behind their wall. Here I was, celebrating the same occasion, but hidden behind my curtain. And just fifty metres or so separating us.

I began to regret my reticence. They were nice people, I knew. He was solid and reliable and purposeful. She was quiet and sweet and sensitive. They were my kind of people. If only I had broken the ice earlier. Now there was so much ground to be made up. Yet, at the same time, even though they were unaware of it, we had so much in common. The wall. They knew it from one side, I knew it from the other. I began to see it not so much as a barrier between us, but as a meeting-point. It was the thin line between pieces in a puzzle, the frontier on which both pieces become intelligible. Or perhaps it was like those optical puzzles in which you see the profile of a beautiful young woman or an old hag, but never both at the same time. I tossed these analogies around in my head, hoping to arrive at one I could share with them, an opening line I could call to them as I emerged from around the wall and took my first real steps into their lives. Eventually I decided to take a cup instead and ask for some sugar.

They were on the verandah, as I thought, drinking beer. They looked up as I crossed the lawn, suspiciously perhaps, although I couldn't see their expressions clearly in the blue gleam that the TV set in the lounge threw on them.

'Good evening Mr Groenewald, Mrs Groenewald,' I called, approaching them at a pace I thought they would appreciate, neither too fast nor too slow. 'I wonder if you could help me?'

He rose from his chair, put the beer on the table, and took one step to the edge of the verandah. She sat back in her chair and crossed her legs.

I stopped just below him but I spoke to her. 'I'm making a trifle and, you know how it is, I've run out of sugar for the custard. Could you spare me a bit, just until tomorrow?'

She rose quickly, took the cup from my hand, and went into the house. I took a few steps after her, drawn by the flickering blue of her retreating back, but he stepped towards the door, as if to block my path.

I was disappointed. I had hoped to gain access to the house, to measure their space against my imaginings. I heard the familiar fanfare announcing the six o'clock news. If only he would invite me in to watch the news with them: that would give us many opportunities to discuss the state of the country, the newest trouble spots, local and abroad, and get to know one another. But he made no move. I realized quickly that the more important opportunity was right in my hands – to discuss the wall with its maker. She, after all, had as little to do with the wall as a trowel or a piece of string. It was just as well she had left us alone.

I turned slightly, so that my pose suggested that I was watching the wall.

'I've been following your progress with interest,' I said. 'Perhaps you have seen me? I live right across from you.'

'No,' he said.

'It's a fine wall,' I went on undaunted. After all, hadn't they been invisible to me for months, even years (I couldn't remember whether they had moved in before or after me). 'A very fine wall indeed. A little high perhaps. A little forbidding.'

'I would make it higher,' he said, 'but there are municipal regulations.'

I began to feel uneasy. He hadn't invited me to sit, so I perched on the edge of the verandah.

'Have you built a wall before?' I asked.

'Many times,' he said. 'More times than I care to remember.'

That threw me. I was going to say that he was doing a good job, for a first attempt. But perhaps I would never have reached that line anyway, for it struck me then, with a sense of loss, that I couldn't see my house at all from this side. It had vanished completely. The sky above the wall was a blank, moronic space, as high as the stars. There was nothing in it that would provide comfort to a human heart, that would fill a human eye. The world beyond the wall was empty: there was not even a world there. Perhaps my house would be visible from the verandah? I stood, hoping to find a way up. But he had moved, while I was musing, to the top of the steps, and was looking back over his shoulder through the open window at the flickering television screen. The curtains were open. You could see right in. I moved towards the steps.

Just then she came out with the cup of sugar. She handed it down to me. It was very full and a few grains spilled onto my fingers.

'I'll replace it tomorrow. Thank you,' I said.

'Please don't bother,' she replied.

I had to leave. The lawn seemed vast. I crossed towards the hard edge of the wall, behind which the world was slowly materializing again. I had an extraordinary sense as I walked, somewhat stiffly, with the sugar trickling onto my fingers, that no eyes were on me. No one was watching me. I wanted to look back, but I couldn't. I couldn't confirm such an obvious insult.

I was mad as hell. I was in my lounge, where everything was still the same. I was mad as could be. I smashed up a chair. Still the rage wouldn't leave me.

I smashed up a table. Then I started to feel better, pacing around among the splinters with a bottle of Scotch in my hand. Who the hell did they think they were, treating me like a dog? Who the fuck were they anyway? Lunatics, blind people, fat slobs, smug shithouses.

I should have gone right into their house and smashed up a few things. That would have been perfect, with the news in the background. I would have shown them unrest and rioting and burning, in three dimensions. I would have given them wanton destruction of private property. I would have given them hell in the eye-level oven, and stonings with the bric-a-brac from the room divider. And then I would have left them uneasy calm after yesterday's violence.

But was it all worth it?

I sat down in the surviving chair and thought about it more carefully. They were such perverse people. What were they planning to do behind that ridiculous wall? Volkspele? Nude braaivleises? Secret nocturnal rituals accessible only to people in helicopters?

Fuck them. I had to tidy up.

17 August

The wall is almost finished.

I have not been thinking about it much. Of course, since the unfortunate incident with the sugar I've had to avoid them, to spare us all embarrassment. I have been going to work early and coming in late – and always careful to avert my gaze. Yet, out of the corner of my eye, as it were, I've watched the wall edge malevolently towards the end of the trench. There is not much space left for it to cross: scarcely a metre. That will be done next weekend and the betrayal will be complete.

I am no longer interested in them. They have blurred into the background out of which they came. But, for the sake of symmetry, I have decided to record the end of it all, the laying of the final brick. It seems necessary. Then I can be done with this journal.

24 August

He is almost finished. He is building the last panel from the garden side. I have watched him slowly obliterated by his wall. Now all I can see is a pair of hands reaching up.

I imagine that she is there with him, holding a bottle of champagne. No doubt I will see the cork flying up to the stars.

But is there cause for celebration? No. Is there reason for building when things are falling down? No. Is there reason for drinking beer when people are starving? Probably not. Do two people and a bottle of champagne make sense when citizens are pitched against soldiers, when stones are thrown at tanks? Does private joy make sense in the face of public suffering?

There he begins the last course of bricks. How bored I am with the tired repetition of gesture. How bored I am with the familiar shapes of words. How bored I am with this journal. It's just a wall. That must be clear by now. Even a child could see it. And the words that go into it like bricks are as bland and heavy and worn as the metaphor itself.

He lays the last brick. But I have the last word.

THE END

Later that same evening:
I am writing simply because I cannot sleep. And the reason I cannot sleep is that those bastards across the road are having a party. A wall-warming, I suppose. The music is too loud. And the buzzing of voices! They have strung coloured lights in the trees. Candles are burning in paper bags on top of the wall. I would phone the police, but I have already smashed the telephone.

I would gather to me, if I could, the homeless and the hungry, the persecuted, the pursued, the forgotten, those without friends and neighbours, to march around the wall. We would be blowing paper trumpets left over from office parties, and banging on cake tins, and raising up a noise to wake the dead and bring the wall tumbling down.

8 September

Today there was something new attached to the wall: a FOR SALE notice.

17 September

Today a SOLD notice.

2 November

Today they left.

I went across and stood on the pavement to watch their household effects being put into the truck. It is all as I expected: the knotty pine, the wicker, the velveteen, the china, the cotton print, the plastic, the glass, the stainless-steel, the beaten copper.

I stood right next to the truck with my hands on my hips. I dared them to meet my eye but they seemed not to notice me, or not to care. They put a few boxes on the back seat of the car and they followed the pantechnicon. I watched until they disappeared.

The wall looked ashamed of itself.

I went back home.

9 November

The new people have moved in. They are simply people carrying boxes and banging doors. Good.

Today the municipality pruned all the trees in our suburb. The sky has opened up. The wall turns its back on the street. It is a beautiful sunny day. I must get out.

And I must remember to take a stroll past the wall some time and see if I can spot my brick.

HOLDING BACK MIDNIGHT
Maureen Isaacson

The night is shooting past. It is bright jet and hot. The air is as smooth as the whiskey we sip on the verandah of the old hotel that has become my parents' home. We are safe from the faded neon and slow-moving traffic lights outside. The bubbles of fifty chilled bottles of champagne are waiting to spill as we touch down on the new century. In our own way, we each believe that from that moment on nothing will ever be the same.

Anything could happen at midnight. President Manzwe has said that he has a surprise for us. What can it be?

'Cheers!' shouts my mother. Old opals shine dully against her sagging lobes, her webbed neck. She is flushed, like a dead person who has been painted to receive her final respects.

'Cheers!' echoes her friend Ethel.

Smoke and disillusion have ravaged their voices. Their tongues are too slack to roll an olive pip. They walk slowly among the guests, in silver dresses that were fashionable once. They teeter on sling-back stilettos. They offer salmon and bits of fish afloat on shells of lettuce leaves.

Don't the people at this party ever think about AIDS? Out there in the real world, they give you cling paper gloves in restaurants lest you should bleed from an unnoticed cut. Waiters wear them. Doctors. Environmentalists, like my husband Leon and me. The lack of sterility makes me queasy tonight.

'What is the time, Dad?' I ask.

'Be patient,' he says.

Hopefully the moment we are waiting for will release him from the grip of history. History is ever-present in my father, like the patterns that shimmer from the chandeliers over the cracked walls. It is trapped in the broken paving outside this hotel where angels of delight once fluttered eyelashes as if they were wings at white men. History hovers, with the ghosts of the illicit couplings that once heated the hotel's shadowy rooms. It is funnelled through my memory.

Here comes my Uncle Otto, ex-minister of Home Affairs, glass in hand. Looking at his ginger moustache, I am seven years old again. I am sitting on his lap at the bar. Don't tell your mother, he is saying. His hand is on my knee. I feel the closeness of flesh. Angels are rubbing themselves against the men. Men against angels.

'Why angels?' I want to know.

'Because they take the white men to heaven,' says Uncle Otto.

Like the street names that have been removed for their Eurocentricity, my parents and their friends are displaced. They do not understand the new signs. Their silhouettes glide across the garden, outlining their nostalgia. Through the shrill chirp of the crickets, I catch the desolation in the voices. The talk of lifts that no longer work, of the rubbish that piles up. There goes our old dentist Louis Dutoit and his wife Joyce, speaking of 'Old Johannesburg'. For all the world we are still there. Except for Leon and me of course. We could not have married in the old days, him being coloured and all. Doctor Dutoit would not even have filled Leon's teeth.

How graciously they tolerate us now. We have breezed in from our communal plot in the outer limits of the mega-city these people are too afraid to visit.

'Not without an AK-4777 rifle,' my father has said.

Instead they ruminate in this, the last of the shrunken ghettos that began to decline when cheap labour went out. Not for them the spread of shebeens and malls that splash jazz from what used to be poverty-stricken township to the City Hall. The place we now call Soweto City. Connected by skyway and flyway, over and underground, as steady as the steel and the foreign funding on which it runs. Talk about one door closing. The Old Order was not yet cold in its grave and the place was gyrating, like a woman in love.

And the people out there? There are millions of us – living the good life advertised by laser-honed graphics that dazzle the streets. We are fast-living. Street-wise. Natural. We till the land. Our food is organic. See this party dress? It's made of paper. Tomorrow I'll shred it. Recycle later.

I thank heavens for Leon. I envy him his equilibrium. Forgive and forget. That's what he said before we came here tonight. His kind of thinking has helped me cope with the effect my parents have on me.

'Thank the Lord Leon's surname is also Laubscher. Some people will never know,' is all they said when I told them about our marriage.

Dad is the perfect host. But earlier this evening his sentimentality got the better of him when Uncle Otto reminded him of the New Year's Eve parties, five times the size of this one, held at our old house. Foreign diplomats, caviar, black truffles in Italian rice. Now he embraces Ethel. One-two. One-two. He dances a little jig with her on the verandah, cooled by the breeze that fans the palm tree. I squirm, reminded of the way he used to cavort when the hotel was in its prime.

'I'm a miner at heart,' he used to say, insisting that the place was a private sideline of no consequence.

Was anyone fooled into believing it was anything but a thriving business? We had more maids than rooms that needed polishing in our double-storey house. My parents had owned three game farms and four cars A relic of the Old Regime, my father will never forgive the New Order for destroying his lifestyle. I am sure that in his dreams he still sells the kisses of angels to those who would cross the forbidden colour line by night, endorse it by day.

'Would you like to dance?' asks Paul Schoeman, once the minister of Law and Order. 'Mona Lisa ...,' sings Nat King Cole. I shuffle. Our feet collide. He holds me close, looks into my eyes and says, 'How can you live in the native township?'

I am unable to persuade old Schoeman that the change has brought with it a downswing in crime. I say all the things my father will not hear. But like Dad he does not grasp a word about redistribution. About progress. How can they when they insist without blinking that English and Afrikaans are still the official languages?

'You talk too much,' he says and pulls me towards him, gripping me so tightly that my left nipple sets off his security panic button, the kind my parents pay a fortune to wear round their necks. A siren wails. Up here on the verandah, men remove the fleshy fingers they have been rolling over their wives' naked, sagging backs. The whites of the wives' eyes show. Paul Schoeman grabs my breast. I scream. I put my hands to my ears. I want to block out the wailing. The barking of the Rottweilers. The jibbering of the guests. Four armed response security guards appear. Their sobriety creates a striking contrast.

They are not amused when my father says, 'False alarm. Who let the dogs out?' Leon is nowhere to be seen.

'Have a snack,' mother offers. It is anchovy, tart and salty.

'Is it nearly time for champagne?' I want to know.

'It won't be long now,' says Dad, as if he were meting out a punishment.

'What is the time?' shouts someone. One minute to midnight, says my watch. My father pours me another whiskey.

'Be patient,' he commands. Any minute now, I tell myself.

'To the year two thousand!' I shout. 'To the future!'

'There is nothing to look forward to.' Dad's voice is weighed down. Now two of him are saying, 'This is the future.' The thick curl of his cigar smoke throws me back into a time when I believed that he had power over the planets. Now I am starting to believe that my father is actually capable of holding back midnight. I want to call the security guards with their military boots and pistols to return.

'Do you want to see the real danger we face here tonight?' I will ask. Then

I will see what they can do about the fear that washes this party like a backward-moving current.

I am standing alone when it happens. The blackness of the sky is split as fire crackers explode brightly into two million broken stars. An ethereal chorus resounds above the voice of Nat King Cole, above the marabi jazz that plays on Station Nnwe in the background. As the heavens shift, time dissolves and my rapture rises.

Down below, the profusion of papyrus plants, the beds of lobelia, chrysanthemum and wild hydrangea, the lawn that is overrun with weeds are illuminated by an unearthly light. 'Happy New Year!' Leon embraces me from behind. 'Did you hear what Manzwe said?' he asks.

From a great distance, I hear my father saying that there is still one minute to go.

The South African short story: A historical overview

It is arguably in the genre of short fiction that South African literature has most consistently excelled: three of South Africa's most prominent writers in English (Pauline Smith, H. C. Bosman and Nadine Gordimer) built their reputations substantially from writing short stories; and a host of others – including W. C. Scully, William Plomer, Jack Cope, Doris Lessing, Dan Jacobson, Es'kia Mphahlele, Bessie Head, Sheila Roberts, Ahmed Essop, Njabulo Ndebele (to name just a few) – have used the short-story form extensively.

The history of the South African short story goes back further than is generally assumed. Stories with recognisable South African settings, characters and preoccupations appeared in literary journals like *The Cape of Good Hope Literary Magazine* in the 1840s. Two of the earliest book collections of South African tales, however, are R. Hodges's *The Settler in South Africa and Other Tales* (1860) and A. W. Drayson's *Tales at the Outspan, or Adventures in the Wild Regions of Southern Africa* (1862). Olive Schreiner was the earliest female short-story writer of note with her *Dreams* (1891), although she was preceded by the lesser-known Marguerite de Fenton (Marguerite Mostyn Cleaver) with her *Tales Written in Ladybrand* (1885) and Mary Anne Carey-Hobson with *South African Stories* (1886). Schreiner's 'Eighteen-Ninety-Nine' (1923, c. 1906), about the devastating effects of the Second Anglo-Boer War on the Boer women in particular, stands out as one of the most powerful and moving short stories of this early period.

The late nineteenth century saw a proliferation of short-story collections, many of them demonstrating in their titles their affinity with an oral milieu, which was a strong tendency in the early South African short story. Some examples are J. Forsyth Ingram's *The Story of a Gold Concession and Other African Tales and Legends* (1893), W. C. Scully's *Kafir Stories* (1895) and his *The White Hecatomb and Other Stories* (1897), Ernest Glanville's *Tales from the Veld* (1897), H. A. Bryden's *Tales of South Africa* (1896) and his *From Veldt Camp Fires: Stories of Southern Africa* (1900), and Percy FitzPatrick's *The Outspan: Tales of South Africa* (1897).

Among this group of early writers, Scully and FitzPatrick are the only two whose short stories have been re-issued. Selected stories by Scully have appeared in Jean Marquard's useful edition entitled *Transkei Stories* (1984). Several of the stories assembled by Marquard contain elements of oral culture; it is evident in the pieces that make up her selection, in fact, that Scully had an abiding interest in oral history and folklore. Sir Percy FitzPatrick's *The*

Outspan (re-released in 1987) is an outstanding example of the kind of colonial fiction occasioned by the presence of the motley band of expatriate adventurers who flocked to the South African diamond- and gold-fields in the last two decades of the nineteenth century. The title story employs a fictional narrator and evokes the fireside ethos of the oral tale.

Perceval Gibbon raised this 'fireside-tale' genre to new heights in his collection of stories *The Vrouw Grobelaar's Leading Cases* (1905). In comparison with Scully and FitzPatrick, Gibbon demonstrates a far greater skill with literary artifice and the art of storytelling, and this technical skill is accompanied by a more complex social vision. His use of a storyteller figure – the redoubtable Vrouw Grobelaar – is not sporadic or opportunistic as it is in the case of the other two writers. The result is a well-crafted collection of compatible stories anticipating Pauline Smith's *The Little Karoo* (1925) and Bosman's *Mafeking Road* (1947).

Pauline Smith's *The Little Karoo* is probably South Africa's earliest collection of short stories to achieve lasting recognition. Each of the ten stories included in *The Little Karoo* (two were added to the original eight of the first edition) exemplifies Smith's remarkable ability to capture the stark, elemental quality of her rural Dutch characters and the ponderous Biblical cadences of their speech, the harsh oppressiveness of a life spent wresting the barest of yields from the reluctant earth, the austerity of their Protestant faith and the tragic dimension in their human fallibilities. So compatible are the stories in terms of theme and setting that they have been profitably read as a 'cycle'.

In the stories of R. R. R. Dhlomo, whose work of the late 1920s and the 1930s can be taken to represent the emergence of black South African short fiction, there are traces of a residual orality, although these are masked by a heavy reliance on Western literary models. A pioneer of short fiction by black writers, Dhlomo's numerous stories and journalistic sketches of life on the mines in the 1920s and 1930s appeared in the black newspapers of the time. A selection of his pieces has recently been edited by Tim Couzens and published as *20 Short Stories* (1996).

William Plomer's stories appeared in *I Speak of Africa* (1927) and *The Child of Queen Victoria and Other Stories* (1933). The title story of the second volume is one of his best-known and, as its title suggests, concerns the dilemma of a traditional Englishman whose attraction to a young African woman in rural Natal threatens to disrupt his conceptual and moral universe. A selected edition of Plomer's stories appeared in 1984.

Herman Charles Bosman is probably South Africa's most popular short-story writer, and his stories have appeared in numerous collections over the years. Among these are *Unto Dust* (1963) which includes his artful 'Old

Transvaal Story', *Bosman at His Best* (1965), *A Bekkersdal Marathon* and *Jurie Steyn's Post Office* (both 1971), all edited by Bosman's pupil and literary executor Lionel Abrahams. The appearance in 1981 of his *Collected Works* (also edited by Abrahams) confirmed Bosman's stature in the world of South African literature. The efforts of another notable Bosman scholar, Stephen Gray, have resulted in *Selected Stories* (1980), *Bosman's Johannesburg* (1986), and *Makapan's Caves and Other Stories* (1987) which has the distinction of being one of Bosman's rare successes on the overseas market.

Mafeking Road (1947), however, is by far Bosman's best-known collection, and was the only one to appear in his own lifetime. Bosman's storyteller figure, the wily backveld raconteur Oom Schalk Lourens, features in all but one of the stories in *Mafeking Road*. Schalk Lourens was first introduced to the South African reading public in 'Makapan's Caves' (first published in 1930), which memorably begins: 'Kaffirs? (said Oom Schalk Lourens). Yes, I know them. And they're all the same. I fear the Almighty, and I respect His works, but I could never understand why He made the kaffir and the rinderpest'. From the very outset, then, Bosman was to make use of his very distinctive brand of irony to undermine white assumptions of superiority, a technique that has not always been properly interpreted by all readers of the Schalk Lourens stories. Between 1930 and 1951 dozens of stories appeared in the Schalk Lourens sequence, most of which have been taken up in posthumous collections of his work. The later 'Voorkamer' stories, which feature a number of narrators in a 'conversation-forum' format, also testify to Bosman's consummate skill as a storyteller.

The trajectory of the South African short story from the 1860s to the 1950s parallels the demographic shifts from countryside to city that were occasioned by the mineral discoveries of the late nineteenth century and subsequent industrialisation and urbanisation. The effects of this demographic shift can be traced in the changing texture of the short story over this period. From stories which have a predominantly rural setting, and which bear a close relationship to oral lore, legend and small-town gossip, the South African short story of the 1950s and after is urbanised, increasingly fragmented in nature and predominantly social realist in mode.

The best-known post-war story writers who worked in this mode are Alan Paton and Nadine Gordimer. Paton is renowned for what is possibly South Africa's single most famous novel, *Cry, the Beloved Country* (1948), but some of the biting social realism and pathos of his novel are contained in the short stories in *Debbie Go Home* (1961) (also published as *Tales from a Troubled Land*) and *More Tales of South Africa* (1967).

Nadine Gordimer is South Africa's most prolific and successful short-story writer. Some fifteen collections of her stories have appeared over the years, beginning with *Face to Face* in 1949. Others include *The Soft Voice of the Serpent and Other Stories* (1952), *Six Feet of the Country* (1956), *Not for Publication and Other Stories* (1965), *Livingstone's Companions* (1971) and *Something Out There* (1984). Selections of her stories have appeared as *Selected Stories* (1975), *Crimes of Conscience* (1991), and *Why Haven't You Written? Selected Stories 1950–1972* (1992).

As is the case with her novels, Gordimer's stories trace, in penetrating and often painful detail, the effects of South African politics and society on the individual. A powerful example is 'Six Feet of the Country' which explores the contradictory emotions of a white farming couple when a young man, an illegal immigrant from Rhodesia, dies of pneumonia on their farm. (See the commentary section, pages 146–147, for more discussion of this story.)

In 'The Train from Rhodesia', another famous Gordimer story, a young white woman on a train which has pulled into a small country station haggles with an old black man who has a wooden carving of a lion the girl desires. The old man's price is too high and the girl, while recognising the artistic merits of the piece, turns him down. As the train pulls out of the station the girl's husband triumphantly presents her with the carving, which he has acquired for less than half the price the old man asked. With the 'heat of shame' rising through her body, the girl turns her back on her bewildered husband, utterly disgusted and wearied by his inability to understand her genuine appreciation of the work of art and her shame at having acquired it in such a degrading manner.

Another prolific writer is Dan Jacobson, whose stories have appeared in several collections over the years including *A Long Way from London* (1958), *Beggar My Neighbour* (1964), *Through the Wilderness and Other Stories* (1968), *A Way of Life and Other Stories* (1971) and *Inklings: Selected Stories* (1973). One of Jacobson's best-known stories, 'Beggar My Neighbour', is about a young white boy who befriends two black children and later has to come to terms with the harsh implications of rigid racial segregation which consigns the children to disparate futures largely determined by race.

Stuart Cloete achieved brief popularity with his many collections, among them *The Soldier's Peaches* (1959), *The Silver Trumpet* (1961), *The Looking Glass* (1963) and *The Honey Bird* (1964). Jack Cope's reputation by contrast, also established in the 1960s – by his *The Tame Ox* (1960) and *The Man Who Doubted* (1967) – is more solid, largely as a consequence of his deeper engagement with the worsening social relations in the South Africa of the time. Doris Lessing was another writer of this period, her African stories appearing in *This Was the Old Chief's Country* (1951), *The Habit of Loving*

(1957) and *African Stories* (1964). These stories deal mostly with the lives of the white colonials of Rhodesia. Her well-known 'Witchcraft for Sale' (from *This Was the Old Chief's Country*) demonstrates her acute awareness of the racial prejudices and insecurities of this society.

Among black writers, the pioneering work of R. R. R. Dhlomo was followed, in 1946, by the publication of Es'kia Mphahlele's first collection of stories *Man Must Live and Other Stories*. This heralded an era of unprecedented literary activity among black writers of the 1950s and 1960s, most of which centred around the magazine *Drum*. The short story (often taking the form of a magazine column or anecdote) was the dominant genre of the period, and *Drum* published the bulk of these stories, including those by Nat Nakasa, Can Themba and Casey Motsisi. Posthumous collections of stories and sketches by these writers have appeared under the titles *The World of Nat Nakasa* (1975), *The Will to Die* (1972, 1982) and *The World of Can Themba* (1985), and *Casey and Co.: Selected Writings of Casey 'Kid' Motsisi* (1983). *Drum* magazine itself is significant in that it ushered in a new era in black writing and black self-awareness, and its contributors laid an important foundation for later black writing in South Africa. Mphahlele was the most prolific writer of the era. His classic 'Mrs Plum', which appeared in his *In Corner B* (1967), deftly explores the lives of black servants in relation to their privileged mistresses. His *The Unbroken Song: Selected Writings* appeared in 1981.

The magazine *Staffrider*, which first appeared in the late 1970s, was *Drum's* more radical successor. Like *Drum* it spawned a wealth of talented black writers, many of them writers of short stories. Mtutuzeli Matshoba, Mbulelo Mzamane, Mothobi Mutloatse and Njabulo Ndebele are among the writers whose work first appeared in *Staffrider* and whose collections of stories were later put out by the publishers of the magazine, Ravan Press. Matshoba's *Call Me Not a Man* (1979), Mzamane's *Mzala* (1980) and Mutloatse's *Mama Ndiyalila* (1982) share a concern with presenting the life of black people in starkly realistic mode, and often incorporate elements of African oral culture in an attempt to shrug off Western literary influence. Ndebele's *Fools and Other Stories* (1983) has enjoyed more sustained success than the collections of his *Staffrider* contemporaries. His stories are rich in minute detail and vividly evoke township life as seen mainly through the eyes of a young and sensitive protagonist.

Another highly accomplished story writer is Bessie Head, whose *The Collector of Treasures* (1977) is set in a village in Botswana and successfully employs many techniques and devices germane to the oral milieu of the village. Head's stories engage effectively with the issues that emerge in

Botswanan village life: tribal history, the arrival of the missionaries, religious conflict, witchcraft, rising illegitimacy and, throughout, problems that the women in the society encounter.

Other accomplished story writers of the 1970s and 1980s include Christopher Hope, Ahmed Essop, Peter Wilhelm and Sheila Roberts. Hope's witheringly satirical view of apartheid South Africa is well represented in his *Private Parts and Other Tales* (1981, 1982), which includes his 'Learning to Fly', a mordant fable about the changing of the guard in the state security apparatus. Essop's *The Hajji and Other Stories* (1978), *Noorjehan and Other Stories* (1990) and *The King of Hearts and Other Stories* (1997) examine in fine detail and with gentle irony the life of the Asian community in and around Johannesburg. The issues that Essop explores are those that beset the day-to-day life of a community squeezed by the interests of the dominant racial groups in South Africa. Wilhelm's collections include *LM and Other Stories* (1975), *At the End of the War* (1981) and *Some Place in Africa* (1987). Roberts's *Outside Life's Feast* (1975) and *This Time of Year* (1983) explore the frustrations and prejudices of her working-class white protagonists with an uncompromising frankness and commitment to detail. Her *Coming In and Other Stories* appeared in 1993.

Cape Town's District Six, demolished in the 1960s, is the setting for a number of short stories, among them stories by Alex La Guma, Achmat Dangor, James Matthews and Richard Rive. Rive's well-crafted stories, collected in *Advance, Retreat: Selected Short Stories* (1983), mainly explore the effects of South Africa's racial laws on the individual. Dangor's writing centres on the iniquitous effects of racial segregation and forced removals, themes that are explored very powerfully in his award-winning prose collection *Waiting for Leila* (1981). The title story of *Waiting for Leila* is a novella which describes the demolition of District Six and features the drunken, degenerate Samad struggling to come to terms with the errors he has made in his life. Another story, 'Jobman' (which became a short feature film), concerns a deaf-mute farm worker who is brutally hunted down and killed on a Karoo farm after he comes back to reclaim his wife.

The contemporary South African short story manifests a fascinating diversity of techniques. The social realism so prominent in the 1970s and 1980s has given way to metafictional experimentation in a variety of forms. Predictably, this development involves a further movement away from forms of story writing which draw on oral culture, the milieu in which the South African short story first emerged. The voices heard in Ivan Vladislavić's *Missing Persons* (1989), for example, are those of alienated city-dwellers, cut off not only from forms of community embedded in the oral tale, but even from the communality of neighbours across the fence. Vladislavić's off-beat vision is consolidated very effectively in his *Propaganda by Monuments and Other Stories* (1996). Zoë Wicomb's story-cycle, *You Can't Get Lost in Cape Town* (1987), explores a South African girl's childhood and the contradictory emotions experienced by her protagonist who ends up positioned uncomfortably between home and exile. The style of her stories is bold and experimental. Maureen Isaacson's *Holding Back Midnight* (1992) is a similar display of imagination and linguistic skill. Her stories range widely in scope – from a depressingly believable projection of South Africa on the cusp of the millennium, to a portrait of regulation-bound life in ice-bound Sweden, to descriptions of growing up as a young Jo'burger in the free-wheeling seventies.

The astonishing diversity in style evident in the recent South African short story makes for rewarding reading. One encounters the tale sprung from oral origins, with distinct folkloristic undertones; the story written in the tradition of realism, with a heavy dose of social realism; the narrative fragment rendered in the spirit of journalistic reportage; the fantasy tale which reaches back into the past of myth and legend and that which looks forward to the kind of fictive experimentation loosely termed 'magical realism'. The genre of the South African short story has undergone a renaissance in recent years and the signs are that the form is destined to play a major role in bodying forth South Africa's future in imaginative terms.

Notes on the authors and commentary on the stories

The commentary that follows has been written to open up avenues for exploring the stories. Some interpretation is offered, but this is not intended to be comprehensive and merely suggests a few ways of approaching the stories. Where possible, cross-references to other stories or sources are noted to enable the reader to explore connections between the story in question and other works by the author or by other authors. In addition, extracts from critical commentaries on the stories are quoted and their details appended for the purpose of further reading.

Herman Charles Bosman (1905–1951)

Born near Cape Town, Bosman spent most of his life in the Transvaal, and it is the Transvaal milieu that permeates almost all of his writings. In 1926 he was posted as a newly-qualified teacher to the Marico district. He spent only six months there, but the experience provided him with the material for some 150 'Bushveld' stories. In July 1926, when he returned on vacation to the family home in Johannesburg, he became embroiled in a family quarrel and shot and killed his step-brother David Russell. The death sentence he received was later commuted to a ten-year prison term; he was released on parole after serving four years of this sentence. He spent some years working in London before returning to South Africa in 1940 and working as a journalist and editor. His major works include *Mafeking Road* (1947), his prison memoir *Cold Stone Jug* (1949), *Unto Dust* (1963) and *Willemsdorp* (1977). His *Collected Works* appeared in 1981.

'Old Transvaal Story' (1948)

'Old Transvaal Story', as the author-narrator of the story himself notes, is actually a rewriting of the Schalk Lourens story 'The Gramophone', which first appeared in May 1931 (collected in *Mafeking Road*). In 'The Gramophone' Schalk describes the troubled relationship between Krisjan Lemmer and his wife Susannah, which ends up with Krisjan murdering his wife and burying her under the voorkamer floor. This story in turn appears to have had its origins in Bosman's experiences in prison, where he encountered a fellow-prisoner who had killed his wife and buried her under the dung floor of his dining-room. The man was then beset by a group of friends who sprang a surprise party and he was forced to proceed with the party and pretend that nothing was amiss. This tale is recounted in 'Rosser', a story which went unpublished in Bosman's own lifetime and first appeared in 1958 (collected in *Ramoutsa Road*, 1987). W. C. Scully's 'Ukushwama' (1895) is also acknowledged by the narrator of 'Old Transvaal Story' as a source. A still earlier potential source, argues Vivienne Dickson, is Poe's 'The Tell-Tale Heart' (first published in 1845), in which a clearly deranged first-person narrator recounts his minutely planned and executed murder of an old man who lives with him. This all suggests that the tale has variations in numerous folk traditions in various parts of the world, and is therefore not 'original' to any one writer.

What Bosman does in 'Old Transvaal Story' is artfully merge a discussion of the Transvaal's 'only ghost story' and its 'only murder story' with a variation of his own on these 'many-told' tales. In this variation, moreover, a 'love story' of a sort is also told. The passage of the fifty-odd years between Scully's story and Bosman's re-telling has some interesting effects on the narrative texture of the tale. Where Scully's story is told rather ingenuously, with Scully clearly attempting to exploit all the standard devices of the ghost story to enthral his reader, in Bosman's rendering the artifice of the tale is foregrounded. Bosman thus sends up the genre of the 'ghost story': his conversational, light-hearted tone runs directly counter to the atmosphere that traditionally envelops the rendering of a ghost tale, and where a storyteller would normally attempt to conjure up suspense in the opening part of his tale, Bosman addresses the reader directly. Eschewing the customary device of his narrator Oom Schalk, he lures the reader into believing that a discursive rather than narrative piece will unfold. Of course, towards the end of the piece Bosman changes gears and the story ends climactically.

Stephen Gray describes Bosman's technique very accurately: 'Bosman knew, as every fiction-writer knows, that the art of writing is based on creating an illusion which must appear, in the reader's eyes, as real ... His on-going commentary on the practice of fiction intrudes quite frequently as you read along, as he explains himself, backtracks, apologises, insists that it is only a trick after all. Often he actually explains the trick to you, only to pull another one later.'

Bosman, H. C. 'The Gramophone'. *Mafeking Road*. Cape Town: Human and Rousseau, 1998: 92–97.

—. 'Rosser'. *Ramoutsa Road*. Ed. Valerie Rosenberg. Johannesburg: Ad. Donker, 1987: 92–94.

Dickson, Vivienne Mawson. 'The Fiction of Herman Charles Bosman: A Critical Examination'. Ph.D diss. U of Texas, 1975.

Gray, Stephen. 'Introduction'. *Selected Stories*, H. C. Bosman. Cape Town: Human and Rousseau, 1980: 7–16.

Meihuizen, N. 'Bosman and Self-Conscious Fiction'. *Literator* 12.1 (1991): 35–42.

Poe, Edgar Allan. 'The Tell-Tale Heart'. *Tales of Mystery and Imagination*. 1845. London: OUP, 1953: 336–342.

Scully, W. C. 'Ukushwama'. *Transkei Stories*. Ed. Jean Marquard. Cape Town: Philip, 1984: 38–50.

Nadine Gordimer (1923–)

Born in Springs, Gordimer has spent most of her adult life in Johannesburg. She began writing at an early age and published her first collection of stories, *Face to Face*, in 1949. Her first novel *The Lying Days* appeared in 1953 and was followed by *A World of Strangers* (1958), *Occasion for Loving* (1963), *The Late Bourgeois World* (1966) and *A Guest of Honour* (1970). Her novel *Burger's Daughter* won the CNA Prize in 1979, but it is *The Conservationist* (1974) – joint winner of the Booker Prize – that really established her reputation as a novelist. (For a listing of her story collections, refer to the overview essay on pages 139–140.) Her achievements as a writer culminated in a Nobel Prize for Literature in 1991.

'Six Feet of the Country' (1956)

Gordimer's remarkable skill in capturing the many nuances in human relationships – whether these relationships be those of master/servant, husband/wife, or black/white – is brought sharply into focus in this story. As the tale of the unfortunate dead black man unfolds, and the bureaucratic ineptitude of South African officialdom becomes more and more evident, we also become aware of the growing tension between Lerice and her husband, the narrator of the story.

Martin Trump argues that the story is a fine example of how Gordimer 'has perceived a common element in the degrading way in which black people and women are treated in her society'. By illustrating the narrator's indifference both to the black people around him and his wife, Trump argues, 'Gordimer offers a piercing indictment of the kind of patriarchal attitudes which maintain or at least lend support to the iniquities of the apartheid society'.

Gordimer can also be seen to be more subtle than this. She clearly portrays the presumptions and casual arrogance of her narrator, but she also understands his predicament. He has to act as mediator between a disenfranchised and oppressed black underclass and a white (mainly male, Afrikaner) class of officials. And he is not entirely unfeeling in his relations with his black staff. He is, Gordimer appears to be suggesting, neither entirely good nor entirely bad, but, like all people caught in the cleft of racially divided South African society, compromised by his race and class position.

Graham Huggan argues that 'the major source of irony in the story can be traced back to the narrator's failure to recognize that ... his own patriarchal values are complicitous with the more obviously divisive and inhumane practices of the apartheid state'. Huggan goes on to argue that 'neither Lerice nor Petrus is given an opportunity to give their side of the story, and when the opportunity would seem to arise, they are immediately cut off, or accounted for, by the narrator'. For Huggan, Petrus's dead brother becomes 'a metaphor for an apartheid regime which withholds the identity of its subjects by denying them a sense of place'.

Stephen Clingman draws attention to the underlying significance of the treatment of Petrus's brother after his death: 'six feet of the country cannot be granted to blacks, even in death. South Africa is a white man's country in which the basic dignities, in death as in life, are not to be afforded to blacks.' He also points to the way in which Gordimer takes up the theme of the black body buried on a white farm in a more sustained and complex way in her novel *The Conservationist*.

Clingman, Stephen. *The Novels of Nadine Gordimer*. Johannesburg: Ravan, 1986: 140–141.

Driver, Dorothy *et al. Nadine Gordimer: A Bibliography*. Grahamstown: NELM, 1993; London: Hans Zell, 1994.

Gordimer, Nadine. *The Conservationist*. 1974. Harmondsworth: Penguin, 1978.

Huggan, Graham. 'Echoes from Elsewhere: Gordimer's Short Fiction as Social Critique'. *Research in African Literatures* 25.1 (1994): 61–73.

Trump, Martin. 'The Short Fiction of Nadine Gordimer'. *Research in African Literatures* 17.3 (1986): 341–369.

Richard Rive (1931–1989)

Born in District Six, Rive was educated at the University of Cape Town and at Oxford University, where he wrote a thesis on Olive Schreiner. His novel *Emergency* (1964) was banned in South Africa. His stories are collected in *African Songs* (1963) and *Advance, Retreat: Selected Short Stories* (1983). His autobiography, *Writing Black*, appeared in 1981.

'Rain' (1963)

Rive's story achieves two things simultaneously: it is an impressionistic evocation of the social milieu of District Six as Rive himself knew it, and it is also the individual tale of the woman Siena and her hopeless quest to find the lover who has deserted her. The names of the two are suggestive. Siena is close to the Italian 'sienna', the name given to the red-coloured earth mixed to form a pigment used in paint, and hence suggesting a quality of earthiness, which is entirely consistent with the portrayal of the woman as a hard-working, trustworthy country girl. Joseph, on the other hand, has a name with ironic connotations: Siena meets Joseph in a church, and this suggests the connection with the Biblical Joseph – reliable father and trusty carpenter. The Joseph we encounter in this story, however, is utterly different: he abandons his innocent and trusting woman when he gets bored, and resumes his philandering ways.

Siena's plea ('Please, baas!') to the abrasive shop-owner, Solly, to allow her to shelter from the rain in his shop initially appeals to his desire for power over others. In his response he mirrors the large-scale response of the apartheid state to the poor and disenfranchised. We do witness a change in him at the story's end, however, when Siena has found Joseph only to lose him again – this time to the police. The intrusion of the forces of 'law and order' is momentary, but the reader is aware that their presence is part of the callous and indifferent state machinery that would later decree that the entire area of District Six be demolished in the interests of 'slum clearance'. In this thumbnail sketch of District Six, Rive deftly evokes the texture of life in the slum.

Eileen Julien points to the story's concern to convey a mood rather than explore the minutiae of individual experience: 'events play a minor role in the story's overall effect for the emphasis is on the mood created by the downpour which echoes the betrayed woman's loneliness and the blunt edge of city life'. The 'ultimate meaning' of the story, she concludes, 'is the morass of city life, its callousness and fragmentation and the tragic isolation of those who have ventured into its midst'.

In a way that strikingly reflects aspects touched on in the story, Rive described the milieu of District Six in a memoir written in 1979. His remarks also suggest something of the anger felt by people who grew up in the area and later witnessed its destruction: 'Last year I was driving through the scarred landscape of what had been the scenes of my boyhood. Bloemhof Flats still stood, and St. Mark's Church stretched solitary and defiant, and my stone-built primary school lay in ruins, and the Fish Market and Star Bioscope were gone, and Globe Furniture where a vicious gang used to meet had disappeared, and the Swimming Baths and Maisels Bottle Store were no longer there. Where were the crowded street-corners where we played around lamp posts in the evenings with the South Easter howling around us? And where were the musty Indian stores smelling of butterpits and spice? And the Fish and Chips Shop with sawdust on the floor and the plate-glass windows steamed over with the heat from the boiling oil? All these were gone because mean little men had seen fit to take our past away.'

Julien, Eileen. 'Of Traditional Tales and Short Stories'. *Toward Defining the African Aesthetic*. Ed. Lemuel A. Johnson *et al*. Washington: Three Continents Press, 1982: 83–94.

Rive, Richard. 'Caledon Street and Other Memories'. *Staffrider* 2.4 (1979): 46–49, 61.

Es'kia Mphahlele (1919–)

Born in Pretoria, Mphahlele was educated at schools in Pretoria and at the University of South Africa. His early life is recounted in *Down Second Avenue* (1959). In the 1950s he worked for *Drum* magazine before going into exile in Nigeria. In 1965 he moved to Kenya, where he published *In Corner B and Other Stories* (1967). After spending some time teaching in the United States he returned to South Africa in 1978. From 1983 to 1987 he was Professor of African Literature at the University of the Witwatersrand. Other major works include *The Unbroken Song* (1981) and the autobiography *Afrika My Music* (1984).

'Mrs Plum' (1967)

In her study of the works of Es'kia Mphahlele, Ursula Barnett quotes a letter to her from the author in which he remarks that 'Mrs Plum' was 'the best thing I ever pulled off'. It is certainly Mphahlele's most widely discussed and anthologised story, and justifiably so: it is an acute and subtle interrogation of white liberalism in South Africa by a black narrator whose steady growth in knowledge and understanding allows her to prise apart the liberal ideology of her employer and to expose the hypocrisy and injustice that it contains.

At the opening of 'Mrs Plum', Norman Hodge comments, 'Karabo is cast as a seemingly naive narrator, unconscious of what she is saying or thinking. Yet the reader soon realizes Mphahlele's mastery of narrative voice: he is able to show a character coming into contact with an unfamiliar environment, gradually learning about it, and at the same time, he uses Karabo's reactions as a means of illustrating some of the absurdities in South African white social protest.'

In his article, which explores 'Mrs Plum' in relation to three other stories that 'prefigure' it ('We'll Have Dinner at Eight', 'The Living and the Dead', and 'The Master of Doornvlei'), Damian Ruth argues that Norman Hodge 'makes too great a claim for Karabo: we do not at the end of the story have a character with "a total awareness of self"'. Nonetheless, he agrees that the story has the qualities of a bildungsroman (a work charting the growth and development of its main character) and stresses the story's emphasis on the enlarged understanding of its protagonist: 'it is specifically a story of how a black South African maid develops to a point where she sees through a white liberal madam and comes to a particular understanding of her socio-economic position in the society she enters'. At the end of the story, he concludes, 'Karabo opts for manipulating the oppressive structural expression of the relationship' with Mrs Plum: 'Karabo certainly has grown up and learnt; Mrs Plum obviously hasn't'.

Barnett, Ursula. *Ezekiel Mphahlele*. Boston: Twayne, 1976.

Hodge, Norman. 'Dogs, Africans and Liberals: The World of Mphahlele's 'Mrs Plum''. *English in Africa* 8.1 (1981): 33–43.

Ruth, Damian. 'Through the Keyhole: Masters and Servants in the Work of Es'kia Mphahlele'. *English in Africa* 13.2 (1986): 65–88.

Bessie Head (1937–1986)

Born in Pietermaritzburg's Fort Napier Mental Institution, her mentally unstable mother Bessie Amelia Emery (née Birch) having been placed there after falling pregnant, Head grew up in foster-care and in a mission orphanage in Durban. After working as a journalist in Cape Town and Johannesburg she went into exile in Botswana in 1964, where she wrote her major novels *When Rain Clouds Gather* (1968), *Maru* (1971) and *A Question of Power* (1973). Her stories were collected as *The Collector of Treasures* (1977) and *Tales of Tenderness and Power* (1989). Plagued by ill health and mental instability, she died suddenly in Serowe, Botswana, at the age of 49.

'Heaven is not Closed' (1977)

Of interest in this story is Head's use of a storyteller figure, the old man Modise, to tell the story of Galethebege's life. This says something about the oral culture of the village of Serowe and Head's attempts to capture aspects of this culture in print. The story arose from an interview which appears in a chapter of Head's social history, *Serowe: Village of the Rain Wind* (1981), dealing with religion in the village. The bare bones of the story are all in the interview: Segametse Mpulambusi describes her grandmother's conflict with, and withdrawal from, the London Missionary Society church. It was possibly the interview context in which Head first encountered the story that prompted her to introduce the device of the storyteller when she retold the story in a fictive mode.

Through this device the author is able to present all the familiar components of an African storytelling ethos: a camp-fire setting, an old and wise narrator, a known and intimate audience, an ending which provokes re-evaluation and comment. The reader is introduced to the texture of village life by being drawn to the camp-fire, as it were, by the storyteller's compelling technique (the storyteller here being both the character, Modise, and the authorial voice).

It is interesting, however, to see that the author breaks into the narrative of

'Heaven is not Closed'. She employs the device of the storyteller to evoke the flavour of village life in a tangible way, but does not restrict herself to what would conceivably be told by a person of Modise's age and context. By evoking the traditional oral storyteller within the text of a modern short story, the story's structure works double-edgedly to give a sense of that which it describes. The story conveys its meaning, in other words, in two ways: by what is said, and by how it is said.

Kenneth Harrow draws attention to Galethebege's role as mediator between two opposed male principals – the missionary, who represents European mission-Christianity, and Ralokae, who represents Tswana tradition: 'Galethebege's interviews with the missionary were intended to bridge the gap between the two men and the two customs each represented. Instead, she finds herself trapped between the missionary's interdictions and her husband's adamancy. She had hoped, by means of the passage of love through her, to overcome the conflict between the two men – to mend the rift between their institutions with their two sets of customs. She had sought to achieve a "compromise of tenderness", but instead of providing the occasion for a flow of love, thus satisfying the people's "cry for love" engendered by the intrusion of colonialism, she becomes herself the occasion for hatred. Seeking to unite, she is excluded.'

Sara Chetin describes 'Heaven is not Closed' as a story of 'one woman's attempts to re-enter [paradise]'. For her, Galethebege has been denied a 'mythical home' and searches for 'ways of repossessing it'. The 'simple and good heart' of Galethebege, she goes on, 'is not enough to combat the dual patriarchal institutions of religion and marriage' and she therefore 'dies carrying the burden of all human suffering while symbolizing the hope for redeeming the human race'. In the story, she concludes, 'Head explores how an individual's inner sense of integrity and beliefs are often at odds with the society's rules which impose a conformity on the community and stifle individual self-fulfilment'.

Chetin, Sara. 'Myth, Exile, and the Female Condition: Bessie Head's *The Collector of Treasures*'. *Journal of Commonwealth Literature* 24.1 (1989): 114–137.

Harrow, Kenneth W. *Thresholds of Change in African Literature: the Emergence of a Tradition*. London: Currey; Portsmouth: Heinemann, 1993.

MacKenzie, Craig. 'Short Fiction in the Making: The Case of Bessie Head'. *English in Africa* 16.1 (1989): 17–28.

Ahmed Essop (1931–)

Born in India, Essop came to South Africa in 1934 and later studied at the

University of South Africa. He taught at various schools in and around Johannesburg, but left the Education Department responsible for 'Indian Affairs' after a dispute. Thereafter he took up clerical work and began writing. His *The Hajji and Other Stories* (1978) won the Olive Schreiner Prize. His other collections are *Noorjehan and Other Stories* (1990) and *The King of Hearts and Other Stories* (1997). He has also written two novels, *The Visitation* (1980) and *The Emperor* (1984).

'The Hajji' (1978)

The element of internal conflict is central to this story. Hajji Hassen's tranquillity is disrupted by the supplications on his brother Karim's behalf by Catherine, his brother's girlfriend. He is torn between a wounded pride at his brother's rejection of his family and his transgression of socio-racial codes and, on the other hand, a genuine love for his younger brother. This provokes the story's crisis, which begins with the news of Karim's illness and continues – punctuated by each failed attempt to change Hassen's mind – until the story's end.

Salima's inferior status in the household is illustrated very early on when Hassen shouts at her to answer the phone. His recent trip to Mecca, which, ironically, should have made him more understanding and humane, has merely alerted him to 'novel inadequacies in her'. She is later compared unfavourably to Catherine, to whom Hassen is physically attracted despite the fact that she represents everything he deplores: sexual freedom, an independent lifestyle, and – most importantly – the temptation that has drawn Karim away from his family and community. Another central irony in the story is the common understanding between Salima and Catherine: they are (literally and figuratively) worlds apart, and yet they achieve a better understanding than the brothers, who should be so close.

The news of Karim's death appears to have a cathartic effect, yet this swiftly gives way to Hassen's sense of ongoing personal crisis. He begins to see himself as the hypocrite the community would see him to be. The breaking of the dawn on his walk out of the city heralds the beginning of a change in attitude. His memory of Karim is activated by his prodding of a stick at the crevice in a rock. The flood of grief he feels and his prostration of himself on the rock is the turning point in his crisis. He hastens back to the city, strikingly at odds with the workaday bustle of traffic, to find that personal resolution is forever to elude him. He has changed his mind too late, and the community, oblivious of his presence, conducts the funeral without him.

Norman Hodge remarks that the story 'has the basic starkness and simplicity of a classical tragic structure and mode; compassion for the central character trying to overcome his own pride and bitterness is counterbalanced by the reader's awareness of Hassen's glaring weaknesses of personality. And the author is aware of what Hemingway called the "little things", the almost unnoticed details of description which contribute greatly to the final effect.'

Jean Marquard describes the broader socio-historical significance of Essop's stories in the following way: 'Those who know Johannesburg remember Fordsburg as the Indian section of town, a place of smell and colour, teeming with life, an oasis near the centre of the city. Inevitably the System intervened; Group Areas proclaimed the destruction of Fordsburg and the Indian inhabitants were moved out of town. Houses were demolished, businessmen and traders were forced into new premises and residents were removed to Lenasia, a large, dreary township bordering Soweto, twenty miles from central Johannesburg.' Essop's achievement, she goes on to remark, is to have captured this milieu in his writings: 'In *The Hajji and Other Stories* he has composed unique portraits of Indian life in South Africa combining a generous, fluid viewpoint with amused irony, at the same time keeping a balanced perspective on the violence and injustice of South African life.'

Hodge, Norman. Review of *The Hajji and Other Stories*. *English in Africa* 5 2 (1978): 81–82.

Marquard, Jean. Review of *The Hajji and Other Stories*. *Staffrider* 2.3 (1979): 60–61.

Christopher Hope (1944–)

Born in Johannesburg, and educated at the University of the Witwatersrand and Natal University, Hope has lived and worked as a writer in London since 1975. A prolific writer with a wry and distinctive style of satirical humour, his works include *Private Parts and Other Tales* (1981, 1982), *Kruger's Alp* (1984) – winner of the Whitbread Literary Award – and *The Hottentot Room* (1986). His autobiographical work *White Boy Running* appeared in 1988.

'Learning to Fly' (1981)

The sub-title, 'An African Fairy Tale', offers some indication of the kind of story 'Learning to Fly' is. 'Fairy tale' suggests something mythical, magical, belonging to the realm of make-believe. This dimension of the story collides comically with its weighty subject-matter: oppression under the apartheid regime and the various methods of torture associated with its Security Police. 'Black humour' would be a fitting description of the story's mode. It is undeniably funny, but its engagement with the suffering and hardship endured by black people under the apartheid regime makes the story both humorous and horrifying.

The story is told from a narrative present which is located in an imaginary post-apartheid period (remember the story was written in the mid-1970s). It thus predicts – in its dark and ironic way – the downfall of the apartheid regime and also exposes the follies and errors perpetrated by the regime. At its core 'Learning to Fly' is a satirical treatment of the ridiculous beliefs and practices of apartheid. By making them appear ridiculous, Hope is protesting against them. The furtive and sinister operations of the Security Police constitute the dark heart of the apartheid regime, and Hope exposes their sheer stupidity and irrationality.

It is worthwhile noting, however, that a 'fairy tale' often contains a moral or lesson that must be extrapolated. In this case, Hope seems to be warning against a perpetuation of the follies and injustices of the apartheid regime by the revolutionary regime that succeeds it. Note, in this regard, Jake Mphahlele's agreement with Colonel du Preez that black people are indeed the 'children' of their white masters, and that they 'owe' them 'everything'. Is the warning here that the new regime may replicate the practices of the old, merely substituting black victims with white ones?

Geoffrey Hughes interprets the story in this way: 'Hope's criticism of "the system" is quite unambiguous, but he shows himself to be a genuine liberal in finding not only apartheid, but all forms of political coercion, ideological tyranny and their extremist exponents absurd, unjust, unscrupulous and lacking in humanity.' The end of 'Learning to Fly', he concludes, 'has the same twist as *Animal Farm*: the revolution does not bring moral rebirth'.

Hope has commented as follows on the kind of fiction South Africa has provoked: 'While one does sometimes have a feeling that in every sense it seems to be a surreal country, South Africa does operate without any real sense of substance and concreteness. My impression has always been that one fell asleep round about 1948 ... and we parted company with reality – we embarked on a night-time adventure – a surreal and curious nightmare of our own choosing and of our own direction, which has so emptied the conventional terms of their meaning that we can no longer address each other in any of the languages which seem to apply, except the languages of dream and nightmare, and, of course, the language of violence.'

Hope, Christopher. Interview with Phil Joffe in *English in Africa* 16.2 (1989): 91–105.

Hughes, Geoffrey. Review of *Private Parts and Other Tales*. *Contrast* 14.3 (1983): 90–93.

Sheila Roberts (1937–)

Born in Johannesburg, Roberts studied at the universities of Pretoria and South Africa. She left South Africa in the 1980s to live and work in the United

States, and has been Professor of English at the University of Wisconsin-Milwaukee since 1987. Her first collection of stories, *Outside Life's Feast* (1975), won the Olive Schreiner Prize. Her novels include *He's My Brother* (1977) and *The Weekenders* (1981). Her other collections of stories are *This Time of Year and Other Stories* (1983) and *Coming In and Other Stories* (1993).

'This Time of Year' (1983)

Roberts begins her story about human isolation and despair with an evocative description of the autumnal landscape which appears to enclose her main character, Hannah. The alternating pattern that becomes established in the story – now a focus on the character, now one on the natural world outside – suggests that Roberts sees the fate of her characters as inexorably tied to the larger rhythms of the outer world. (This, of course, is also suggested by the story's title.) Another interesting technique is her use of seemingly inconsequential details – like the reference to the old woman who has come to 'help out' the Vosloos – which are skilfully woven into the fabric of the narrative; only later will their significance become apparent.

Hannah's compulsive musings on the reasons for, and significance of, Mary Vosloo's death (note her observation that she is the same age as Mary was when she hanged herself) show her awareness that her fate may be similar unless she chooses to sever ties with the past – and her former husband. Like the seasons, Hannah stands poised on the threshold of change. She knows that her future hinges on the decision she will shortly have to make about remarrying Sam. As the details of her former life with Sam unfold it becomes clear that she is in danger of following the same route to financial ruin and familial disintegration experienced by Mary Vosloo. The sordid details about Sam and their former life together that filter into the narrative accumulate to provide a compelling portrait of suffering and deprivation.

Her decision at the story's end not to remarry Sam triggers a release of emotions. Her earlier indecision provides the story with its narrative tension and her cathartic laughter at the end dispels this tension. She has chosen, and chosen wisely. She has chosen life above degradation, potential above stifling limitation, hope above despair. Spring is evoked at the story's close, and the story thus ends on a triumphant, celebratory note. The intervening winter will be endured; she will plant vegetables and trees in the spring. As Peter Wilhelm suggests, however, her choice has been made in circumstances which are far from ideal.

Wilhelm characterises 'This Time of Year' as belonging to a feminist strain in Roberts's work: 'The commanding qualities here are lamentation, rage and resistance. Life – even in its lurid South African colours – is not patronised, along with its slimy or redundant personnel. Instead, the women at the centre of these tales are capable of moving beyond, or thinking through, their predicaments. In 'This Time of Year' the choices are bleak – but, fully presented, we can understand that there is no "best" decision, only compromise around an enduring focus of integrity.'

Roberts herself has commented on the story's underlying humour and optimism: 'the woman decides not to return to her husband and has some glee imagining him having to ride his bike in the rain, because he's lost his licence. She has this feeling of being home again and reconciled with the life that her father will provide on the farm, and they'll paint the farm in the spring. These are not great triumphs, but the break-up of her marriage is also not the end of life.'

Wilhelm, Peter. Review of *This Time of Year*. *English Academy Review* 1 (1983): 121–123.

Roberts, Sheila. Interview in *Between the Lines: Interviews with Bessie Head, Sheila Roberts, Ellen Kuzwayo, Miriam Tlali*. Ed. Craig MacKenzie and Cherry Clayton. Grahamstown: National English Literary Museum, 1989: 31–57.

Njabulo Ndebele (1948–)

Born in Western Native Township near Johannesburg, Ndebele moved with his family in 1954 to Charterston Location near Nigel, a small mining town south of Johannesburg, which is the setting for most of the stories in *Fools and Other Stories* (1983). He studied at the University of Botswana, Lesotho and Swaziland (BOLESWA), Cambridge University and the University of Denver. In 1991 he was appointed Professor of African Literature at the University of the Witwatersrand. He resigned as Rector of the University of the North in 1998, a position he held from 1993. His essays have been collected as *Rediscovery of the Ordinary* (1991).

'The Test' (1983)

The title of this story suggests that its protagonist will undergo a trial of some sort. As the story unfolds it becomes clear that what young Thoba experiences is a rite of passage: he is on the threshold of young adulthood and the story charts an important moment that marks his passage from childhood to adulthood. Thoba is tested in three arenas: by his peers, by the community at large, and by his parents.

Among his peers, he struggles to assert himself by measuring himself against the older boys, Vusi and Simangele. When they make it clear that he is beneath them, he turns to someone his own size – Mpiyakhe. He runs out into the rain without his shirt on, and in so doing issues an unspoken challenge to Mpiyakhe. His struggle to gain the acceptance of his peers is complicated by his class position: Mpiyakhe articulates the view that the others have of him – that he is a 'higher-up', that his family are '[s]ofties'. He longs to have the cracked feet of the other boys, and to run freely in the streets without shoes on.

In the community at large, the women in particular are perceived by Thoba as impeding his transition to young manhood. When he runs past the crèche, he imagines the matron looking out at him and saying, 'There is my little man'. In this way, he marks in his own mind his departure from his childhood. Later on in his run he encounters the women getting off the bus. By this stage he is exhausted and on the verge of tears. The women gather around him and, significantly, it is his trousers clinging to his body that become the focus of attention. The significance here is that he believes that the women are humiliating him by implicitly mocking his manhood (he is very self-conscious about the fact that the outline of his buttocks and penis is visible because his trousers are wet). He musters his energy and sprints away: 'It was the most satisfying sprint, for it was so difficult, so painful. It had led him out of humiliation.'

He also strives to break free of the influence of his parents, who envelop him in all the trappings of protected, middle-class existence. We note the stress placed on education in his life (while all the other boys are free to roam the township at will), the emphasis on wearing shoes, keeping warm, keeping out of trouble, coming home when the weather looks threatening. It is particularly the mother's role in all of this that he resents. When she protectively puts her arms around him, he 'allowed himself to be embraced, all the while wishing his mother had not done that. It made him too helpless.' And when, at the beginning of the story, he worries about whether he should run home before the rain comes, it is his mother's insistent warnings about keeping warm and dry that preoccupy him. Significantly, after he has undergone his 'test', and arrives home cold and tired, he gets into bed without doing his customary chore of making the fire: 'Let his mother do whatever she liked with him. He would not make the fire.' He has completed his test: he has begun to break the protective maternal bonds that impede his progress to manhood.

Brenda Cooper makes the point that Ndebele is 'one of the very few black South African writers to portray consistently the significance and complexity of class differences within the township'. Why Thoba undertakes 'the test' in the first place, she argues, is that 'he comes from a more educated petty bourgeois class than most of his friends. He has, therefore, to prove that he is as rough and as tough as they are.' Thus, she concludes, 'the pranks and agonies of childhood and growing up are played out within concrete realities of apartheid and of class struggle'.

J. M. Coetzee points to the polarity of 'street' and 'home' in Ndebele's stories: '*Street* and *home* are in fact the two opposing zones in which Ndebele's stories are played out. The home is a zone of order and security, usually created by the hard work and self-sacrifice of a woman. The street, contested by criminal gangs and police patrols, is a zone of disorder and insecurity, though also of vitality. Between these zones Ndebele's children move, trying to satisfy the demands of the home without transgressing the norms of the street.'

Coetzee, J. M. 'Tales out of School'. *New Republic* 22 December 1986: 36–38.

Cooper, Brenda. 'The Value of the Pearl: For Now or Forever? The Question of the Universal in a Materialist Aesthetic'. *English Academy Review* 4 (1987): 91–114.

Zoë Wicomb (1948–)

Born near Van Rhynsdorp in Namaqualand in a remote Griqua settlement, Wicomb was educated at the University of the Western Cape and Reading University in England. She lived in Britain from 1970 to 1991, when she returned to South Africa to teach at the University of the Western Cape. She has since returned to Britain to resume her academic career there. Her *You Can't Get Lost in Cape Town* (1987) is a collection of inter-related stories which centre on the character Frieda Shenton.

'A Trip to the Gifberge' (1987)

This story is the last in Wicomb's sequence of stories and deals with the return home of her protagonist Frieda Shenton (although the name is never explicitly mentioned) after many years in Britain. It probes at the issues of exile and homecoming, of living a life outside the constraints of parental control and coming home to confront them again. In its adroit switching between past and present, the story provides a rich insight into the interior world of a young woman struggling to break free from a background that threatens to engulf her again.

The moment of her arrival at the airport and her experience of encountering accents and attitudes that have not changed with the passing of years are deftly rendered. Wicomb shows considerable skill both in capturing the inflections of Aunt Cissie's speech and also in exposing the mindset her words betray. We realise very early on, then, that this story will explore the disjunction between the protagonist and the environment to which she has somewhat reluctantly returned.

This disjunction takes the form of disparities in political views, attitudes to protocol and decorum, and, in general, outlook on life. The protagonist re-enters a world of limited horizons and ambitions, but the one novelty is her mother's new-found forthrightness and assertiveness. In the trip that the mother insists on undertaking, mother and daughter achieve an unexpected re-union symbolised by their falling asleep together on freshly plucked 'Hotnos-kooigoed' in an abandoned shepherd's hut in the mountains.

Just before this occurs, the protagonist playfully insists that her mother use the term 'Khoi-Khoi-kooigoed' to describe the bush, and her mother acquiesces. This is further demonstration of the rapprochement between mother and daughter, but it also points to another dimension in the story: the distance between the protagonist and her family as regards their differing levels of awareness of the complicity of language in social and political control.

Sue Marais addresses this issue in her article on Wicomb's stories: 'Frieda is ... brought to an understanding of the ever-increasing gulf which separates her from her immediate relatives . . . their sense of belonging and permanence is premised on the fact that they unquestioningly take language at its face value.' The sentimental homilies and clichés they utter, Marais concludes, 'gloss over the harsh realities of apartheid, of dispossession and racial segregation, which have actually determined their existence'.

Dorothy Driver also draws attention to the different kinds of knowledge possessed by mother and daughter: 'Speaking with an apparent authority (gained through education, political know-how, and travel), Frieda criticizes her mother for wanting to plant a protea in her garden, since the protea stands for the Afrikaner nationalism in whose name people like the Shentons have lost their land. But Mrs Shenton takes the protea as her own in a way it cannot be for white settlers . . . Book-learning gives way here to a different kind of knowledge. And so it is, at the end of the story, that the narrator takes direction from the Southern Cross, as if re-entering the world of her Griqua ancestors who lived in the hills and doing so without jettisoning science.'

Wicomb has herself commented on the story as follows: 'In a sense the trip to the Gifberge is a metaphor for all sorts of things that [the mother] was barred from; and [the father] had had a very silly excuse for never taking her on that trip ... In a sense I have to kill off the father, in order for her to speak.' The mother, whose death was reported in earlier stories in the sequence, is brought back to life for a very specific purpose, Wicomb observes: 'the resurrection of the mother is a metaphor for returning: it's a homecoming, in both the physical and [spiritual] sense'.

Driver, Dorothy. 'Transformation Through Art: Writing, Representation, and Subjectivity in

Recent South African Fiction'. *World Literature Today* 70.1 (1996): 45–52.

Marais, Sue. 'Getting Lost in Cape Town: Spacial and Temporal Dislocation in the South African Short Fiction Cycle'. *English in Africa* 22.2 (1995): 29–43.

Wicomb, Zoë. Interview in *Between the Lines II: Interviews with Nadine Gordimer, Menàn du Plessis, Zoë Wicomb, Lauretta Ngcobo.* Ed. Eva Hunter and Craig MacKenzie. Grahamstown: National English Literary Museum, 1993: 79–96.

Ivan Vladislavić (1957–)

Born in Pretoria and educated at the University of the Witwatersrand, Vladislavić lives and works in Johannesburg as a writer and freelance editor. He has developed a reputation as an iconoclastic writer with an innovative and humorous style. His first collection of stories, *Missing Persons* (1989), won the Olive Schreiner Prize and his novel, *The Folly* (1993), won the CNA Prize. His most recent book is *Propaganda by Monuments and Other Stories* (1996).

'Journal of a Wall' (1989)

Vladislavić's bizarrely funny story is anchored in the incongruity of someone devoting so much attention to the trivial event of a neighbour building a garden wall. The diligence with which the narrator records the event verges on the pathological. And yet the humour of the story is located partly in the reader's shock of recognition: contemporary South African city-dwellers, we realise, are perhaps only a few stages away from the pathology displayed by Vladislavić's narrator.

As the story progresses the narrator's intense isolation becomes more and more apparent, and when his emotional investment in the event of the wall-building is not rewarded by closer contact with his neighbours he becomes violently angry and retreats still deeper into himself. It becomes clear that Vladislavić's satire is directed chiefly at the walls that divide us in modern urban society.

At the edges of the story the daily horrors of life in South Africa during the 1980s obtrude, and this gives the story its satirical depth. The disproportionate amount of attention paid to the building of the wall, on the one hand, and the violence and tragedy of life in the townships just a few kilometres away, on the other, is in itself a tacit criticism of the psychic dislocation of many South African city-dwellers.

Verna Brown describes this skewed state of affairs as 'the word . . . substitut[ing] for the experience'. She says the following about Vladislavić's collection as a whole: 'In his exploration of the missing persons of a dislocated society, Ivan Vladislavić, with a wit sometimes pawky, sometimes mordant and often outrageous, explores the intimate connections between the tragic and the comic. He holds the satirist's distorting mirror up to "our very strange society" so that, in Arthur Koestler's words, "the reader is thus made to recognize familiar features in the absurd, and absurdity in the familiar".'

The notion that we all at least partly occupy the world inhabited by Vladislavić's narrator is suggested by. Alf Wannenberg in his review of Vladislavić's stories: 'Vladislavić's world seems at first very different from mine. It has many familiar features, but in mindscapes strange to me. Exploring it, I discover more in common with my world ...' Vladislavić, he concludes, systematically juxtaposes 'impressions and association of ideas to create a world in which reality is manifest in a form of fantasy, dream – indeed, nightmare'.

Brown, Verna. Review of *Missing Persons*. *English Academy Review* 7 (1990): 127–129.

Wannenberg, Alf. Review of *Missing Persons*. *New Contrast* 18.3 (1990): 82–84.

Maureen Isaacson (1955–)
Born in Johannesburg, Isaacson studied at the University of the Witwatersrand and spent three years living and working in Sweden. She works as the literary editor for the *Sunday Independent*. Her *Holding Back Midnight and Other Stories* appeared in 1992 and established her reputation as a short-story writer.

'Holding Back Midnight' (1992)
Set in the last minutes before midnight, 31 December 1999, Isaacson's story impressionistically sketches South Africa on the cusp of the new millennium, where women wear recyclable paper dresses to parties and where everyone uses paper gloves in restaurants to prevent the transmission of AIDS.

But it is Isaacson's probing of the past that is most telling. Her parents and their friends – among them cabinet ministers from the old regime – refuse to relinquish the past, and as the story unfolds the attitudinal differences between the narrator and this older generation emerge quite clearly. This older generation is not able to 'read the signs'. Misinterpreting the new freedom for anarchy they protect themselves with security measures (panic buttons, guard dogs, armed-response personnel) and retreat into nostalgia.

While the main character professes an optimism for the future, however, the story has a dark undertow: it is difficult to decide, finally, whether the rubbish piling up and the lifts not working are real or greatly exaggerated – and, if real, whether they are symptomatic of a general malaise or merely a minor blot on the 'good life' that the narrator professes to live.

Dorothy Driver observes that Isaacson's stories 'subvert the dichotomies of the past'. They use 'intricate tonal and perspectival shifts to render the complexities of being "white" at this moment in history'.

Driver, Dorothy. 'Transformation Through Art: Writing, Representation, and Subjectivity in Recent South African Fiction'. *World Literature Today*. 70.1 (1996): 45–52.